The Rising Fire

The Rising Fire

Reachers Series Book 4

L. E. Fitzpatrick

Copyright (C) 2019 L. E. Fitzpatrick
Layout design and Copyright (C) 2019 by Next Chapter
Published 2019 by Beyond Time – A Next Chapter Imprint
Edited by Alicia Ramos
This book is a work of fiction. Names, characters, places, and incidents are the product of the author's imagination or are used fictitiously. Any resemblance to actual events, locales, or persons, living or dead, is purely coincidental.
All rights reserved. No part of this book may be reproduced or transmitted in any form or by any means, electronic or mechanical, including photocopying, recording, or by any information storage and retrieval system, without the author's permission.

In memory of Winetta Starr

Come all you good workers,
Good news to you I'll tell
Of how the good old union
Has come in here to dwell.

Prologue

Ten years ago

It was nearly two in the afternoon. Si Daniels swirled the melting ice in his glass of Scotch. He perched awkwardly against the hotel bar, one hand on the counter, the other whiling away another hour on a single drink. Daniels' feet twitched anxiously, scuffing his old leather shoes against the parquet floor. Once upon a time, the shoes were a quality purchase, much like Daniels' suit and the semblance of a haircut he didn't seem able to part with. But, like the Grandchester Hotel that housed him, they'd all seen better days. By chance the hotel had found itself on the right side of the border when the wall went up thirty years earlier. The cheap rooms and concrete views attracted a clientele more accustomed to life in the slums, needing a base of operation while they conned their way across the capital. Daniels was such a guest, lingering between what was beginning to feel like two worlds, trying to find a way home that didn't end in poverty.

A burner phone sat in front of him. He checked it every few minutes, growing more anxious with every disappointed glance. Two days ago, he'd put feelers out around the city looking for a buyer interested in stolen security software. That had been his second mistake. His first was accepting a job from ViperCorp Securities in the first place. But Daniels wasn't in a position to be turning down work. He had debts to pay, two families to subsidise, and a gambling habit that overwhelmed both.

The prospect of a temporary respite to his financial hardships dazzled him, distracting him from the obvious signs this was going to go south. The biggest being that a respected security company would enlist a third-rate thief to secure a product that was worth millions. The second was the target, Jay Stanton. Stanton was supposed to provide them with the program he had designed—until ViperCorp had retracted their generous deal three weeks ago and Stanton told them to go to hell. One double-cross always leads to another. Now Daniels had a computer program he didn't understand, ViperCorp tearing apart London looking for him, and no buyer to save the day.

From the back of the bar, Charlie Smith kept an eye on Daniels over the top of his newspaper. He knew all about Daniels' woes, and it wasn't difficult to see where the thief's future was going. Charlie checked his watch. His brother would already be in Daniels' room. In a few minutes he would crack the safe there. And then Charlie would finish his drink and leave the Grandchester and London for good.

"You in the mood for some company?" The female voice made him start.

When Charlie looked up, a woman was leaning over him, her breasts spilling from her tight dress as though they were coming up for air. She smiled, cracking the creases in her heavily applied makeup. She was holding on to her beauty, but it wasn't enough to hide the severity in her eyes. She'd approached Charlie because he was in an expensive jacket and she'd seen him buy a drink from a wallet full of notes. Unlike Daniels, Charlie was at the top of his game.

She twisted herself to present her best angle. Charlie put her in her forties, twice his age and an expert in her trade. He entertained the idea of paying her to distract Daniels, to buy John enough time to get the job done. It was too risky though. If anyone came snooping around later, they'd connect the woman to Daniels, and inevitably Charlie to the woman. The last thing he needed was another corrupt, ruthless corporation hunting them down.

He opened his mouth to respectfully decline, when he saw Daniels bolt for the door. Charlie jumped up after him, pushing past the whore. He grabbed the door at the exit and turned in the lobby, expecting to see Daniels hit the stairs. The steps were empty. He looked left instead, catching the man fleeing out the hotel's main entrance. Charlie launched himself forward.

A heavy cloud of smog had settled on the city. Vehicles chuntered over the road, clogging at the entrance to the border control. To Charlie's right, he caught Daniels weaving through the cars and reaching the opposing pavement. Charlie chased after him. He thrust into his jacket to grab his phone. They'd checked Daniels' pockets an hour ago, and he was clean. He had no vehicle, no safe house. The only place he could have kept the program was the hotel room, so why was he running? Charlie pulled his phone out and punched the menu key. A force hit him from behind, hurling him across the road.

When he came to, his face was pressed into the tarmac. Slowly, on his hands and knees, he panted into the sidewalk. His fingers brushed plastic. He looked and saw his phone, smashed and sitting in a puddle of brown water along with a set of false teeth. He frowned and raised his head. In front of him an old man sat gawping, empty mouthed. His grey eyes fixated on something behind Charlie. Confused, Charlie turned back to the Grandchester—what was left of it.

A smoking skeletal structure stood in its place. The upper floors had disintegrated downwards, swiping away two sides of the building with them. Smoke and dust blossomed in their stead. If Charlie hadn't chased after Daniels when he did, he'd still be inside. He'd probably be dead. Then it dawned on him. John was still in Daniels' room.

Bystanders helped the old man to his feet, recovering his teeth from the pavement. Charlie wasn't in the mood for help. He scrambled to his feet before they could reach him, ignoring the pain in his arms and legs from the fall. There was no serious damage, nothing that would stop him racing back to the Grandchester and pulling his brother free.

Sirens blared around him. They were in London; the response time here was quick. There would be police coming, and they'd want to ask questions. Charlie hesitated, knowing if he ran to help, the authorities would catch him.

Before he could make up his mind, red and blue flashed in his line of vision. Seconds later bodies were being pulled from the rubble. Charlie was still staring, his clothes betraying his proximity to the blast. He backed away from the crowd, from the police looking for witnesses, before anyone could spot him. There was a car park across the street littered in broken glass and dust. He grasped the railings shielding him from the emergency services and looked back at the hotel. Logically, John couldn't have survived. He was three floors up. Now there were no floors, just one pile. John had to be buried in there. But if Charlie concentrated, if he reached out with his mind, he could sense his brother inside. As impossible as it was, he was sure his brother was alive.

More bodies were pulled from the rubble. Eight dead. Charlie scanned the scene, looking for signs of movement within the carnage. He toyed with his broken phone, trying to piece it together and finding it as ruined as the hotel. It was getting dark, and he was starting to doubt his earlier confidence. He concentrated again, reaching out to see if he could sense a stronger presence. John was still there, still moving, still fighting. At least Charlie believed he was.

A rumble rattled through the building. The firefighters inside fled, escaping seconds before the building gave out and imploded. There was no way anyone inside could still be alive. There was nothing left. Charlie felt his hands start to shake. He couldn't even comprehend the possibility of a life without his brother. He glared at the firemen, surrendering to the catastrophe, not knowing what to do.

"Been waiting long?" John said from behind him.

When Charlie turned, John was standing there, as though he'd been there the whole time. There was debris on his clothes and a small gash on his head, but nothing to suggest he'd just survived a building collapsing on him. He looked at Charlie, expectant and smug.

"How the hell did you get out of there?" Charlie was so overwhelmed he pushed John back, then grabbed hold of him to make sure he wasn't hallucinating.

"Crawled mostly," John said with a shrug. He pointed at his trousers. "Knees are fucking threadbare."

There was a commotion outside the hotel. The police were pushing the crowd back, trying to isolate the area. John tipped his head. It was time to leave. Side by side, they headed back towards their car, parked three streets down. Charlie tried to play it cool—he tried to pretend he was as nonchalant as his brother—but minutes earlier he'd been waiting for John's body to be pulled from the rubble, and now he was striding through London like he owned the place. He had so many questions, starting with the most important.

"Did you get it?"

John's hands were stuffed deep into his pockets. A faint blush rushed up his cheeks. And if Charlie weren't already in a state of shock, he was about to encounter his brother being embarrassed. Incredible as his survival was, he'd been in the Grandchester for a reason. John was a perfectionist, and empty pockets were unacceptable.

"No."

"No? What do you mean no? What happened?"

"The fucking building blew up," John snapped.

"So it's still in there?"

"No. But I know where it is."

Charlie looked at him expectantly, but John had already moved on. Charlie watched his brother slip deeper into the London shadows. If John knew where the program was, then they would find it. They'd get the job done. They were the infamous Smith brothers; they always got the job done. He fastened his jacket and went after his brother.

1

Charlie pressed against a frost-covered pine as the sun retreated. He peeled back his gloves to check his watch; the night air chewed on his exposed skin. The second hand rotated twice. He nudged his brother. John hooked his rifle over his shoulder and pulled his balaclava down. In three strides he disappeared into the woods. Charlie checked his watch again. Time to go.

Thirty miles of forest stretched in front of him, interrupted only by a single undocumented dirt track slicing between the trees. At the end of the road a twelve-foot barbed wire gate and fence encircled a three-mile-wide dip in the terrain. The site was marked only with a battered Private sign hanging loosely across the gate, pretending that the road beyond was nothing but a dead end. Charlie knew better. The fence was intact, the gate locked. What was the point in maintaining defences if the road led nowhere?

He moved forwards. The brace on his weak leg bore the weight of his descent. The pain in his hip and back was irrelevant against the importance of this final job. His boots struck the tarmacked road, and twilight embraced him. A sudden hush settled on the surrounding wilderness. Charlie sucked in a breath and waited.

Nothing.

No warning shot.

No rush of guards coming to capture him.

His attention flicked left to his brother's hideout. Then right to where he knew Rachel would be waiting. He checked his watch a final time. On cue an engine rumbled through the trees behind him. Half a mile down the road, Roxy was covering their escape. But Charlie had no intention of escaping. This was it for him. And he was ready.

His boots crunched on the frozen tarmac as he advanced on the gate. To his left a concealed camera pointed at the entrance. If it was being monitored, they would know he was coming. *Let them know.*

He counted his steps. Three more and he would be visible. He looked to the growing shadows—they were on his side—and moved forward.

The silence deepened. His heart quickened. He pulled his gloves off and pressed his hands against the metal framework of the gate. It was sealed with three electric bolts. Charlie closed his eyes and let his mind wander. Like a current, his powers surged through the gate, reading every twist of wire, every supporting frame. He travelled through its mechanics, learning it, understanding it. Controlling it. He found the operating system, his mind merging with it. And then he was the gate blocking his path. He twisted his hand sharply. The fuse box blew, the locks releasing. He let go of the gate and swiped his hands apart. With a violent creak it flew open and clattered against the fence.

Charlie stood, exposed. An open target for a lazy shooter. The air rattled in his body. He waited. Waited for the alarm. The soldiers. The bullets.

But there was still nothing.

His lips parted, another plume of breath twisting in front of him.

He took one final look at the shadows and stepped across enemy lines.

The track devolved into mud and stone, hugged by a lower tree canopy. The darkness deepened until he was surrounded by an eerie emptiness. The cold worsened, sinking through his clothing, penetrating his body to his bones. The moment stretched forward, the black seemingly infinite. And then it was suddenly lifted. The woodland broke and a concrete structure was exposed.

The sight of it hit Charlie hard. He was unable to move forward, the wind knocked from his body. The broken, vengeful man was suddenly gone. In his place was a terrified boy, staring at his worst nightmares unfolding. He blinked, concentrating on the pain in his back, reminding himself who he was and why he was here. This is not the place, he assured himself. This could not be the place they incarcerated him all those years ago. The structure was square and unmarked like the building from his childhood, housing an identical single, fortified entrance. But the laboratory he was held in was made vulnerable by a rocky incline, climbable by two young boys with nothing to lose. Here the ground where the incline could have been slumped, petering off to a small, stinking pond. This is not the place, he assured himself again. This is not the place.

Charlie squared his feet, stretching his back before the building. He would not be intimidated. He would coax them out of the bunker, and John would pick them off.

As he neared the building, he flexed his fingers, savouring the power he could wield. He reached out, feeling for anything threatening. Weapons, vehicles, machinery. He sensed nothing awaiting him. But that couldn't be right. If this was an Institute laboratory, it would be protected.

The stretch of tarmac that circled the building was now fully exposed and empty. Charlie was dumbfounded. Last week the road had been full of military vehicles. At the very least there should have been a handful of base vehicles parked up.

Charlie stopped walking, hit by a cold, unsettling thought. What if they were waiting for him? What if they had known he was coming for a long time? What if they intended to capture him and resume their experiments? There was still time to turn back, and for the first time since arriving in the forest, he was considering it. He wasn't afraid to die, but he was never going to be their lab rat again.

His fingers brushed the grenade in his pocket—he wouldn't be taken alive—and he continued on.

When he reached the bunker, he placed a hand against the metal door. His powers surged through the building, but he could get no sense of what lay beyond. The stillness seemed to deepen the harder he focussed, until he was part of the building, sitting in a place out of time and space.

"Where is everyone?"

He spun, drawing his pistol. Rachel raised her hands, unimpressed.

"Don't shoot."

Charlie almost cried. His heart was racing. The gun trembled in his hand, and he stuffed it back into his hip holster.

"Don't sneak up on people," he said.

"Hey, you told me to sneak in behind you. It's not my fault you're easily spooked." She examined the door, frowning. "Aren't we all supposed to be dead or dying about now?"

"Apparently it's our lucky day."

"Think they're waiting for us inside?"

Charlie nodded. It was the only place they could be.

He loosened his shoulders, feeling the wave rocket down his back and into his weaker leg. He could do this. He would do this.

"Ready?"

Rachel nodded, the uncertainty he felt reflected in her eyes. They were both here for revenge, both willing to die for it and both afraid of what could meet them inside. He pressed his hand against the metal door and allowed his powers to explore. The lock had been sealed electronically, but Charlie struggled to find a current he could surge. Instead he found the manual override, an internal heavy-duty lock on the back of the door.

The lock clanked hard. Heavy hinges creaked, and the door stretched open. The noise ricocheted into the long, dark corridor before them.

Charlie gasped, overcome with a sense of vertigo. This was all too much like a bad dream. He touched the wall to steady himself, listening to the deafening silence swallowing his breaths. *Where are they?*

Rachel peered in. "Well, doesn't that look inviting." She fished out her flashlight and shone it into the black. Illuminated, the entrance wasn't any more welcoming. The walls were scuffed and scratched, the floors stained with brown track marks. The corridor housed a single check-in point to the left, a small cubicle which should have been constantly occupied, recording the movements of everyone entering and leaving the facility. Beyond that was a seemingly inactive lift. Charlie was starting to get a bad feeling in his gut.

"Ladies first?" he offered.

Rachel glared at him and pushed him forward. He took out his own torch and crossed the threshold. *Run. Get out of here.* The panic sounded like a chorus in his mind. As if the echoes of all the Reachers lost here were united in trying to compel him to save himself. He didn't believe in ghosts, just regrets. And he carried too many of those to turn back now. This was his fight. He wouldn't shy away from what awaited him.

He shone the light into the check-in station. There was an empty pencil pot beside a mouldy cup of coffee on the desk. Scraps of paper carpeted the floor. As Rachel covered him, he bent down to inspect them closer. The jotted notes were unintelligible clusters of numbers and codes. Nothing he could make sense of. He gestured for them to move forward towards the unfunctioning lift.

"If the lift's out, where are the stairs?" Rachel asked.

Charlie pressed his hands against the closed doors and eased them open, exposing an empty shaft. Empty save for a ladder running the length of the cavity. It was exactly as he remembered it, except this time he would be going down and not out to freedom like before.

It was impossible to know how far the cavity went. In his laboratory there were six floors that he knew of. It was possible this was even deeper.

"Wait until I get to the next floor, then follow me down," he told her.

He crawled inside and grasped the ladder. The climb down was clumsy. His leg brace struck the ladder, each step creating an overture for his descent. If they were waiting, they would know exactly where he was, but he could do nothing about that now. He hung outside the lower floor. It was far too late to go back. He put his hand against the metal and forced the doors open.

Another empty corridor stretched in front of him. He shone his torch, exposing a row of open rooms. If they were still here, they were dragging out the game and having fun with him.

Rachel's feet struck the ladder. He waited for her to join him. He was willing to take on an army alone, but not the emptiness of the place. Only when she stood behind him did he feel any confidence to move forward.

Rachel was lucky. She had never been in an Institute facility, although she'd come close once—too close. The atmosphere of the building wasn't affecting her as much as it was him. She surged ahead, poking her head in the nearest doorway.

"What are these rooms for?" she asked.

"In the one I was taken to, this was the staff floor. Offices, common room. That kind of thing."

"Well, I suppose you need somewhere to unwind when you've had a hard day torturing kids," Rachel said and gestured they should keep going. She was right to keep up the pace. The longer they stayed here, the more unsettled he would get.

He moved to the next room, the ajar door concealing the inside. He kicked it open and waited for the shot, or shout, or anything. When he shone his torch into the space, he found an abandoned desk sitting there alone. There were marks on the walls and floor, signs of recent life, but no indication of who worked here or what they did.

They moved on to the next and the next. Each one similarly vacant. Some housed discarded furniture, others were totally barren. Cabinets had been emptied. Computers cleared away. A stray monitor remained fixed to one wall, cables dangling like the legs of a hanged man. There were nails remembering pictures, wear marks around doorways. A coffee machine sat on the opposing wall of what had to be the common room, the pot burnt and cracked.

Rachel nudged one of the discarded chairs with her foot. "This doesn't make any sense. We saw them. They were here two days ago. Where the hell have they gone?"

"I don't know."

Thunderous rumbles shook the corridor, reverberating across the walls like gunfire. Charlie swung around. Halogen lights ignited in blasts. *Bang. Bang. Bang.* The lift gave out an agonising groan. Rachel pressed herself against the wall. She nodded at Charlie. He went first.

He twisted his body into the corridor, raising his weapon at the lift. The lights fizzed and flickered. The corridor was plunged into darkness. A second later the lights ignited again. The lift doors opened.

Charlie waited for the gunfire. For the hordes of soldiers to charge at him. He was ready. He could do this. He wanted this. *Come on.*

His brother stepped from the lift, into the open, and quirked his eyebrow. An amused twitch twisted his mouth. Charlie lowered his weapon and exhaled. He wasn't sure his chest could take any more false alarms.

"Who's watching the entrance?" he asked.

"I called Roxton over to cover us. Not that we need it. The whole place has been abandoned. There's no one here, just a shallow grave by the generator, probably about five men inside."

"Reachers?" Rachel asked.

Charlie understood everything from the look John gave him. They had seen what the Institute did when they abandoned facilities first-hand.

"Non-essential staff," John explained. "Still in their uniforms. Single shot to the back of the head. Nice to know the Institute are creatures of habit."

If he closed his eyes, Charlie could still see it. The porters and janitors, all standing outside the facility, executed one by one by men they had worked alongside for months.

He kicked at the wall with his braced leg, furious with his timing. This was supposed to be his final stand, the moment he faced his greatest enemy. He was prepared to die here. But not to wait. Not to reset and begin hunting all over again.

"Do you think they knew we were coming?" Rachel asked.

"No, they'd still be here if they did," Charlie said. "Something else must have happened. Maybe someone compromised the location. We found them; others could too."

He rubbed the growing weariness from his face as the adrenaline started to subside. The building was still hiding rooms. Beneath his feet would be a cell block, little white spaces to house unfortunate Reachers. Beyond that, the hub of the operation, the laboratory. If there was no one here, those places would be similar husks, but Charlie was compelled to see them. This was not the place he and his brother had been incarcerated, but it was similar enough. If nothing else was to come of today, he would stand outside the cells a free man.

The lift seemed to slow the further down they travelled. Charlie wondered if this was all an elaborate game. Whether the doors would open and he would be greeted by a small army now they'd convinced themselves the laboratory was deserted. It was wishful thinking. There would be no fight. All that awaited him here were ghosts and bad memories.

The doors opened, and the corridor lights blasted into life. The smell hit Charlie first. It was unmistakable. Rachel took the lead, decomposition drawing the former doctor out of her. Charlie brought up the rear, the walls of this latest corridor being all too familiar.

Again, the rooms were all open. He counted eight. Eight rooms for eight solitary Reachers. Five of the beds still had bedding; the other three were stripped. Each room only housed one prisoner, a change from Charlie and John's time. John moved into the nearest cell, his steps just slightly more hesitant than normal. He looked to Charlie in the doorway, and his jaw clenched. John was a grown man now, but Charlie could still see the young boy he'd been paired with, and he was reminded again of why they had come here.

Towards the back of the corridor the smell got worse. The final door led to a shallow staircase, opening to an examination room. The sight of it made Charlie's stomach lurch more than the smell. How many times had he been restrained in a room like this? How many doctors had cut him, electrocuted him, poisoned him? His hands were shaking, and he was furious with himself for wavering. It had been years ago. They shouldn't still have this hold on him.

The equipment had been stripped from the room, leaving only rust marks and stray wiring hanging over the metal stretcher. And on the stretcher, beneath a yellowing sheet, was the source of the smell. The body had already begun liquefying, dissolved innards pooling on the tiled floor near the drainage grate. Rachel approached, her constitution ironclad. She peeled back the sheet, exposing the body of a teenage girl.

Her head had been shaved, exposing purple welts, bruises from countless experiments. There was no way to tell what kind of Reacher she was, whether she'd been telepathic like Rachel or telekinetic like Charlie. In the end it didn't matter. This was the fate for them all if they got caught.

Rachel turned to him, colour draining from her cheeks. She had come so close to being on that slab herself. Charlie had saved her, but the potential still bothered them both. It wasn't just Rachel. The girl could have been his daughter. And once again he found himself grateful Lilly had been killed before they could bring her to a laboratory like this.

In a storage shed on a farm in Wales, Charlie had file after file of other fallen Reachers. Their fates mirroring that of the girl on the slab. He carried them all with him, taking the burden of their deaths because he had survived. So many faces. So many names. What was the girl on the slab's name? Where had she come from? Would they ever find out?

"Take some pictures," he told Rachel. "We need to document this."

2

The light bulb was swinging. Back and forth, a pendulum over the dying Union man. His blood spattered over the antique printing press, dripping onto the anti-government pamphlets scattered on the floor. The printer's fingers twitched in a puddle of blood and ink and dirt. His face was pressed into the floorboards, his last breaths clogged with paper dust. Then he was gone, the moment as swift as the assault on his office. Five enforcement officers pointed smoking automatic rifles over him. Their victory had been spoiled by yet another anticlimactic bust. Union men favoured words over weapons. The fight was starting to become a slaughter.

There were other targets. The Union had stores and offices all over S'aven. There was no point wasting time on a lone rebel and an archaic printing system. Time to move out. Then something stirred in the shadows of the back room. The squad froze, eyes alert, watching the darkness hungrily. Their steps were cautious as they advanced. Guns poised, flashlights dancing over a cluttered storeroom, amphetamine-fuelled fingers vibrating against triggers—this was what they lived for.

Boxes had been dumped by the back exit, blocking the only escape anyone inside might have. The space was small, only large enough for two of the squad to fit inside. Their torch lights spiralled and caught the terrified eyes of a girl hiding under the cardboard. She shrieked and tried to cower back into the rubbish.

She was pretty, in an emaciated, grief-stricken way. No older than fourteen, her tears stained with ink; she would be their reward.

Mark Bellamy was leading the squad. He stood at the head, the alpha, and felt the lust build around him. He raised his hand before anyone else tried to claim the girl. A wave of disgruntled passivity rattled through them. Mark threw his rifle over his shoulder and snatched the girl by her bony wrist. She yelped and cried, twisting in his grip. With her free hand she clawed at him, scraping her filthy nails at his face. He slapped her. The sound surprised them both. The girl lowered her head, her braids covering her face, shielding her from further assault.

"Go on without me," he said. It was an order, not a request. He knew the nature of his unit. They would relish the opportunity to destroy the girl with their desire. Unleashed, they would be uncontrollable. But Mark had the girl, so Mark called the shots. He drew her closer to his chest, breathing in the smell of machine oil and ink. "I'll make my own way back."

There was another potential site for Union propaganda distribution and another opportunity for more helpless girls to savage. S'aven was nothing if not filled with potential. And these were S'aven's elite. These men could—and would—do anything.

With renewed purpose they filed out. Mark waited, listening to their steel-capped feet clomping out onto the street. An engine ignited—their transporter—and then pulled away. As the sound faded, he exhaled and released his grip on the girl. She dropped to the floor, scampering away from him, but he stood between her and the exit. There was nowhere to go. He breathed deeply, returning to a semblance of rationality, then removed his helmet.

The act liberated his thoughts—his real thoughts—and he shed the persona of the law enforcer.

He looked at the girl. Really looked at her this time, without intent or insinuation. The effects of this night would stain her future like the blood on the pamphlets. Mark couldn't save her from what lay ahead. He could only help her in this moment. And maybe afterwards she would be alive to do something more. Maybe she would survive this rotting town.

He crouched down, allowing her to look him in the eye. She was small for her age, like most of the kids in S'aven.

"What's your name?"

She didn't answer. Despite her emaciated form, there was defiance in her eyes.

Another trait of the S'aven youth.

"My name's Mark. I'm sorry for hitting you. I had to make them think I'm like them. But I'm not going to hurt you again. I promise. I'm going to help you. It would make it easier if I knew your name."

She considered it. Her big brown eyes flipped from Mark to the body over his shoulder. Then she pushed back her braids, meeting his gaze with more bravery than anyone in the unit would ever know. "L-lacy. My name is Lacy Mooney." Mark cursed inwardly. He knew the name too well.

"Was he your father?"

Her eyes filled with water as she nodded. It meant the dead man was Leroy Mooney, the second most important man holding the Union together. His death should have been avoidable. The building was supposed to be empty. Mark had leaked the plan two days ago and, unlike other strikes, this had run by the clock. He understood that the printing press was immovable, its Victorian weight and size cementing its place in the unsuitable office. Surrendering the building meant giving up a means to distribute information. But there was no need to die over a machine and certainly no reason to bring a child here. Mark didn't need any more blood on his hands, and he was putting a lot on the line trying to keep innocent people safe. What was the point when men would wilfully sacrifice everything for an unwinnable fight?

"We need to get out of here. Let's move these boxes and get going."

Lacy rose to help. Her cardigan was thick, but Mark could see how unnaturally thin she was beneath it. He'd lived through food droughts before, but the current situation in S'aven was starting to scare him. Food was being purposely withheld from the people in an attempt to control them. It was a dangerous game and one the authorities would regret playing. Mark moved Lacy aside and did the work himself. She couldn't afford to waste her strength, and the station provided him with more than enough rations.

With the back door clear, he was able to map a path to the canal. The rest of the unit should have made their way to the next raid site, but there was a chance they'd been inspired to commit more trouble in the area. Avoiding the main roads, he took the back alleys and weaved around the ramshackle homes lining the gardens to the old, dilapidated townhouses.

A gag-inducing stench haunted the canal. Death had arrived in S'aven, gathering disease-ridden bodies beneath the thick water that cut through the town. A cholera outbreak had hit the worst of the slums. If things didn't improve soon, it would spread, and the canal would be abandoned for bigger dump sites. Mark held his breath as he walked. Lacy seemed used to it.

A mile down the canal he took a sharp left, veering into the darkest part of the street and into Union territory. These homes were well built and strong, created for the once-privileged Union workers. But since the riots, the local council had cut off the electricity and water, forcing them into premature decay. In full uniform, being spotted here by either side would be a death sentence. Mark took three brisk strides around the back of an old flat block, down a set of concrete steps, and prised open the door to the basement flat entrance. A single solar light beckoned him towards a green door. Mark nodded at Lacy and knocked.

There was always a possibility this was a trap, and as long as the inhabitants of the next room remained hidden, Mark wouldn't relax. He clenched his fists, hand hovering over his Taser in case he should need it. The door opened. Lacy's uncle, Carson Mooney, stared back at him.

Mooney was an unlikely leader. He was in his early forties, grey creeping across his face and head with surprising sympathy. He was average height, average weight, commonly dressed for his common flat. And yet, beneath the normality of a typical Union man, there was something about Mooney. A light behind his eyes, a way he looked at the world that changed perceptions. He ignited something powerful within his own people. It was frightening. And it was inspiring. He was a man Mark was reluctant to disappoint, but bringing Lacy here would undoubtedly affect him.

Mooney took in his niece, her cheek swelling from where Mark had struck her, and closed his eyes, knowing his brother was dead. He didn't seem surprised.

With a wave of his arm, he ushered them inside, closing the door behind them and shutting out prying eyes. In her uncle's territory, Lacy seized her opportunity and put herself behind Mooney for safety. She linked her hand with his, and her trembling started up again. Mooney patted her shoulder.

"We got fresh water today. Go clean up, yeah? Let us talk." He gestured to the only other door in the room and waited for Lacy to go. She threw one more glance at Mark. He'd helped murder her father, but he'd made good on his word. What would she possibly think of him now?

Mark waited for her to close the door. "What were they doing there? I told you we were coming. Nobody should have been in there."

"Leroy wanted the leaflets printed. He thought he could do it in time."

"Well, I hope those leaflets were worth his life."

"We don't have weapons to fight you with. All our power comes from words. Leroy knew this. The Union is… was his life."

"And his daughter's life?"

Mooney glanced back at the closed door. "He lost his wife a week gone. Sickness got a hold of this town and has done for us all. Leroy hasn't been thinking straight since. I should have… I should have stopped him going. I was preoccupied. There are others who want to move the Union against the police. They're watching their kids dying. It's all I can do to keep us united and contained."

Mark was too aware of the tumultuous situation in the town. His squadron were relying on the growing tension. Peaceful protest could only last so long. Soon it would overspill into real, punishable violence, and the police measures could become more severe. All it took was careful prodding: cutting food, stopping amenities. The right raid at the right time.

Mooney held out his hand, his palm scarred from years of manual labour. "I appreciate the risk you took in bringing her here. You didn't have to. We'll remember."

Mark wondered if Mooney would be so grateful if he knew Mark's next stop would be filing a report with the Institute. He wondered if Mooney would shake his hand knowing his superiors were responsible for the growing disease and the rising unrest.

"I have to go. I'll be in touch." He shook Mooney's hand, feeling a fraud. Then he left. He didn't want to see the girl again. He wished he didn't have to see any of this again.

Rain fell in thick, icy sheets as he stepped outside. He closed his eyes and water poured down his face, nipping life into his pallid skin. He was tired. Tired of S'aven. Tired of the job. Tired of the unrest. But there was still so much to do. There was always so much to do. And he was on his own. The only man in S'aven who really knew what was going on.

Two months ago the Institute had shut down PCU, and his one-man department was thrown to the wind. He had entertained the idea of getting out of the south altogether, heading up to Blackwater and seeing if he could pick up work with the police force there. But, although the Institute were done with his department, they were not done with him. They were losing a grip on the police presence in S'aven and, with the unrest getting louder, they wanted a man on the inside. No, they wanted a man on both sides.

Now Mark flitted between a corrupt police force and an underground political revolution. He'd listen to briefings, then tip off Mooney; listen to Mooney's speeches and ideology and report everything back to the Institute. The work was pulling him in all directions—and yet, at the same time, he was gaining more clarity about the world he wanted to create around himself. There was potential in S'aven, potential for real change, and he was a man orchestrating so many instruments, a secret conductor in this war song.

3

Rachel gasped into consciousness. The air was tight. The darkness, suffocating. She tried to move and found her arms and legs bound and stuck. *Shit, shit, shit.* As her heart raced, her breath quickened. This was how she died, strapped to some rusting hospital gurney, choking like a beached fish. She gulped in air and flailed against her restraints. There was an unexpected give, and she started to roll. She slammed into a warm body to her right. He grumbled and elbowed her back into her own spot. Rachel gasped again, the nightmare dissipating with each glug of air.

For a moment she lay motionless, calming her heart. *You're free. You're free. You're free.* She repeated the phrase over and over, a mantra of reassurance. With the clarity came a flood of tears. She stifled the reaction and wriggled out of her sleeping bag to wipe her face. It was just a dream, but it could so easily have been her future. Three months later and she still couldn't shake it.

She sat up, pulling her knees to her chest, and stared into the darkness. Her fingers traced familiar patterns on the floor. The van had been scuffed and battered before they acquired it; now she knew each scar by heart. This was her vehicle, not the Institute's. She closed her eyes and breathed deeply. Underneath the heavy smog of Roxy's liquorice smoke ingrained in the metal, she could make out the mud and damp permeating Charlie's clothes, while a faint trace of John's aftershave lingered over everything, a memory of what civilisation smelt like.

Beside her, Roxy grunted and snorted before resuming his snoring. The sound grew louder with each exhale, rattling the van walls. Rachel reached out, her fingertips running over the curve of Roxy's shoulder. She touched the weave of his jumper; the hole at his collar, then the one at the seam. Finally, her fingers found the small burn mark on his chest from the cigarette he'd dropped last week.

"If you must, darling, but be gentle," he muttered.

And then the nightmare was over. She cursed inwardly at her melodrama. It wasn't like she had been tortured as John and Charlie had. The Institute only captured her for a few hours, and for most of them she was unconscious. Then all that happened was being put in the back of a transporter; it wasn't exactly cause for anguish. The others had rescued her long before she could come to real harm, and yet in the dream she was always alone. Charlie and John were missing; Roxy was dead. And she was a prisoner with a lifetime sentence in hell.

Her heart quickened, and she knew she couldn't start dwelling on those types of thoughts again. If she was going to get better, she had to move on. When they destroyed the Institute, the nightmares would stop. Or she'd be dead. Either way, there would be resolution. She just had to be patient.

Roxy snorted again. It was her cue to leave. She grabbed her winter coat and shuffled forward. She'd become adept at manoeuvring silently in the cramped space, not that a little rummaging or a small bomb raid would disturb Roxy. A sharp blast of cold air slapped her cheek as she opened the door. She leapt out quickly and fished a hat from her pocket before shutting Roxy away for a couple more hours.

The cold crept in at her sleeves and collar, clawing at the aches in her body and culminating in her shoulder. She rubbed at the gunshot scar and flexed the muscles there. It was approaching dawn, black trees studded against a purple canvas, and she could just make out a twist of cloud threatening to blot out the morning sun. In readiness, Charlie had made his own light. A small fire crackled in camp. It was the first they'd allowed themselves since coming out here. They had taken refuge two miles east of the Institute base and what felt like a hundred miles from anything else. Before, a plume of smoke would have given away their position. Rachel couldn't help but wonder if now Charlie was hoping the fight would come to him.

He sat hunched over the flames, under two heavy coats and a thick hat. Only his hands were exposed, cradling a half-empty cup of tea. His leg brace had been discarded the moment they returned to camp. In its stead, his crutch rested at his side. If the cold was rattling her body, it would be wreaking havoc on his. She pressed her hand on his shoulder, and he offered her a distracted smile. He was sat on a strip of discarded tarp and shuffled up so she could keep dry too. As they pressed tightly together, her hand automatically found his.

Touching Charlie, or sometimes just being near him, could settle her nerves. As she felt his bare palm on hers, the worries about sleepless nights and cold cell blocks quietened. For the briefest moment there was only the two of them, and she felt strong again. Charlie offered her his tin cup of lukewarm tea and powdered milk.

"Any sugar?"

"Ran out two days ago."

She took the cup anyway. It wouldn't be long before they were out of milk too, and she was sure the others were helping themselves to her share behind her back. Her palate deserved a hit of lactose before winter.

"Can't sleep?"

"Roxy's snoring again." It was better Charlie didn't know about the nightmares. He had enough demons to fight on his own without taking on her battles as well. "I think next time John's going to make him bring his own van."

"Next time?"

The question hung between them. Would there be a next time? This was supposed to be their last stand, the grand finale. Only half the cast hadn't shown up, and the show was a bust. What were they supposed to do now? It had taken months to find the Institute facility, and that was only because she had been on her way to it when she was rescued. If the Institute were moving on from old laboratories, they could be anywhere in the country.

"We have to do something," Charlie said. "Otherwise we're just running with no end in sight."

Before she met Charlie, Rachel's life was entirely about running. Her father had been insistent: you keep moving, you're always ready to go. She was prey, staying stationary only for as long as the wind blew clear. She fled the war in Red Forest as a child, fled the convent at the cusp of womanhood, and had escaped Safe Haven three years ago. But she was tired of running. She was tired of having her life dictated by a stalking wolf perpetually haunting her in her peripheral vision. It was no way to live.

"How do we even find them?"

"If I knew that, we'd have hit the road by now."

It wasn't like him to have no heading. Even when things went really south, she'd always been able to count on him to lead them somewhere. Then she remembered how the laboratory had affected her. Charlie's history was deeply rooted in the Institute facilities. How could he walk away from such a place and think clearly? She squeezed his hand. "How are you doing after yesterday?"

With a broken smile, he shrugged. "I'll live to fight another day."

When they first met, he was popping prescription painkillers to numb his grief after his wife and daughter were murdered. Moving in a daze of survival and surrender. With her help, he'd sobered up and stayed clean. But it was a balancing act. Under their weathered exteriors they were both still so fragile. It would be easy for him to slip, and if he did, she was sure she would slip with him.

"I am okay," he reassured her. "It's not what I wanted, but it's not going to ruin me. I promise you."

Charlie was a very good liar. He had kept his addiction hidden from Roxy and John, but she could always read him. He meant what he was saying now, even if he didn't keep his word later. She rested her head on his shoulder. A slow tingling grew where their skin met, their powers weaving around each other. The connection they shared was growing stronger.

"What was it like for you? Going back there, I mean."

"Like walking through a bad dream. It wasn't the same place, I know it wasn't the same, but it was so similar. The cells, the operating room. It had the same smell, the same feel about it." Charlie chewed on his lip, struggling with his next sentence. "There's something I need to tell you, Rach. I don't think I can go back there again."

She raised her head in surprise. His feelings made sense, but him admitting them so early showed real progress. "It's okay."

"It's not though. How am I supposed to fight them when I'm too afraid to even confront them? They killed Sarah and Lilly—rage should overcome my fear—but as soon as I stood outside that place, I was a kid again. It's pathetic."

"Charlie, it's not—"

"Really? You weren't freaking out. It was nearly you strapped to a bed and left to die. You coped. And John didn't even flinch."

She was about to confess and tell him why she'd fled the van. Then she realised he wasn't supposed to be sitting here on his own. John was supposed to be keeping watch with him.

"Hey, where is John?"

Charlie waved his hand dismissively. "He went to fill up the water."

"Have you spoken to him about this?"

He prodded the fire with the end of his crutch. "And tell him what? That after all these years of planning—of promising him we'd take back what they took from us—I can't go through with it?"

"Well, he's going to need to know eventually."

Charlie shook his head. "No. I owe him this. After everything, I have to be as strong as he is."

"I'm not sure it's strength with John, just dogged determination and stubbornness. He just fixates on a plan and executes it."

He let out a sad laugh. "You've not got that wrong. Did I ever tell you about our time at the Grandchester Hotel?"

"I don't think so."

"It was this three-star travel stop for people crossing the border who preferred a stopover in London over S'aven. I was sitting in the bar, tailing this thief, Si Daniels, while John raided his room. Then suddenly the guy bolts out of the place. Back then I was a lot faster on my feet, and I made it out across the street when the whole building explodes. John inside."

He smiled to himself. "I watched the response team pull out body after body and then, a couple of hours later, John taps me on the shoulder. There was a bit of dirt on his shoulder, a small cut on his forehead, nothing else to even hint that he was in that building. Except maybe a smugness about him. I guess it's just like what happened last summer."

The inspiration behind the nightmare sparked in Rachel's memory. John had faced the Institute to save her, and he'd taken a knife to the gut for his trouble. He shouldn't have survived—Rachel had been sure he wouldn't. She was an out-of-practice trauma doctor, not a surgeon. And yet he had. He got better. He got stronger. And he didn't hesitate when it came to coming back here.

Rachel swallowed a growing lump in her throat. She didn't want to think about recent history. Not when the wounds were still so fresh.

"So how come the hotel blew up?" she said before they deviated from safe territory.

"John wouldn't admit it, but I think he set off a trap. It would explain why Daniels bailed when he did. And why John blamed himself for the job going to shit. The building blew up in his face, and all he cared about was the job being a bust. So much so that the same night he leaves me to finish it. We were after this computer program, and it turned out to not even be in the hotel. But John tracked it down, brought it home. All while I went out of my mind with worry."

"He left you behind?"

Charlie's face darkened. "John's sense of duty is paramount. He was given a job to do, and he made sure he did it. That night he disappeared, and I didn't see him again until morning, program in hand. We got paid and got the hell out of London. And as we were driving away, all I could remember thinking was that John could do anything if he set his mind to it. It was the first time I ever even considered we might be ready to take on the Institute."

"So why didn't you?"

"We crossed the border, and that morning I walked into church looking for Darcy and met Sarah." He turned to the fire, the flames flickering in his sad eyes. "She was handing out Bibles like a regular member of the congregation, but she'd been helping Darcy with forged IDs for Reachers on the side. The moment I saw her, I forgot everything. I'm not sure John's ever really forgiven me for it. We were working so hard, for so long, to get ourselves ready, and I detoured off the path the first chance I got."

"It was for a good reason. You fell in love."

"I screwed up. We were going to war, but instead I brought that war home—to my family."

"Don't think about it like that. You got to experience real happiness, even if it was fleeting. Maybe the likes of me and John breeze through government dungeons because we're more at home there than we are in real life. Maybe if we had experienced what you had, our cold hearts might thaw a little."

It was her turn to look away. She wasn't even sure where her words were coming from. It had been a long day. Charlie was staring at her. Even with her back to him, she could feel his eyes pressing into her head, trying to unravel her. She took a moment, put on her playful smile, and nudged him in the ribs.

"Or maybe we're just better at putting on a brave face." She kissed his cheek. "Don't worry. We'll figure this out. I'm going to go talk to John. You never know, maybe he's stressing about telling you the same thing."

She left Charlie and the warmth of the fire, stepping cautiously through the undergrowth before her façade slipped.

Rachel was a city girl at heart. Her time in the wilderness was normally spent fleeing for her life. It was rare she got the opportunity to lose herself amid the trees. Without the threat of the Institute lurking nearby, she found she could take her time. There were no houses for miles around and no resources worth pillaging. It was entirely possible they were the first human visitors to this place in decades, maybe even centuries. It was a thought that brought her comfort, thinking that this could belong just to them, that there were places out there they could have all to themselves.

The ground dipped, revealing a thin river cutting through the trees. The gap in the foliage allowed pink light to fall on the water, illuminating a figure knelt at the edge of the bank. He was shirtless, his pale skin glowing against the shadows as he dipped his hands into the water. They'd all been living on top of each other for weeks; she'd become immune to discovering them in private moments. And yet there was something about this encounter that felt like she was intruding.

John pulled his razor blade from the water and ran it over the curve of his jawline. He flexed his shoulders, the muscles over his arms and torso rippling with the effort. He was unusually relaxed, his gun with the rest of his clothes, away from the river and out of easy reach. As he dipped the blade in the water a second time, he paused.

"You're not supposed to be up yet," he said.

Rachel coughed, feeling like some perverted voyeur spying on him. She propelled herself forward and nearly fell into the river. She was embarrassed and could feel it burning in her cheeks. It was silly—she'd only caught him shaving; it was nothing compared to some of the sights Roxy had subjected her to this week. And yet this was John Smith standing in front of her half naked, in the middle of such a mundane task. John Smith, who could walk away from explosions. Who would come to rescue her or Charlie whenever they got into trouble.

She realised he was looking up at her, waiting for an explanation.

"I, eh, I couldn't sleep." A breeze skimmed the river, and she shivered despite her winter jacket. "Bloody hell, John, aren't you freezing?"

He shrugged. "I've been colder. I take it Charlie's still sat by the fire like an old cat." "Purring and everything."

He went to put his razor away and paused. "You can borrow it, if you want to?"

"You're kidding, right? I'm keeping all the insulation I can get. This winter is going to be brutal. Why are you even bothering? It's not like there's anyone here to impress. Unless you like being out here in the cold."

John pressed the razor into a tight leather pouch. "Every morning I wake up stinking of Roxton's filthy socks. That van is fucking ripe. It's bad enough we have to sleep in it. I'm not smelling it for the rest of the day too."

He had a point. They were all so used to the squalor, she didn't even notice it anymore. She hated to think how revolting she must look and smell. Her clothes were days old, and she couldn't remember the last time she'd done more than wash her hands and face. She bent down and tested the water flowing downstream. It was painfully cold.

"Maybe I'll put a pan of water on the fire before we go back to civilisation," she compromised.

John smirked as he fished his shirt from the bank and lifted it over his head. As he raised his arms, the thick, red scars on his abdomen stretched. Three strikes blemished his otherwise perfect skin. A severe reminder that, despite what Charlie thought, he wasn't indestructible. It felt like only yesterday she was stitching him up, her hands covered in his blood. *How the hell had he survived?*

He cleared his throat, and she realised he'd caught her ogling him once again. "Sorry, I didn't mean to stare. I just haven't seen them for a while. It looks like they're healing well. Can I?"

She ran her hand over the scars, feeling the ridges of the old injury. "I can't believe they've healed so quickly."

"I followed doctor's orders."

He had. A month's bed rest without complaint, but that couldn't be the reason his recovery had been so miraculous. She opened her mouth, ready to ask him why he thought he was still walking, when he pointed at the largest of the three scars.

"This one is a fucking disgrace. I could have done it neater with my eyes closed."

She took the hint. He didn't want to talk about the hows and whys. Not tonight anyway.

"Well, next time you're spilling your intestines all over the back of the car, you can sew them back in yourself."

"There isn't going to be a next time." The confidence was rich in his voice. Like his brother, he meant what he said, but unlike Charlie, John's words were his doctrine. He regarded her for a moment, then fastened his shirt. "What about you?"

She rubbed her own shoulder as her gunshot wound began to ache with the attention. The last year had taken its toll on them all.

"It's healed about as well as yours. I think, all in all, I'm fighting fit."

"And yet you're up two hours before watch."

"Roxy's snoring."

"Roxy's always snoring. I thought you'd have figured that out, given you always volunteer to take the same watch."

The connection she shared with Charlie was based on powers she didn't really understand. It wasn't the same with John. There was only understanding between them, and sometimes it surprised her how well he knew her.

"Nightmares back?"

"They never went away. Would you believe the noise helps? I wake up and hear him grunting beside me, and I don't panic. Or not as much anyway."

"And trying to go back to sleep is impossible," John said with a knowing look. He dusted the back of his coat before putting it on.

"After everything you've been through, I'm surprised you can even close your eyes at night."

He shook his head. "I don't really dream."

"What, not at all?"

They were skirting dangerous territory again, trying to decipher who or what John Smith was, but she felt she had to press on, especially since he knew all about her.

"What was it like, going back to a laboratory like the one you grew up in?"

"You don't want me to answer that."

"Let's say I do."

He picked up his gun and slipped it into the back of his belt. Then he sighed and looked at her with eyes heavy with regret and anger.

"It was like going home," he said and walked away.

4

From his bedroom doorway, Carson watched his niece finally succumb to sleep, the rise and fall of her emaciated chest just visible under his worn bed sheet. With his brother gone, she was all he had. And he was all she had. Lacy deserved better than a grief-stricken uncle to help her make it through the winter. She deserved a proper home, not a corner set aside in his one-bedroom basement flat. They all deserved more. Lacy was just another orphaned child in S'aven. He was just another bereaved father, brother, husband. There were no complete families left in town.

He made to close the door and caught one final look at her. With the covers pulled tightly to her chin, he could almost believe it was Danelle in bed, that his only daughter had lived past her third birthday and was resting soundly asleep. If he allowed himself to dally in the fantasy, he'd pretend he was waiting for his wife to return from the market with a piece of meat for Sunday. Sundays were days for gathering, when Leroy would bring his family over and they'd eat and argue and laugh. Carson could pretend that this world was just a nightmare and he still had a family and hope.

"Uncle?"

The dream was over. Carson sighed, almost in relief. What was already lost could not be taken away from him again.

For the fourth time that evening, Lacy sat up. She clasped the bed sheet in her fingers, beads of sweat forming on her bony forehead. Carson instinctively passed her a cup of water from the windowsill. It was the last of his supply. In the morning he'd have to queue with the other families now he had a child to support.

He sat on the bed beside her. "What's wrong?"

Lacy's wide eyes scanned the damp-stained wall in front of her. "I forgot where I was," she murmured. She sipped at the water. Everyone in S'aven had become so accustomed to the rationing it was automatic.

"Do you want to try and sleep again?"

She shook her head, and he had no intention of pressing the issue. Some battles weren't worth the fight.

"Are you hungry?"

They were all hungry, but Lacy shook her head. He offered his hand anyway and lifted her from the bed. Her body was dangerously light, just bones and heartache. He took her into his living space and placed her in the only armchair there. When she was settled, he removed a tin of protein from his depleted stock and slopped it into a pan to heat on his gas stove. He was used to skipping meals and donating his rations. Now he had Lacy, he would need to be more careful.

"It's chicken flavour, your favourite," he said.

The brown, jellified gloop popped and spluttered on the heat. The cans came in a variety of flavours, chicken being the least disgusting but no more palatable than decade-old dog food. Carson was sure the protein had never even met a chicken, which made the salty, mulchy aroma even more disturbing. He prodded at the block until it softened. The trick to getting it edible was heating it up just right. Too hot and the taste would be bitter, too cold and jelly blocks of awful would explode the moment they hit your mouth. He dipped his finger into the pan and pulled out a bowl for Lacy from the countertop.

Her enthusiasm for the meal matched his own, but she was a S'aven girl, and all S'aven children knew the importance of eating when they got the chance. Nothing could be wasted, not even dubious government-issue protein.

Carson watched her eat, ignoring the growls from his own stomach. Old men like him were used to going hungry. He had days before he had to worry about his health ailing. Lacy was the vulnerable one. She was already underdeveloped, small for her age with no fat to spare for the winter months.

She ate with methodical eagerness, and Carson was reminded of his brother sitting in a similar way when they were both boys. *Watch your brother*, his mother would say. And Carson would. He would sit and watch Leroy, two years his junior, consume everything he could find and still complain he was hungry.

Just like her father, Lacy ran her finger around the bowl until it was clean. She lowered her head, fatigue setting in once again.

"Why didn't the police kill me?" she asked when she was finished.

Carson knelt beside her. "Is that what's bothering you?"

"They killed my dad. I thought they would kill me."

"They probably would have. But Mark Bellamy, the man that helped you, he's not like the other police. He's my friend."

This was the first time Carson had told anyone about his relationship with Mark. He hadn't even told Leroy, for fear of his brother's outrage. The police were violent, ruthless and callous in their attacks. Even in peacetime, it was better to keep them at a distance. Like most Union men, Leroy had a deep distrust for them and anyone working with the government. But maybe if he had known, maybe he would have taken Carson's warning more seriously.

Don't bother with the rest of the leaflets. It's not safe. There could be another raid. We'll just use what we have.

"Dad says—said the police aren't our friends."

"In most cases your dad was right. But most police aren't like Mark Bellamy."

"He killed my dad. He was there when they shot him. He didn't even try to save him."

Carson took the bowl from her and placed it back on the counter.

"Let me ask you a question. Who was Leroy Mooney?"

"My dad."

"Now ask me the same thing."

She frowned. "Who was Leroy Mooney?"

"Leroy Mooney was my little brother. He's not a father to me, or a brother to you, but he's still both of those things at the same time. We think of him as what he is to us as individuals, but a person is more than just one thing. There's people out in the street that would tell you Leroy Mooney was a determined, intelligent, and righteous Union man. One street over, I know there's a man who will tell you Leroy Mooney was a scoundrel and a cheat. He was all those things and more. Father and brother. Friend and foe. All at the same time, all different depending on whoever is with him."

"I don't understand."

"In this world, we are never just one thing. Several of the police officers that murdered your dad were probably dads themselves."

"That doesn't make it right."

"Of course not. But it makes things more complicated. We look at the police like they're monsters. Why wouldn't we? They do some monstrous things. But it's not necessarily all they are. Then you get people like Mark Bellamy, who are being told to be one thing but become something else. He is a man with the Union at his heart. He believes in us and our cause, but he's also a policeman. And he can't stop being a policeman, not with things the way they are right now. So he has a uniform and he follows orders, but he also helps us when he can."

"He shot my dad. They all shot my dad."

"If your dad was told to shoot Mark Bellamy or let you starve, what do you think he would do?"

Lacy pressed her lips together.

"Listen, Lace, this doesn't change what happened. It doesn't make it better. But this world is not straightforward. And you must always remember that what you think about anything could be a very different story in someone else's view. It's important we look further than our own front door before we act."

"Then does the government have good reason for starving us like they're doing?"

Carson smiled at the question. It was just what his brother had asked him when they'd had a similar conversation.

"Think about it from their point of view. They see us as dangerous—frightening even. They are accustomed to a way of life, and we are proposing to threaten it. We are standing on the other side of the wall and telling them that they must share. Demanding it."

"But they have so much."

"They will only see how much they have when they realise how little we have. It doesn't necessarily change things, but we're no better than they are if we only care about our own interests."

"We're going to go to war, aren't we?"

"I don't know. There's a lot still to decide. And it's certainly not something you need to worry about."

A sudden banging on his front door made them both start. Lacy grabbed his hand, holding him at her side in terror.

"It's okay," he said, recognising the curt rhythm rattling the frame. "I know who it is."

He prised himself free and grabbed the door before it was hammered through. Riley Banks, another of their London bin crew, stood in front of him. Riley had been a huge, hulking man; now he was like a withered tree, a piece of rusting cable holding up his trousers, his jumper flapping in the wind.

"Shit, Cars, is it true?"

It was strange to think that a year ago Carson, Riley, and Leroy were laughing and singing their way through London's refuse. Hard work, good pay, decent homes; how suddenly everything can change.

"It's true," he said.

"Leroy. Man, I don't believe it. Not—" Riley saw Lacy and stopped.

"Lacy's living with me now," Carson explained.

Riley gave her an awkward smile, something bordering on sympathy and encouragement and ending with a pronounced grimace. Riley was a dedicated Union man, but he left the public speaking and propaganda to the Mooneys. He was happier guarding a door, keeping watch for police, than engaging with folks.

At least let me send Riley out with you.

"I should have been there," Riley said.

"He was insistent he didn't need you." Carson rubbed at the curls on his head in frustration. There was a ball inside of him that wanted to sob and scream. His brother was dead. It hurt so much he couldn't allow himself to feel it. There was still so much to do and no time to waste mourning those gone. Not when all their lives were on the line. Leroy died fighting a battle. Carson owed it to him to finish what he started.

"They destroyed all the leaflets he made," Carson said. "Do me a favour: go around the houses, spread the word we need to recycle what we've got, re-purpose anything we can. Word of mouth, anything we can do to keep the meetings running."

"Sure thing."

"And then come back here and sit with Lacy. Leroy got me a spot on the radio yesterday. I have to go."

"Radio? Really?"

"Leroy was an ambitious man. He reckoned if we could get on the air it would make spreading the word easier. Starr Talks apparently wants me to go up against Hargreaves-Smith in a battle of words."

"That governor in charge of the border? Well, that's going to be embarrassing. That twat can't string two coherent sentences together. You're going to wipe the floor with him."

"I hope so." Carson didn't match Riley's confidence. He could talk and he could believe in himself, but without his brother's ingenuity in his corner he couldn't imagine how they were going to possibly get anywhere.

5

When Charlie had awoken the day after the Grandchester bombing, his ears were still ringing. He stretched, the couch beneath him groaning in protest. He kicked out his leg to stir his brother, but John's sleeping bag was empty. Charlie sat up, spraying the sofa with dust from the hotel. He needed to shower. But first he needed to find his brother.

He stepped over a carpet of takeaway containers and anime porn and checked the kitchen. Staying in Jay Stanton's mother's basement wasn't ideal, but Jay did have a state-of-the-art coffee machine that had placated John most mornings. Charlie expected to find him there, soothing his bad temper, ready to regroup and rethink. They still had a job to do, and it was going to take more than a collapsed building to stop them—at least that was what he was planning to start with in his pep talk.

Only John wasn't nursing the coffee machine. Charlie scratched his head, displacing more dust and dirt from yesterday. He went back to the sofa, found his phone wedged between the cushions, and called John. Straight to voicemail.

"Hey, where the hell are you?"

His chest started to tighten. He hadn't checked John for injuries when they got back. He could have a concussion, an internal bleed, anything. And he knew what John was like. If he was in pain or distressed, he wouldn't ask Charlie for help. It wasn't in his nature to play patient; he'd try to fix himself. Charlie already could see him crawling out into the city streets, his body giving out in some alleyway somewhere.

He grabbed his boots and heard the basement door open and close. When he looked over his shoulder, John was standing there holding out his hand.

"Done," he said. He gave Charlie the memory chip they were supposed to have recovered the day before.

"How did you get this?"

John shrugged with a smirk. "Coffee?" He disappeared into the kitchenette at the back of the basement.

Charlie charged after him. "Seriously, how did you get it? You found Daniels, right? Is he still alive?"

John washed up two cups from the counter, seemingly undisturbed by the thick brown coating staining the sink. He put them under the coffee machine and switched the machine on. There was an unusual swagger in his movements, a relaxed cockiness he probably deserved after all that had happened yesterday. "Is Jay going to pay us today?"

"When he wakes up."

"Start making some noise. I want to get moving."

"What's the hurry?"

"London's a shithole." He thrust a cup of coffee at Charlie.

"Then I guess it's time to move out."

"Seems that way." He looked up expectantly.

Charlie felt a sinking feeling in his gut. John's good mood suddenly made sense. He was ready, and he expected Charlie to be too.

He'd made a promise to John, a promise he repeated night after night when the skies were cold and the land was black: one day they would have their revenge. One day they would return to the Institute and tear apart the cells that had confined them. He promised that those who had tortured them, experimented on them, would be given no mercy. The Institute would feel the brunt of their creation, and they would repent all they had done. But Charlie wasn't ready, and he dreaded disappointing his brother.

They got paid. Eventually. They hit the road. John's good mood continued, Charlie's plummeted. They had deviated from their path before. Right at the start, weeks after their escape, when John had wanted to fight, Charlie pulled his brother away. They were too young, too inexperienced. What was the point in returning to the Institute only to be recaptured? Much better that they develop their skills, become something nobody could predict.

So they grew up roaming the country, picking fights with gangs and violent men, honing their skills. And on the way they met Father Darcy, who brought the boys back into civilisation and opened Charlie's eyes to their real potential in the world.

Potential was something to work towards.

Potential was another diversion.

Charlie had deviated again, finding work stealing and tracking and manipulating. They made money. They made connections. Their reputation grew, and Charlie's ego matched it. He couldn't help himself—he was having too much fun. His ambition got the better of him; he wanted to do more, to try more. Going after the Institute became an afterthought. But not for John. Never for John.

"Hey, let's go see Darcy before we move out," Charlie said as they cleared the border check.

"What for?"

"We've got a bag full of money. He'll appreciate it."

"Just leave it at the drop point."

"Look, I want to see him, okay?"

Reluctantly John took a left off the border lane to the old station housing Darcy's nomadic church. Charlie unclipped his seat belt. John kept the car running.

"You're not coming?"

"I'll go get supplies. No point in hanging around here longer than we need to."

Charlie decided to let his brother's church phobia slide. A couple of minutes alone with Darcy would help settle his panic. He grabbed the bag, hopped out the car, and jumped back as John revved the engine and sped off.

Charlie didn't subscribe to religion, but he did find comfort in Darcy's counsel. He stepped into the makeshift church, as always a prodigal son. The chairs circling the altar were all different, all battered. Each accommodated a different style of Bible. Religious texts were hard to get hold of these days. A woman was laying them out, humming an out-of-tune song he thought he should know. She was covered with a thick cardigan, her hair pinned up clumsily. He coughed and she turned, expectant rather than startled. In a matter of moments, all of Charlie's worries were tossed aside. This was Sarah, and he'd divert his whole life for her.

The memory still made Charlie shiver. He closed his eyes, savouring that first meeting, before it dissipated. He'd let Sarah down; now he was going to do the same to his brother. He would have to tell John the truth. He couldn't do it. He couldn't go back to another Institute facility. And he would have to suffer all of John's frustration. That didn't bother him. His big concern was what John would do once he'd calmed down.

John's entire life had been driving towards one purpose. If Charlie took that away from him, would he accept defeat? Or would he be defiant? Charlie couldn't imagine his brother without his need for revenge. John's life had never existed without the Institute. What would he have if Charlie took that away from him?

It was all such a mess, and Charlie was furious with himself, with the world, for allowing this to happen. If he hadn't returned to the facility and confronted his nightmares, he wouldn't have realised how afraid he was. But he had been forced to walk those sterile corridors, and now he knew he would never be able to do it again. It had all been for nothing.

God has a reason for everything. That's what Darcy used to say. Bringing down the Institute would be a fitting destiny for them, but it seemed they were no longer fated to storm a facility in one glorious final stand. Although the more he thought about it, the more he doubted their stand would be anything more than a quick, meaningless end. The Institute had already destroyed two of their own bases—would they really feel the loss of a third?

Maybe the quest to go full circle and return to the cells they had escaped from was part of the Institute's plan. Could John's determination be residual programming? If he thought too hard about it, he'd have to work out exactly what his brother was. Territory they all preferred to stay away from.

When Charlie closed his eyes he visualised the white walls and bright ceiling light. He realised with a chill that he had never really escaped. He had kept a part of himself in that cell. He had circled the Institute and had the audacity to be surprised when they caught him again and again. He was an idiot. They both were. They were never going to fight the Institute from within. If their destiny was to take down the organisation, then it needed to be some other way. Glorious. That was the key. But it was still a pipe dream, and until he had something better to offer his brother, he would hide in the passenger seat of their van.

"First hot meal we've had all week, and you're burning it!"

Charlie looked up at John frying off meat cubes on a rekindled fire. Roxy was hovering over his shoulder, critiquing from a dangerous proximity. John threw Roxy a murderous look.

"It's caramelising," he replied coolly.

"It's not a bloody apple, love. You know burnt food gives you cancer." Roxy took out his cigarettes with one hand and tried to fish a cube from the pan with the other.

John rapped his knuckles with his fork. "If you don't fuck off, you won't live long enough to get sick."

"Ow! That really stings, you dolt."

"Dolt? What are you, a hundred years old?" John snorted and returned to his cooking.

Charlie waited for Roxy to retaliate. Instead, he seemed to think better of it and retreated to the van, rubbing his blistered knuckles as he went. He hauled himself into the driver's seat and showed Charlie the already fading red mark on the back of his hand.

"Your brother gets so touchy about his bloody cooking," he said. He regarded Charlie for a minute and then pushed forward the question they were all probably desperate to ask. "So where are we shipping out to next? I don't know about you, but I am itching for a decent pint and a fight that actually, you know, happens."

Charlie still had no heading. He needed more time to think. "I don't know. We might just go back to Wales."

The humour fell from Roxy's face. "Oh, pet, you're having me on."

They were all going to share Roxy's sentiments. In Wales there was a safe house they could ride out the winter in, but it came at a cost. They had already wasted three months recovering there, listening to their hosts constantly bickering. The farmhouse was cramped, the space they were offered little bigger than the back of the van, and under constant rainfall the house was practically a prison.

And yet where else could they go this close to winter?

"All our files are there. We can go through the Institute records again, see if we can't find another heading. Maybe by the spring we'll have something."

"The spring! Now I really do need a drink." Roxy leaned closer, full of conspiracy. He lowered his voice. "You know, we could just do a regular job. Something to keep us out of real mischief for a while. There are so many things worth stealing, Charlie. And we're very good at that. Why not blow off some steam and then head back to sheep-shagger country with a victory under our belts?"

It wasn't a bad suggestion. They had geared themselves up for a big battle, and having an outlet would ease the monotony of the winter months. But going back to their old ways would be a clear sign to John that they were abandoning their mission again. Charlie couldn't do that to him so brazenly. He needed to steer John away from a head-on collision with the Institute and offer him an alternative that satisfied them both.

"No," he said. "We've wasted too much time as it is."

Roxy groaned and flopped back into his seat. He lit up his cigarette and blew rings of smoke in the air nonchalantly, as though he was happy to go along with whatever Charlie wanted. Charlie wasn't convinced. He liked Roxy, but his friend came with his own agenda. He belonged to Sarah. She had brought him into their fold, and now she was gone he couldn't help but question why Roxy stayed with them, especially when they were pursuing an enemy that didn't concern him.

"You don't have to come with us," he reminded Roxy. "This isn't your fight."

"Is this a polite way of telling me to bugger off?"

"No. But the Institute aren't after you. And if you stay with us it'll probably get you killed."

"It'll be better than choking on my own vomit in some S'aven back alley," he said. "Besides, I've already proven I'm a difficult man to kill. Maybe I'll be your secret weapon."

"I can't offer you anything for sticking with us," Charlie said.

"Don't worry about it, love. I know the score. I don't need incentive."

"Roxy, you need incentive to get up every morning. You're not here out of the goodness of your heart."

"No. You're right. Sarah was my dearest friend. I owe it to her to help you. And it's the right thing to do. Also, in case you didn't know, I'm very much at a loose end at the minute. At least with you guys, I get one *caramelised* meal a day."

Roxy gestured at the windscreen. Rachel was bringing them two tins of meat and vegetable paste. She elbowed Roxy's window until he opened it.

"What, no cola? What kind of drive-in are you running?"

"Shut up and eat." She shoved the trays onto his lap and went back to get her own. "I do love it when she gets all domineering."

Roxy dabbed a cube in paste and glanced back up at John and Rachel by the fire. It was subtle. Too subtle to mean nothing. Suddenly his dedication to their cause made sense.

"You two have been getting close." Charlie couldn't conceal his disapproval.

Roxy paused mid mouthful. "What's that, pet?"

Charlie coughed and cleared his throat. He wasn't Rachel's father; he had no authority to interfere in her relationships. "You and Rachel, you seem to be close these days."

"Darling, we spend twenty-four hours living on top of each other. I don't think we have much say in the matter." He shoved another cube in his mouth and regarded the fire again. "Would it be a problem if we did get... closer?"

Charlie didn't know. He had nothing against Roxy personally, and if anyone could handle his antics it was Rachel. But the idea of them together seemed wrong.

"No, I guess not."

"Well, I'm invigorated by your enthusiasm."

This was a conversation that would never end well. Charlie reached for the radio to interrupt them before it went too far. The speakers hissed with violent static, a stark reminder of the barrenness of the northern territories. Then a woman's voice blared into the cabin, making them both jump.

"*Chancellor Hargreaves-Smith, you've been border chancellor since the gates were closed. Can you foresee any possibility the border will be opened before the new year?*"

Charlie tweaked the volume louder. The last time they were in Safe Haven they were stuck in the middle of the first wave of rioting, which sparked the civil unrest. Charlie could still feel the heat from the burning buildings as police and protesters clashed in the streets. They were lucky to all make it out alive. He'd purposely stayed out of touch with the south since. From the sound of things, it was a good decision.

Roxy nudged him excitedly. "You know, Li Starr is a real piece of work. Used to come into the club, she was like a Rottweiler if she smelled a story." He nodded at the radio as if the sound of her voice would back him up.

The woman—Li Starr, apparently—was talking about a new wave of protests, rising from the London/S'aven workforce, after the riots. London's borders had been closed more than open in the past few months, throwing both the city and the surrounding slums into a tense stalemate.

"*The situation in London is such that it will take time before normality is restored. And, quite frankly, the endless protesting and assaults on the border gate are only prolonging the situation. The people of S'aven should be asking themselves what purpose the Union could possibly have in continuing to put unnec-*

essary pressure on London. Their relentless targeting is tantamount to terrorism, and it is not unrealistic to expect a number of so-called Union men to be involved in other terrorist extremism," the border official boasted.

Starr interjected, "What would you say to that, Mr Mooney?"

There was a pause. When the next voice came, it was quieter, calmer, more assured.

"If I may, I'd like to ask the chancellor a question. Chancellor, what did you have for lunch last Tuesday?"

"I don't see how that is relevant," the chancellor replied.

"Perhaps you don't remember. What about yesterday? Or today. It's midday. I imagine you had breakfast. In fact, I am certain when you awoke this morning you had something with your coffee before you started your day. Am I incorrect in my assumption?"

The chancellor made a passive mumbling.

"Would you like to ask me the question, chancellor? Would you like to ask what I had for breakfast? The answer, I suspect you know, is nothing. The last time I ate was last Tuesday. And I'm one of the lucky ones. Since the border closed, London has systematically attacked Safe Haven—"

"That's preposterous."

"After the first week of protests, London emptied our ration houses. After the second, you cut off our hospital supplies. By the third it was our water. Union men and women, S'aven men and women, have been standing in front of the border gate with the audacity to will an end to this madness. The terror does not lie with us. The blame does not lie with us. The state turns to terrorism when it needs to dampen our ambitions. But I put it to you, sir, that London is the terrorist threat in Britain. And it is London that needs to address her behaviour."

There was another pause. A longer one. Charlie stared at Roxy, disbelieving what he was hearing. All media was strictly moderated. This man, this Mooney, would never normally be allowed a public voice to condemn the capital city.

"Did he just say that?" Roxy asked.

"Did they just let him say that?"

"My apologies, listeners, we've gone off topic. Chancellor, let's talk about the threat that the border patrol are currently up against."

The change in subject was too awkward to obliterate the moment Mooney had created. "She allowed him the platform," Charlie said. "This is a step up from sex scandals."

"Oh pet, she was never after sleaze. Li was all about exposing corruption. And she always had a rebellious streak." Roxy clapped his hands in approval.

"Who's this Mooney guy? I've never heard of him."

Roxy scratched at the scraggy beard around his chin, picking out bits of moss and dirt and meat. "You wouldn't have. While we were flitting across the border with boots full of cash, men like Mooney were lining up waiting to cross legitimately. Union drones, that was what we used to call them. Street cleaners, handymen. Useful people London needed and permitted across the greener grass. Mooney headed up the Union that kept them all working. He was a small fish. Bit of a dreamer. If one of our girls got caught in a predicament over in London, he'd help us get her back, but all strictly above board. Of all the people you'd expect to lead the charge, it wouldn't be him."

"It's always the quiet ones. Still, sounds like things are getting rough down there."

Roxy snorted. "Things in S'aven have always been rough. The Union guys are just used to being better off than the rest of the scumbags, and they're finding poverty hard. Can you imagine what they would say if they saw what we just saw? They don't know how kind this bastard world has been to them."

The idea crackled like lightning through Charlie's mind. *What would they say?*

Even Reachers themselves never understood the horror of their fate until it was upon them. Without being subjected to the experiments, being confronted with a long demise and swift execution, without smelling the furnace, it was impossible to comprehend what the Institute was doing. Did the government really know? Or did they just subscribe to the same bullshit scare tactics and leave it in the hands of mad scientists and warmongers? *The state turns to terrorism when it needs to dampen our ambitions.*

What if the girl on the slab were broadcast to every television set? What if all his files were published in the papers? What if they started talking about the truth on the radio? The Institute had done everything they could to manipulate the public, quashing any possible speculation against them. But what would happen if someone exposed them? Someone who had nothing to lose.

"Of course, you'd expect Li to be involved. That firecracker shows up to break all the big stories. Probably the last good journo out there, if there is such a thing as a good journo."

"Do you still have her number? I've got a story for her."

"No offense, darling, but I'm not sure we've ever done anything we should be broadcasting to the country."

Charlie started to smile. "Maybe not yet. But we will." His ambition was growing again, morphing into an epic, exciting plan. He had to think big. He had to think about more than his own needs. And it came to him in an instant. He knew exactly what would shake the foundations of the country and turn everything on its head.

6

The eastern shoreline had become a graveyard of discarded plastic. Piles of refuse bleached in the winter sun, their vibrant colours ebbing with the departing waves. A strip of road stretched over the beach and out to sea. The morning was bitterly cold, the view across the ocean just visible against the mist. A shadow perched on the horizon at the end of the bridge, a distant, forgotten island. Scarlet flexed the growing stiffness from her hand and slammed the car into gear. The sea was slipping away, the old road beckoning her forward. She hit the accelerator, kicking up sand and plastic debris in her wake.

As she drew closer to the island, the structure beyond the monument became visible. Sheets of glass and metal hid behind the ancient stonework: the island's secret, the new heart of the Institute. Before, when she was just a project, the Institute was fragmented, built up of contradictory theories and ambitions, sandwiched together by a government obsessed with Reachers. Individual, independent facilities had been scattered all over the country, buried deep in secure bunkers under the protection of mad scientists and even madder soldiers. But the intention had always been to consolidate, to amputate failure and regroup in one dynamic hub once the time was right. Now was the time.

Scarlet felt a stirring of anticipation whenever she returned to the island. This was, after all, what she was made for. And yet a nagging pain in the back of her skull stifled all her excitement. She felt the tide lapping at her vehicle, threatening to close in on her, and she contemplated that this might well be the last time she challenged the waters.

The road rose as it approached the monument and the secrets inside. To her right, she caught the glint of an armed guard trailing her position. She pressed a call through on her phone, transmitting a code exclusive to her. The passageway would be clear. She surged ahead, and seconds later the island was hers. Shadows moved from the stonework, soldiers keeping watch. She pulled up the car and clenched the steering wheel.

The pains were worsening. Cramps in her arms and legs accompanied an almost constant throbbing up her back. Inside they would have medicine to ease her condition, but they would also be tracking her doses and how frequently she was beginning to rely on them.

The wind whipped at her face when she opened the door, the clouds in the sky churning black. Scarlet marched steadily against the weather until she reached an opening in the wall. A solitary soldier awaited her. She was known to them all by sight but still presented her finger for scanning. He waved her through.

She crossed the open courtyard just as the hail struck. The building resting within the abbey was sealed with another fingerprint scanner. Most of the soldiers guarding the surface had never seen what lay in the depths of the island, and she felt curious eyes watch her as she disappeared inside.

The new facility was supposed to be a break from tradition, but despite the modernity of the structure, it followed a familiar Institute pattern. The floors beneath the ground were built in layers: rooms for personnel, rooms for administration. Then, in the bowels, were the Reachers, those important enough to be retained in the grand downsizing.

Scarlet's heels smacked harshly on the floor as she made her way to the lift. She waited until the doors had closed before she rubbed the tension at the base of her skull. The lift seemed slower than usual, drawing down her precious seconds. When it opened, she hurried through the corridor, pushing a junior scientist to the wall when he got in her way.

The man she needed was at the back of the facility. The door was open, welcoming—as welcoming as the facility got anyway. She launched herself at it as though her limbs were about to betray her. It was melodrama and foolishness, but she knew only too well that desperation lay in her future, even if it wasn't quite upon her now.

The man she sought was sitting in the office. He was small and stocky, a thick layer of white hair covering his skull. His skin was unnaturally pale, his eyes wide and grey. His name was Khosh, and Scarlet had known him all her life. He looked up at her blankly.

Scarlet felt a strange apprehension overcome her. She could deny what was happening to her body for a little longer, but she'd seen others do that, passing the point of no return before they needed to. She didn't want that. She wasn't built for waste. And she still had a mission to complete.

"I need another top-up," she stated.

Khosh's shoulders slumped. He bowed his head, defeated. "Already?"

She understood his disappointment. She was his last surviving subject. Her death would determine his great project a failure.

"Have the headaches started?"

"Yes. But not the tremors."

"I thought we might make another year." He pushed at the pen on his desk.

Khosh had watched ten subjects die over the past decade, some quicker than others. When he'd discovered the defect, that their bodies had become dependent on the cocktail of chemicals that elevated them into perfect soldiers, it was too late. They were all infected. All damaged. Over time he had managed to extend the lives of some, but it came to nothing in the end. The grand plan of his old mentor, Mary Smith, was over. And his continuation of her research was a bust.

Scarlet pulled up a chair from the other side of his office. "It may not happen as quickly as the others."

"Your body is going to perish regardless."

"Not if I bring back John Smith."

When Khosh had inherited Mary Smith's project and subjects, he hadn't even picked up John Smith's file. The boy was no longer part of his research, and it was up to the army to hunt him down. But Khosh soon learned that John Smith was more than a plucky escapee. There were tissue samples, bloodwork, detailed records that showed John responded differently to the others. He existed without reliance on medicines and elixirs. He was special. He was essential to finding the perfect being the Institute were seeking.

"You're weaker now."

"Only physically. I can still think clearly, and I know John, I know his weaknesses.

His brother, all we have to do is—"

"When the board learns of your condition, you will not be allowed to leave."

Scarlet pressed her lips together in annoyance. They couldn't pull her away now.

Soon John would show his face again. She needed to be ready. "Then don't tell them."

"They're our superiors."

"And when I get John Smith back here, everything they have been working for, everything you've worked for, will click into place. We'll have it. We'll have what we need."

"If you die—"

"I won't."

Khosh held up his hand to silence her. "If you die, your body must be recovered."

He was right. Even dead, Scarlet would betray secrets.

"Then I'll take Johnson with me. If anything happens to me, he can make sure I am disposed of correctly."

Khosh twisted in his seat.

"Without John's body, how long will it take to perfect the virus without any side effects? Years? Look at this country. Do we have years to waste? This is our chance to fulfil our potential. You know I'm right. And you know that I will bring him in. This time I'll find a way. Whatever it takes."

Khosh took a key from his pocket. He turned his back on her to open the cabinet behind his desk. He pulled out a small vial of clear liquid. It seemed strange that such an insignificant thing could be the key to her survival. Methodically, he pressed a needle into her arm, and in an instant her body was starting to relax.

"Do you even know how to find the brothers?"

"Johnson's in S'aven now. I'll join him there. The brothers will pass through eventually."

"You better hope they do it in the next few months. I give you seven at the most." Scarlet nodded. Seven months was plenty of time.

7

"You want to do what?" John's attention was fixed on Charlie. He sat forward, shoulders tense, jaw clenched. A tiger ready to strike at its prey.

Charlie refused to waver under his brother's piercing stare. He believed in what he was saying; he just had to convince John. "I'm going to head down to S'aven and open the border."

A crease dented John's forehead. His eyes narrowed, searching for something in Charlie. "What?" he repeated. He shook his head and turned to the others around the camp to share in his disbelief.

Charlie stood his ground. He had a great power, a power that had so far been squandered on petty crime and a fool's revenge. But he could do more. He could open the border between London and S'aven and change everything. He could show everyone what Reachers were capable of. He could change the world for his kind.

But first, he had to convince his doubtful brother.

"We want to destroy the Institute. Not just for what it did to us, but for what it does to all Reachers. But we've been thinking too small. Taking down a laboratory isn't going to mean jack shit to them. They've killed more of their own people than we ever could."

"So what? We just give up?" John snapped.

"No. We think bigger and cleverer. We've been seeing the Institute from the cell we were kept in. But they're far more than that. They're part of the government, part of London, of the fucking elite. If we want to take them down, we have to hit them where it will hurt them most."

There was a slight softening in John's eyes. He was interested, if not convinced.

"All of their power comes from fear and propaganda. The lies they tell about us keep us separate from the rest of the world. We've spent all our lives in the shadows, believing it was only a matter of time before someone reported us. And that's because they got in our heads. We're so used to running, we've never even considered the possibility of standing our ground, of being who we are."

"And opening the border will do this, will it?"

"People in S'aven are desperate and dying. They need something, *someone* to come and change things. If we ally ourselves with them, they could unite with us against the Institute. Their attitudes towards Reachers could change. If we open the border, we show them our power and we give them our respect—and in return they support our cause."

The tension in John's face was back. "You've lost your fucking mind. They'll just call you a terrorist, and this time they'll be right."

Charlie grabbed his wrist. "Not if we make the Institute files public. If we time it right, it will be more effective than any physical assault we can launch. Think about it, John. Darcy always said we had a purpose. What if it was more than just revenge? What if we're supposed to open the border and change this country for good?"

"Don't bring Darcy into this. He was more deluded than you are." John sucked in a breath. This was difficult for him. Charlie was asking him to forget their whole plan, the idea that had fuelled them both for so long. And he was asking just as they had got back on the right track. John had been begrudgingly patient, letting Charlie have his family instead of going straight after the Institute. Too much time had already been wasted, and now Charlie wanted to divert away permanently, to scrap their plans altogether. He expected John to walk away, treat Charlie to a few days of brooding silence before he saw sense.

But John had changed over the past few months. Instead of meeting Charlie's proposal with stubborn hostility, he seemed to be considering it.

"Can you even do it?"

"I don't know. Possibly. What have we got to lose?"

"I'd say dignity, but you lost that years ago," he said.

Charlie hadn't expected to be victorious so easily. He turned to the others, beaming. "So, what do you think?"

"I think you've taken too many hits on the head," Roxy said. "But hey, if it means we don't spend any more time in Wales than we have to, I'm in."

"Rach?"

Standing behind John, Rachel pushed her hands into her pockets. "Have you seriously thought about this, Charlie? If you open the border, what do you think is going to happen?"

Breaking down the border would stop the barrier between rich and poor. It would give S'aven a fighting chance for equality. For liberty.

"It would be war, Charlie. That border comes down, and London and S'aven go head to head. There's no coming back from that. You get that, right? Look what happened when we closed it. The rioting, the anger—that was only on one side. Now you're talking about letting people who have nothing to lose go up against people who have everything and don't want to share."

"The alternative is we let the government have that hand. Do you think they won't open it when it suits them? This whole country is gearing up for war, and believe me, the odds are going to be stacked in favour of the rich and ruthless." The more he talked, the more he felt like he was delivering a prophecy to them. The more opening the border seemed like something that had to be done.

Rachel stared at him, fear and uncertainty shining in her eyes. Charlie gave her his most reassuring, confident smile. He rose and placed a comforting hand on her shoulder. "Trust me. I know what I'm doing."

8

The station shook with commotion. Mark led his team through the front doors into a throng of prisoners and officers. Punches were thrown. Mark felt a boot strike the back of his leg and fell forward. A Union man blocked his way, stopping him from hitting the ground. Mark grabbed him and shoved him out of the way. His riot gear was heavy, drenched in sweat and blood.

He sidestepped into the changing room and exhaled, enjoying a break from the chaos of the station foyer. It was shattered seconds later as the rest of his team piled in behind him. They kicked off their vests and helmets, pushing and shoving each other until their residual adrenaline was spent.

Mark took a seat on the bench and started to unbuckle his steel toecaps.

"Did you see that fucker's nose when the bullet hit it? Fucking hell, that was nasty. Snot and blood. Minging." Fry slumped down at Mark's side and beamed at him. Fry was like an excitable child after every raid. He bounced on the bench, recounting moments he grossly exaggerated until the rest of the team tired and told him to beat it.

"Bellamy, did you see that girl that Doogie got?"

Mark glanced up at Doogie. He was ex-military and barely spoke. If there was a fleeing woman or child, you could always count on Doogie to take them down. He liked to get them in the back, just before they escaped his range.

"And you got that runner. Man, I thought he was getting away for sure."

Mark felt a pause settle on his body. He did kill a man, but he didn't want to think about it in the station. At the station kills were badges of honour, and Mark couldn't engage with that sort of pride. Better to pretend it was nothing until he got home and could confront his shame and grief.

"Fry, do you always have to hover over me when I'm about to get changed?"

The comment sparked a wave of childish mutterings from the others. *Queer boy.* It was enough to launch Fry away from everyone immediately. He pulled open his locker, exposing a collage of abnormally large breasts and buttocks, a blatant statement of misogynistic heterosexuality to anyone who would challenge him.

Mark turned away, facing his undecorated locker and the rust creeping up the shelving there. He dressed quickly, eager to shed his policeman disguise and flee the thin blue line he was forced to walk.

The changing room door opened again, and a new set of officers strode in. A regular beat patrol of eight, all men drifting towards forty with scarred faces and boastful eyes. Their confidence faltered when they saw Mark's team. Like so many in the station, Mark recognised the officers from his days as a lowly PC. But they looked at him like he was a stranger. He supposed he was. PC Mark Bellamy died in a work camp years ago. Agent Bellamy was a force to be reckoned with, a killer, a danger.

"Bellamy?"

When he looked, Doogie was waiting to get past. In the olden days, Mark would have been pushed aside by bigger brutes in uniform. Things had changed. Here he had respect. Doogie, a man twice his size and ten times as ruthless, was waiting for him to step back. Mark stood his ground a second longer than necessary, then let Doogie through.

"You going home, Doogie?" Fry asked.

"None of your fucking business, Small Fry," he said, knocking shoulders with the younger man.

"We should all go for a drink, right guys?"

"A drink where?" Mark said. "Curfew's in place. Everywhere is closed."

Fry frowned. "Shit. I forgot. There must be somewhere."

Mark thought about Lulu's club, flames licking at the velvet curtains. Most places had gone that way.

"The whole town is fucked," Doogie said. "I'm going to bed."

Mark pulled on his jacket. For once he agreed with Doogie. He followed the man out, nodding his head at Fry on the way. Fry was an irritating son of a bitch, but Mark kept everyone onside. When he got out into the open air, Doogie stopped him.

"Hey, I do know a place," he said. "Beer and girls, if you're interested."

He wasn't. "Sorry, mate, maybe next time. I'm beat. I'm going home."

But as he walked away from the station, he realised he was lying to his teammates again. He had no home. S'aven, London, the station, his flat, they were all just locations that tolerated his presence. Soon, he was sure, he would outstay his welcome.

9

Rachel hated S'aven. She hated the cramped tower blocks, stacked full of desperate families working long, unsociable hours. She hated the stinking pollution that lingered over the town in thick clouds of smog. She hated the endless, riotous noise: the sirens, the shouting, the crying. She hated the blackouts. The violence. The desolation. Mostly she hated the fact they were going back there.

S'aven was broken and dying. It had been for as long as she had known it. She had witnessed the first eruptions of dissent when she was starting her first year at the hospital. Over time it had worsened. On their last visit much of the town was on fire, the residents raging in the streets with smashed bottles and lost hope. It was strange to think this visit could end the town altogether.

The van rattled, then struck a deep pothole. She fell sideways, and Roxy fell on top of her. He was heavy and clumsy and managed to elbow her twice before clambering back to his knees.

"Whoopsy-daisy, sorry, pet," he said and resumed his rummaging through the piles of bags pushed in the back of the van. "Aha! I knew he had one."

He pulled a black top from John's rucksack victoriously and pressed it to his nose.

"What are you doing?"

"I have a reputation to uphold in S'aven. It's important I look my best. Now close your eyes, it's about to get sexy in here." He peeled his own T-shirt off and slopped it into John's bag.

Rachel rolled her eyes and wished, not for the first time, that they had a bigger van. Being cramped inside with the three of them for the past month was starting to take its toll on her patience—and sense of smell.

"Do you think Charlie knows what he's doing?" she said.

"Charlie never knows what he's doing."

"That's what worries me." Rachel rested her head against the back of the van, unable to quash the ball of tension in her stomach. "And John."

"Why would we be concerned about John?" Roxy slumped beside her.

"You've not noticed? He's nicer. Easy-going. Has been since he got hurt."

"He hit me with a fork this morning. That's not nice."

"Before, he would have tried to shoot you."

Roxy conceded.

"And he wouldn't have gone along with Charlie's plan. Not this easily. I don't know, neither of them seems right, and this plan is big. Really big."

"You don't think it's a good idea."

"I think it could get us all killed."

"Pet, not to be pedantic, but you were willing to go down fighting last night in an Institute laboratory. What's the difference if you die in S'aven?"

She really didn't want to die in S'aven. That was the difference. "Aren't you worried what will happen to you?"

He shrugged. "I was utterly convinced I wasn't going to make in past twenty-seven. Like a rock 'n' roller. Figured I'd piss off the wrong gangster or die in some bizarre bondage accident. Everything post twenty-seven is an unexpected bonus."

"Which you're choosing to spend cramped in the back of this stinking van with me." That made about as much sense as Charlie's plan. "Seriously, why are you coming with us?"

Freshly dressed in John's clothes, Roxy sat back down. "Honestly? When Sarah introduced me to the Smith brothers, she was convinced they were going to do something amazing. What can I say, I'm a convert and dutiful disciple. Charlie can open the border, and he will. If I'm there, if I see it happening—well, I'll be dining off that story for the rest of my years." He pursed his lips as he regarded her. "You know, I could ask you the same question."

"I can't leave Charlie," she told him honestly. "The bond between us is too strong now. Most of the time I want to slap him, and yet the idea of being away from him, of anything happening to him, scares the shit out of me."

"Would you two ever, you know, become more than friends?"

The question was so absurd she started to laugh. "With Charlie? Hell no. I'm reckless enough to follow him, but I haven't lost all my common sense."

"This Reacher connection sounds very inconvenient."

"Actually, it's pretty good. Being with Charlie is like being back with my sister. I feel complete." She rested her head on his shoulder. "If he does it, he's going to be famous." The possibility made her nervous. Rachel preferred to slip unnoticed through the world. It was the only reason she was still alive. The limelight was dangerous, and Charlie's ego was drawn to it.

"He's already infamous. A little legitimacy might do him some good. He could be like Jesus, only with a duff leg and shittier facial hair."

"Do you think he wants to be famous?"

"I don't know. Sometimes I think he does. Sometimes I think he's sensible. He made a name for himself when he worked in S'aven and London. That's how the Institute caught up with him. One would hope he's learned a lesson somewhere."

"But if there's no Institute…"

The van shuddered to an abrupt stop. A flicker of nervousness passed over Roxy's face. He pushed a wide, fake smile and nodded at her. "After you, pet."

Before she could reach for the door, John was pulling it open. He looked at Roxy, at the shirt he was wearing, and said nothing. The grave look on his face was chilling and made her stomach lurch. She looked over his shoulder at familiar buildings. They were parked outside Lulu's—Roxy's mother's nightclub—at least what was left of it. The main entrance was charred and exposed, the brickwork collapsed and blackened by the fire ignited at the bar. Inside, a season of rain had forced the three floors above to collapse, leaving nothing but a pockmarked ceiling hanging precariously over the scorched dance floor. The fire had spread across the two neighbouring buildings, and vandalism and looting had stripped what was left.

This felt worse than discovering the girl in the laboratory. She knew this club, and she knew what it meant to her friend. She turned to see him standing frozen outside the van. His eyes darted over the skeleton of his mother's legacy, and he paled. They were supposed to find sanctuary here. Roxy had been certain one of his mother's girls would have seized the place as her home and would offer them a drink, if not a bed for the night. Rachel cursed his optimism. They'd seen the club burn; it was foolish to imagine the place was salvageable after that.

She reached for his hand, but he was already walking, heading to the concrete shell to assess the damage. Where he'd once swaggered like a king, he now roamed stunned across what had been the club's stage. Rachel could remember him up there, serenading an audience of drunkards and deviants before the first of the flames took. After that it was a blur of heat and blood. His mother at least was safe, but her home and business were in ruins. Without her, the building was nothing. So where did that leave its heir?

She watched Roxy as he nudged at charred wood with his foot, his usual bravado and confidence wilting in the late afternoon sun. His tangled mess of blond hair covered his face, hiding the worst of his feelings. Rachel didn't need to see it though. She could guess what this sight was doing to him. The Institute had stolen something from all of them, and Roxy's association with Reachers had left him wide open to attack too.

"We need somewhere else to stay," John said quietly to her. "We don't want anyone knowing we're here."

"I'll go speak to him."

Rachel's relationship with Roxy was less complicated than his relationship with the brothers. Roxy had met them through Charlie's late wife, and he still blamed Charlie for Sarah's death. But Rachel came to the party afterwards, and their friendship wasn't tainted with heartache—at least not yet. For all Roxy's flamboyant flippancy, he'd been a pillar for her over the past year. It was only fair she return the favour.

With the brothers out of sight, she made her way into the building. It seemed like a lifetime since she was last in this place. A lifetime since Roxy commandeered the stage, belting out tune after tune with a supporting brass band that was about to be publicly decimated by an erupting riot. A lot of people died that night.

Debris crunched under her heavy boots. With each step the overhanging beams and supports creaked threateningly. She approached the stage, feeling an overwhelming urge to get the hell out of there before the building collapsed. But she stood her ground, hoping to draw Roxy out with her.

"Sweep the floor, restock the bar, and we'll be up and running again as normal," she said.

Roxy blinked as though seeing the place for the first time. His eyes met Rachel's, and he cracked a sad smile. He dusted his hands and jumped down. Rachel winced as the whole building groaned with the impact.

"Doesn't look like we'll be staying here tonight, eh, love?" His bravado was shaking with the surrounding walls.

"You got any other ideas? We need to stay off the radar for as long as possible."

"One, but I don't imagine it looks much better than this place."

Roxy mooched back to the van and tapped on the driver's window. He murmured a new destination to John and got back into the van. Rachel followed him.

"All things must end, right? At least Mother isn't here to see this. It would break her heart," he said as she closed the door on Lulu's.

"Are you okay?"

"I'll survive. I did survive." He took a deep breath and fumbled for his cigarettes. "And Mother did. It was just a building. It couldn't last forever. Nothing ever does."

She pressed a kiss to his face and wrapped an arm around him. "You've still got me and the others."

"Please, pet, I'm trying to get out of this depression."

On the exterior Roxy was all innuendo and foolery, but inside he was deep and complex. The destruction of his childhood home would likely hit him in waves over the next few days. She would watch him closely, like she watched the others. She'd carry him through. After all, he'd carried her often enough in the past.

The van slowed again, and Rachel held her breath. If the outlook was as dire as before, she wasn't sure any of them would be able to cope. It was Charlie who opened the door this time. John was still in the driver's seat, engine running. She blinked in the light. In front of her were rows of concrete storage units. The boxes stretched out in all directions. A breeze carried the acrid stench from the nearby factories that dominated the estate, seasoned with sea salt from the docks. Rachel stepped out of the van and scanned the scene. It was exactly as she had left it two years ago, so why did it feel different?

"You okay?" Charlie murmured.

"Déjà vu," she said.

Roxy grabbed a pair of bolt cutters from their kit. He took a deep breath and gestured them to follow him to the storage unit he'd once rented.

"I'll warn you now, it's not going to be pretty," he said.

As Rachel remembered, last time it was filled with boxes of unsellable pornography, illegal hooch, and a badly stuffed tiger. She'd stayed in worse places since. Roxy cut the lock and paused.

"You know, I reckon I might know a guy who could put us up."

"We don't want anyone knowing we're here," Charlie told him. "This'll do."

"If you insist, love." Roxy pulled the hatch door open. The van's headlights shone inside. Roxy's old clutter had been cleared out. The walls were exposed and scorched black. All that remained was a chair. And tied to the chair was a blackened corpse.

Behind them, drawn to the sight of death, John got out of the van. "Who the fuck is that?" he said.

Roxy scratched his head sheepishly. "Donnie Boom. You remember. Crazy Scotsman, face almost as ugly as his personality. If you remember, he tried to torch mother's place and I was hellbent on revenge. In retrospect, I suppose it was all a bit pointless."

Rachel remembered Donnie Boom. She remembered his scarred, barbaric face as he grabbed her and stuffed her into the boot of his car. She could also remember Roxy selling her out to get his hands on this man. That was a long time ago. So much water had run under the bridge it wasn't even the same river anymore. But two corpses in one week was too much.

"You just left him here?" John said.

"I had no intention of coming back. Two years left on the lease. It was a perfect coffin. And it's still a good spot to hide a van—plus Donnie's not so bad, now he can't talk."

"I'm not staying if he's staying," Rachel said, gesturing at the body.

"I'll get rid of him." John went back into the van and took Roxy's sleeping bag and his machete. Roxy followed him inside and closed the garage door, dampening the sound of the hacking.

Rachel turned away, the smell of charred flesh and decay blistering her nostrils. The journey to S'aven had been long and arduous. She'd foolishly allowed herself to fantasise about a warm shower and proper bed. Another night in their van, sharing a garage with the ghost of one of S'aven's infamous pyromaniacs, felt like a kick in the gut.

"Hey," Charlie said. "I've been thinking about how we're going to do this with maximum impact. I'm going to try and track down this Mooney guy, see if he'd be interested in forming an alliance."

"An alliance? The Union pride themselves on legitimacy. They're hardly going to jump into bed with Britain's most wanted."

"As always, you underestimate my charming nature. I'm going to take John with me."

"Well, that will certainly help the charm offensive," Rachel murmured.

"We'll open the gates, and then we go to ground quick. The Institute will be all over this place. I want to make sure we're clear before they show up. Roxy's going to touch base with this journalist friend of his. He'll give her everything she needs to blow the Institute wide open. We'll watch it unfold from the safety of the farm. Then plan our next move."

She nodded. "You sure you don't need me to come with you? I can make them more amenable without having to wave a gun about."

"No. There can be no question about free will. If you're there, then there will always be an uncertainty about whether you've influenced anyone or not. Besides, we need supplies for the road and eyes around town. You can hide in plain sight and pick up things we can't."

Rachel cast one last look at the garage. A night wandering around S'aven might not be so bad.

10

S'aven had been Roxy's. He was born in the blue room of the infamous Lulu's with a cabaret accompaniment, his birth mother one of the many lost girls who had come to town to seek her fortune and found herself on the game. Lulu's was his childhood home, and when his birth mother left, the lady of the house—the mistress of S'aven—took him on as her heir. He learned to walk on the sewage-filled streets. Learned to talk with bartering punters. The town had contaminated every part of his life, and he liked to think a piece of himself was firmly engrained in the brickwork of this pretty ugly place.

But in his absence the town had continued to grow and change, and this evolution had occurred without him. There were faces he didn't recognise, faces that did not recognise him. Places that had been fixtures in his history had ended, leaving gaping holes in the streets he had once thought of as his own. As he traced familiar paths, his steps became hesitant and cautious, and it dawned on him that this was no longer his home. S'aven would not welcome him as it had once done. His reign was over.

He turned a corner, and his feet scuffed on the cracked pavement. The building in front of him was a ghost of what he remembered. He wanted to see the gaudy sign proclaiming great food and service. He wanted to marvel at the oddly proportioned dragon twisting awkwardly around the words Lucky Charm. But it was all gone. Even the sign that boasted Real Chicken Not Cat was lost. His favourite takeaway restaurant, closed until further notice. Boards were nailed to the outside of the building, broken glass still heaped on the pavement like fresh dirt over a new grave. Rats scurried through holes in the brickwork, victorious now they had won their tenancy over the former owner.

Roxy took a step forward and flinched. A distant explosion bounced across the surrounding streets, and the rats fled. He wasn't immune to bombings, but not this close to the border. He straightened his jacket, keen to be back with Rachel, and dared to cross into rat territory, making his way towards the back of the building and the entrance to the bedsit flat above.

Li Starr was waiting for him, her black bob swaying in the wind. He remembered her being edgy, full of London style and S'aven bravado. And he was relieved to find she, at least, was largely unchanged by the situation they found themselves in. She'd swapped her bold makeup for a single swipe of purple lipstick and traded in her trouser suit for two thick cardigans, but she stood as tall and proud as ever, sucking on a cigarette like she was doing it a favour. When she saw him she smiled, blowing a stream of smoke from the side of her mouth.

"Well, well, well, James Roxton, aren't you a sight for sore eyes."

He imagined at the very least he was a sight. She embraced him anyway, and he found a sudden comfort in the contact. Li was part of his old life. Living, breathing, even thriving in the new world. She was looking well, considering the conditions she was existing in. Her hair was streaked with a grey strand or two, her eyes creasing slightly when she smiled, but little else betrayed her fifty-fifth year. When Roxy was younger he'd harboured a very intense crush on her. If his situation was different, he might have even considered pursuing her again.

"Come on in. I can't promise it will be warmer, but I've got gin."

"Mother's ruin. Lead the way, darling."

She climbed the stairs first, her cardigans parting briefly, exposing a small pistol concealed behind her back.

She was living out of two rooms. One a bedroom, the other a makeshift recording studio kitted out to broadcast an analog signal as well as an online stream. She hesitated at the studio, then closed the door, leading him instead to her personal room and offering him the seat beside her bed. The setting was bleak, ingrained with the smells of fried oil and damp. She poured him a drink in a tin cup and offered him a cigarette from a battered old silver case.

"My brother owns the building," she said, putting one in her own mouth. "Told me if he caught me smoking here, he'd turf me out and take my equipment as a deposit. Coward bailed last week, pinned a note to the door telling me I could wire him the rent payments until he got back." She offered Roxy a light.

"I told him he could go fuck himself. If he wants the rent he can grow a pair of balls and come get it."

Roxy let the sweet nicotine fill his chest. Rationing his smokes had stopped him enjoying them, almost to the point he was considering quitting. This small moment of bliss reminded him how miserable he'd be without them.

"I've been listening to your show. Seems like you're the only voice of reason out there at the moment."

Li dismissed him with a wave of her hand. "Most days I'm the only voice at all. Ratings are dropping every day. Government has been shutting down transmitters all over the country. They want us off the air, but not so swift it looks like I've been shut down deliberately. Soon I'll just be broadcasting to space."

Her worry was good. If she felt like she was on borrowed time, she would be interested in a life-changing story, something that could cement her career in the history books.

Roxy toyed with the cigarette, letting ash singe the stained carpet. "Maybe you will, or maybe you'll experience a surge in listeners."

She pursed her purple lips with intrigue. "Which brings us nicely to why you called me. After your mother's stern words last time we spoke, I didn't expect to hear from you again. But then I've seen the club, what's left of it. Perhaps you have some secrets that no longer need protecting."

Roxy reached into his pocket and pulled out a memory chip Charlie had given him. It contained everything they had uncovered about Reachers and the Institute. Murder, experiments, torture. Right down to the pictures they had taken at the last laboratory.

"Sweetheart, I have something that will blow everything else you've ever covered out of the water." He took her hand and pushed the chip into it.

"Six years ago my best friend was butchered in her kitchen. Her daughter was kidnapped, stuffed into the back of a government vehicle which later crashed, killing her too. They both died at the hands of the Institute."

Li's eyes widened. The chip rested in her palm like a piece of dirty glass.

"My friend was not the first. She wasn't even the second. We've only scratched the surface of what the Institute are capable of, but so far there are four hundred other victims we've discovered. Innocent people, people who did nothing wrong. They're all on there. Institute files, records of what happened to them."

She was paling, the danger of the moment rich in her face. But Li was ambitious too. This was a story, a real story, and Roxy could tell she was hungry for it. "Reachers?" she asked. "We all know what happens to them."

"Believe me, pet, you don't. And you have no idea what Reachers are, nor what they're capable of."

Her fingers closed around the chip. She'd taken the bait.

"Something big is going to happen here, and it will change everything. You now have the answers to all the questions people will want to ask. In a few days everyone will be listening to your voice."

Li necked her gin and poured another. "What's going to happen?"

"You'll see."

"Come on, Roxy, I need more than that."

"You've got everything you need. Look at the files. Get the story ready."

"Jesus, how the hell did Lulu's little boy get himself involved with all this?"

Sometimes Roxy wondered that himself. It started with Sarah, of course, but that part had been over a long time ago. Now it was more complicated. "It concerns people I care about. The Institute needs to be stopped."

"People you care about? Or a particular person you've gotten yourself involved with? Please tell me you're not involved with a Reacher."

Roxy grinned. "Fine, I won't tell you."

"You're off your fucking head."

"Always have been, love." Roxy cleared his throat and knocked back his drink. "In a few days the biggest Reacher event since Piccadilly is going to take place. It's going to be huge, Li. And it will change everything. The story belongs to you if you want it. We're not talking about quick headlines or bloody ratings. We're talking about going down in history as the one who exposed the most corrupt organisation in British history. You could be the woman who told the world what was really happening here."

"Why did you pick me?"

He gave her a knowing smile. "Well, darling, you're this side of the border; that helps. You're a very competent journalist. And aged fourteen I would have done just about anything for you."

She laughed. "If this is what you say it is, I might just let you."

"Will you do it?"

"I will. It will probably get me killed, but we can't live forever, now, can we?"

"Good. I better go." Roxy placed the cup on her bedside table. He kissed her cheek and rose. She caught his hand before he could move away.

"What's your role in all this, James? How deep are you?"

He let out a laugh that sounded strange on his ears. "Don't worry about me, pet. I always walk away in the end."

11

There was a hum in S'aven. It fizzed like electricity through the city, crackling and hissing in secluded corners rife with conspiracy. Areas once populated with crime lords and gangsters now rippled with whispers of politics and revolution. S'aven was transforming, shedding her dried Mafioso cocoon to mutate into something very, very different. Charlie had never seen a hive of activity like this. He remembered streets filled with thieves and murderers. But those scoundrels had been replaced by a new kind of hostility. Disgruntled Union workers, men and women that had once been too good for S'aven slums, controlled these poverty-stricken streets. The closed border had forced them into unemployment—a situation which was starting to become desperate. And desperate times called for desperate measures.

Charlie could spot factions of new Union-affiliated gangs loitering on each corner. They varied in age and appearance, huddling together at strategic points throughout the town, glancing suspiciously about. Despite the tension buzzing off the pavements, there was an eerie calmness about the night, as though the presence of the Union was keeping everything in check. For now.

Union meetings were conducted in public. It was a standard practice, the idea being transparency created trust. It made the Union men easy to find, easy to follow, and easy to disband. Speeches had to be monitored, toeing a line that bolstered their ill-feeling whilst simultaneously upholding the law. Charlie would have had more luck juggling fire. He did, however, appreciate the sentiments of the organisation, even if it was destined to fail.

They found the latest meeting in the exposed interior of an old bank. A bomb had ripped through the building's hull, and years of weathering had softened its edges. What remained was the strength of the building, and what gathered inside was the strength of S'aven.

Hundreds of people wedged themselves as close to a makeshift stage as possible. Charlie could sense their anger, but there was no danger of a riot tonight. This was a stewing pot. Potential only. He pushed his way through the audience, his leg brace hissing with each laboured step. John followed close behind.

On an upturned crate in the centre of the building was a man conducting the audience.

"I know you all are struggling. I see it. I see it in your eyes. You're worried. You're thinking about your kids, the little ones, the sickness we can't seem to shake. And I know those across the border are saying that Union men are prolonging this strike. That we are keeping the gates closed deliberately. Let me ask you, is there a person here that would not willingly return to work the day that barrier is lifted?"

The crowd in unison replied, "No!"

"And I ask you too, is there a man here who is to blame for that border closing?" The answer was the same.

"We, friends, are the casualties. We were loyal to London. And what do they give us in return? Nothing. But we are not nothing. We are not slaves. We are not worthless. Each of you here has a right to work, a right to feed your families. We are more than scraps. We are better than cast-offs. And we deserve more than such. We keep their world turning, and it is time we are recognised."

A cheer reverberated through the crowd. It was intoxicating. Charlie closed his eyes. He couldn't read people like Rachel could, but here, in this moment, he sensed each and every person, and he was with them. He felt a tug on his arm and looked down to see a girl pressing a leaflet against his chest. The face of their speaker was printed on the front. Just the man they were looking for.

He nudged John and gestured to the speaker. "It's him," he said, showing John the grainy picture of the Union leader, Carson Mooney.

Mooney had settled into middle age with little signs of aging or corrosion, which was more than could be said for Charlie. Like the men and women around him, Mooney was dressed in quality clothing that had worn away over the years. But unlike them, his eyes shone with vibrancy and determination. They would follow him because he was strong. Defiant. And he would speak for them because he was truly devoted to the Union and equality in S'aven.

Charlie, even with all his Reacher abilities, would never hold such an audience under his control. He could barely keep his party of three engaged for more than a few minutes. Mooney's power was way beyond anything Charlie had anticipated, and the possibility of working with Mooney was now a necessity.

Charlie looked at the men and women, rapt and awestruck under their leader. The starvation they were surviving, the disease they were suffering, the desperation crushing them would not shackle them to submission. For the first time in his life, Charlie understood how men like Father Darcy could command such a room. It was all about the word, and if the word was true, it would work miracles.

"What do you think?" Charlie murmured to his brother.

John was the only person in the room unaffected by Mooney and his speech. He stood, unmoved, more interested in the crowd than why they were there.

"I think he's going to get a lot of people killed."

Charlie agreed. But revolutions were built on sacrifice, and many of these people would by dead after the first snowfall of the year anyway. Under Mooney's leadership there was a real possibility of change. Charlie couldn't deny that he too was getting swept up in the excitement.

"Brothers, sisters. We've been trudging in our parents' footsteps for far too long. We've carried their loads, allowed our own futures to be tainted by servitude to that city. What can we do now? For ourselves? Nothing. But you think of those you've got waiting for you. Those in need of medicine. Of nourishment. You think of them in years to come and what this world will offer them. People, London's border may be impenetrable, but so are we. United, my friends. We are the Union, your Union. We will endure."

The audience hooted, raising themselves taller with his words. Nothing had changed. They would still go home to the same misery, but this man had invigorated them for another night, encouraging them to survive and return again for another dose of optimism.

Mooney jumped down from his pedestal. Behind him tables were being set up, a queue forming as volunteers started distributing a meagre stack of food crates. Charlie expected a desperate grab for provisions, but the opposite happened. Meals were divided and then quartered until everyone was able to walk away with something. He even saw people surrendering their allocated portions, grateful mothers and fathers sobbing at the generosity.

With the talks concluded, Mooney weaved through the endless faces, shaking hands, making contacts. Some received whispered words, others stern glances. And all the time the pamphlet girl followed him, distributing information.

There was a gap in the crowd. Charlie seized the opportunity and surged forward. He caught Mooney's attention and stretched out his hand before the Union man got spooked. "Those were some powerful words," he said.

"Never underestimate the power of the truth," Mooney replied with caution.

Clad in thick winter coats and boots, Charlie and John stood out. Their closeness to Mooney had caused a tension in the crowd. Who were these well-dressed strangers? These men with violence in their auras? To make any kind of impression, Charlie wanted to speak freely, and for that he needed privacy. He leaned in closer to Mooney, keeping his body relaxed and open.

"My name's Charlie Smith. This is my brother, John. If you could spare us a minute of your time, I'd appreciate a word."

"Are you police?" Mooney stiffened. His eyes darted around his people, checking in with the likely heroes who could sweep in and save him.

Charlie put on his most genuine smile. "We are definitely not police. And it would be in all our interests if the authorities didn't see us together. Like I say, it will take a minute, and afterwards, if it suits you, we'll walk away, never to be seen again."

Mooney nodded at the girl handing out flyers, then gestured that Charlie and John should follow him to the back of the building.

The bank's vault had been blasted open years ago. The door was long gone, the interior metal stripped and repurposed. All that remained was a brick box, wet from a leak in the ceiling above. It stank of piss and worse, but it was private.

Out of sight of his adoring public, Mooney's composure hardened. "If you're not with the police, who are you?"

Charlie appreciated his hostility. Naïve leaders never lasted long.

"We are supporters of the Union, and we would like to offer our services to help you in your effort."

Mooney folded his arms, his doubt blatant. "The Union's always looking for donations from people able to spare a meal or two for the cause. Lots of families in need at the minute; each day things get harder."

"Charity will just prolong the problem," Charlie said bluntly. "You keep them fed and subdued and eventually they'll be too weak to fight. The Union will be over before Christmas. The only thing that is going to save them is getting that border open. If they can go back into London, this fight becomes relevant. London can't ignore you if you're in her garden."

Mooney tightened his threadbare coat. "I see, you're from the border patrol. Well, you're not the first turncoat to try and make money off this. I'll tell you what I told them. We don't trust you, and we don't want your help."

"Mr Mooney, we are not involved with the border patrol. We're not part of the police, or the government, or anything that stands in your way." Charlie raised his hands, and the discarded brickwork on the ground rose with them. "But we can open the border."

Mooney stumbled backwards, his dark eyes wide. He shook his head frantically. "We have no interest in affiliating ourselves with terrorists. Get out!"

Charlie had anticipated this response. The Union were solid as long as they were operating on the right side of the law. Affiliation with Reachers could destroy them, which was why everything needed to move quickly and quietly.

"They called you a terrorist too. I seem to remember you didn't like it. You asked a lot of good questions on the radio. I've got one to ask you. What do you really know about Reachers? I know what the government tells you, how dangerous we are. They're saying the same about the Union at the minute. Don't you think they'll eventually do to you what they've done to us?"

Mooney swallowed, his Adam's apple bobbing nervously in his throat.

"We are all at the mercy of their lies if we don't challenge them. Is that fair on our kids, growing up in a world where they suffer because they are born in the wrong body or on the wrong side of the wall? My daughter has already been murdered at their hands. How many more kids have to die?"

Charlie stepped closer. Each moment they were all together there was a chance someone would spot them. "I can open the border. I can take away the control they have over you. Think about it. You take your people to the gates and suddenly there is no barrier.

London is open to all, as it should be."

Sirens pierced the night air. Time was running out.

"Why would you do this?" Mooney asked.

"I'm tired, Mr Mooney. I've been running my whole life, and it's time to make a stand. We are very different men, but I see the same persecution happening here. As long as we are divided, we are weak. But together, well, men like you and me can change the world."

A closed border had a devastating impact on S'aven—but if that border could be opened at will, if the Union could state the terms of their migration without London controlling them, they would hold the power. Charlie could see Mooney processing the potential of his offer.

"London would retaliate," Mooney said, but it was an afterthought, a small hurdle to conquer.

"Sure, if we open the border and storm the city, but that's not what we're going to do." Charlie flexed his fingers, and the bricks around them began to shake again. He relaxed his hand and sighed into the silence. "Real power is about control. I can open the door. I can take away their blockade for you. But you can choose whether that means war or whether you walk away."

A crease furrowed Mooney's forehead. Charlie couldn't gauge what he was thinking. He glanced at his brother. He'd opted for brawn to back him up, but now he wished he'd brought Rachel instead. She'd be able to read the Union man; she'd know the promises Charlie should make.

"These people aren't used to this hardship," Mooney said. "They know they're dying, and they're afraid. Maybe a grand gesture like the one you're offering would lift them. But you're asking them to put their faith in a stranger. A Reacher. As desperate as they are, they are still law-abiding citizens."

"Would you be able to convince them otherwise?"

Mooney laughed. "It's all I can do to keep them from rioting now. But I confess, I'm interested in seeing what you can do."

That was good enough for Charlie. "What do I need to do to get the others' attention?"

The noise from the bank was dying down, the sirens getting louder. Whatever Charlie could do, it wouldn't be tonight.

"Give them hope. They're tired, they're suffering. And there is no sign of respite. Look at them: they are surviving on quarter rations; they go home to freezing houses, sick families. Where is the hope there? An open border is potential they can't believe in. You want them to follow you to that gate, give them something that proves you are more than a Reacher terrorist."

Charlie understood. Asking them to rise up and challenge London was like asking a beaten man to take one more punch before dying. An alliance built on dependency and desperation would collapse at the first sign of difficulty. But if they believed there was a brighter future, they would never stop fighting.

"Uncle?" the pamphlet girl called from the exposed doorway. "The car's waiting. The police are nearly here."

"Come to our next meeting," Mooney offered. "I'll give you a chance to speak. But I'll warn you, don't expect miracles."

The Union man moved away like a king, back towards his loving people. Those that passed him made a point of shaking his hand and listening to any words he offered them. They adored him. They would fight for him. With power like that, Charlie could have taken over the country by now. But he wasn't made for leading men, and he certainly couldn't be trusted with that kind of responsibility.

When Mooney was out of earshot, Charlie turned to his brother. "What do you reckon?"

"I reckon you're going to get a lot of people killed," John said, stuffing his hands in his pockets.

"Don't be an asshole," Charlie said. "Seriously, what do you think?"

John shook his head. "Criminals I get; these people… what's their end goal?"

"Survival. Just more modestly than the people we're used to dealing with."

"Well, at least they're used to disappointment. It won't be such a shocker when you can't open the border and we all get shot in the head."

"Aren't you in a good mood today. I can do it. I know I can."

"Then why do you need the walking dead backing you up?"

"I don't need them backing me up. I need an audience who will back Reachers over the government. We're talking about changing history. The moment has to resonate with the right people. But first we've got to charm them into backing us."

John shrugged. "We've got a van full of money. You might as well give it to them before Roxton steals it all."

Charlie shook his head. "No, this has to be something bigger. Something more meaningful." And in an instant he had it. "Remember the boat that Darcy used to use to ship Reachers out on?"

"You're fucking joking."

"Same time every week, Spain to England. Think it's still making port?"

"This is not a good idea."

John gave him a look, one of those *Sometimes I wish you weren't my brother* looks.

Charlie beamed back. He had the perfect plan.

12

The change in S'aven hit Rachel in cold shivers as she made her way through town. Her powers made her invisible to those around her but not immune to the degeneration of her former home. S'aven had always been a dark place. A town built on misfortune had no option to be anything else, but this time things were different. She could feel the suffering in the brickwork, the pain rising from the cracked tarmac. S'aven was dying. And despite all this place had done to her, had taken from her, she found she was sorry to see it this way.

Her boots crunched against the shattered glass glittering on the pavement like fresh snow. The shops lining the street were boarded up or kicked in, selling only dust from their ransacked shelves. She twisted her fingers as she walked, hunting for any tormented souls looking to block her path. It was strange. The street was empty.

Even in the bleakest winters, the road heading towards the market was crammed with S'aven locals looking for a scam. She'd regularly fought through crowds of shoppers to get across town. Now the way was clear. She crossed the road and spotted two men hovering at the corner. They stood as though on guard, their woollen hats hiding their weathered faces. They didn't see her—she made sure of that—but surveyed the crossroads shrewdly. She passed them unnoticed and took a left into S'aven's market.

What was left of it.

Day or night, the market had been the violent home of commerce and corruption. Men and women screamed and raved about new stock, knock-offs and rip-offs. Dirty notes were pressed into dirtier hands. Deals were done. Wallets were lifted, thieves were beaten. And amid it all, slum tourists queued for an E. coli burger in a bun. It was never quiet. Never still.

Until now.

Rachel stared at the graveyard of stalls. The wind whipped against stray flags desperately clinging to abandoned frames. Amid the desolation there were pockets of trade. The trinket sellers, the jewellery makers—those that sold things nobody needed—sat optimistically looking for business. As though having no other business in their way would elevate their wares to something beyond pointless.

She walked to the nearest stall, looking at the pitiful display of wired earrings rusting in the display cabinet. The woman operating the stall was old, her fingers thick and swollen with arthritis. She coughed, a dry, empty noise ricocheting across the market place. There was nothing here of use.

The only other option was the ration house.

When she'd lived in S'aven, she opted for rations over haggling with traders every time. But back then money was tight. She lived frugally to keep herself under the radar, to keep a little aside in case she had to get out of town quickly. The government supplied enough reasonably priced protein meals to keep a girl with simple tastes healthy. Once a week she'd join the winding queue and wait patiently for a share of sustenance, ignoring the cramping in her overworked legs and the blisters on her overused feet. God, she was glad those days were over. As the wind strengthened, she pulled her collar up and hurried southwards.

Six blocks down, she rounded another corner and stopped. The ration house was dark. Chipboard panels covered the door and windows, *CLOSED UNTIL FURTHER NOTICE* crudely written in red across them. Rachel felt a chill that ran colder than the wind. Even when things were really bad, S'aven could fall back on the ration house. It was S'aven's heart, keeping the town alive when the other organs failed. She stared at the useless building. The sooner they got out of town the better.

Going back to the van empty-handed annoyed her. Going back to the van at all made her mood entirely sour. She fingered the notes in her pocket and remembered a neighbour from the old days who sold cigarettes and hooch from his flat. If she couldn't bring back proper supplies, at least she could cheer Roxy up.

It was too easy to lose herself in familiar footsteps, tracing a path through her history. A lot had happened since she left S'aven, and yet she could still remember the weight of her legs after a shift at the hospital, trudging through icy puddles of grime to get home. Exhaustion numbed what the cold couldn't, and despite the bombs, despite the thieves, despite the Institute, she always made her way back to her little sanctuary. And now she was standing under the shadow of her former flat block, a stranger to those days.

The tower block and its seven neighbouring sisters filled the darkening skyline. Twenty stories high, hundreds of apartments, thousands of people, all crammed together in one poorly constructed concrete structure. Few people in S'aven could afford the luxury of such a place, but her job in the hospital and Mark's position on the police force had elevated them just above poverty. It had been more than she had ever hoped for, but ultimately it wasn't enough to keep her in town.

Residents moved in and out of the building, faceless people who had once shared her path. She had been one of them before, but that time had passed, and although her life on the road was hard, she was free. She was in control of her own destiny. The futureless men and women shuffled aimlessly about the base of the block—then one caught her attention. His slow stride, the broad curve of his shoulders, the way he carried himself with determined hesitance. It couldn't be. He was living in London, surely. She looked closer. It was him. He moved into the tower, and she had to follow him.

She hurried to the entrance door, catching it before it closed. He was already above her, trudging up the staircase. She bounded after him. He toyed with a set of keys as he walked. Did he live here now? That didn't make sense. When she last saw him, Mark had been with the PCU, working from London for the Institute.

Unless.

When she last saw him, he'd betrayed the Institute. They ordered him to kill Roxy, but he couldn't do it. So he lied to them. He told them Roxy was dead, and they believed him. At least they *had* believed him. Did they now know the truth? Did they know Roxy was still alive? No, that couldn't be the case. If they knew Mark had lied, he'd be dead himself, not demoted to a S'aven flat. Something else brought him here, and she couldn't help herself—she had to find out what.

She shadowed him up the stairs, using her powers to conceal herself. Two floors short of their old apartment, he stopped and curled to the right. When he came to his door he stopped and looked back where he'd come, as though he could sense her following him. She waited, concentrating on staying hidden until he opened the door to an unfamiliar flat and disappeared inside.

Rachel fell back against the wall, her stomach sinking. When she'd thought he was in London, she could pretend leaving him had been for the best. Sure, she'd walked out on him, broken his heart, nearly ruined his life, but he ended up living in London. He was promoted to agent. He had a real shot at a good future.

But if he was back here, his life had come full circle. Back to this monotonous hell.

He didn't deserve to be here. Certainly not alone. And it was all her fault.

Before she knew what she was doing, her hand was knocking on the door. She had no idea what to say to him or if he'd even want to see her. But she knew she'd never be able to leave S'aven if she didn't offer her help.

The door opened. Her breath caught in her throat. Mark stood there, and the air around them changed. He was changed from the memory she carried of him. The childlike naiveté had gone from his eyes. In its place was a knowingness she had ignited, a sadness she had fuelled. And a kindness she never deserved. He stared at her, his face conveying a myriad of incomprehensible emotions. She wondered if she looked similarly dumbstruck. She certainly felt it.

"Rachel," he said, his lips quivering under the weight of her name.

There was a lot to say. Apologies, gratitude, explanations. Anything she could think of didn't seem worthy of the moment. She stepped forward and did the only thing that felt natural. Her arms slipped around his waist, drawing him against her. She breathed in a smell she had forgotten and sank deeper when he matched her embrace. He stepped backwards, leading her inside, and slammed the door shut, sealing them off from the rest of the crumbling world.

They stayed together, clinging to each other until eventually Mark released her. He stepped away, letting out a pensive, nervous laugh. She remembered this side of him fondly. He ran his fingers through his hair, battling his nervousness with uncertainty. It was infectious.

Rachel felt colour rise to her cheeks. She had thought about Mark a lot when they were in Wales. Remembering who he was, imagining who he'd become. Now she was standing before him, and it was like looking at a parallel version of the man she had lived with. So like him and so unlike him.

"What are you doing here?" he finally said.

It was then she realised her being here was possibly the worst idea she'd ever had. She was a wanted woman. If anyone even suspected Mark had talked to her, he would be sent back to the work camps before the first snow fell. She'd put them both in danger for no good reason.

She started to panic. "I don't know. I came to get supplies, and I just saw you here and I had to come up. This was a silly idea. I'm sorry, I should go."

With her right hand she caught the door; with *his* left, he caught her. His hold was gentle but strong.

"Don't go," he said, his voice little more than a desperate whisper. Then his eyes met hers and he seemed bolder. "Not if you don't have to. Stay for a little while. It's safe. I promise you, I never get visitors here."

She wanted to. And not just because she didn't want to return to the van and the tomb-garage with its lingering smell of burnt flesh. She wanted to stay with him for a little longer, to relive the only part of her past she found comfort in.

"I'll put some tea on," he said before she could respond. He retreated to the kitchenette and filled the small kettle with water.

The flat was almost an exact replica of the one they had shared. It seemed bigger, but it only had Mark's possessions, and since his incarceration he'd downsized considerably. When they lived together they had splurged on a bed to fill their living space. It was one of the few indulgences they'd ever allowed themselves. That had been lost when Rachel fled S'aven and Mark was arrested. Mark's flat hosted a small, battered sofa in its place. Rachel sat down there, surprised at how comfortable it was.

She watched Mark make the tea. In their flat the kitchen had been packed with tins and jars that they'd salvaged over the years. Now he was living with two cups and a solitary teaspoon.

"What are you doing back here, Mark? I thought you'd made a life for yourself in London."

The muscles in his shoulders tensed. "A life for myself? No, not in London. London's not a place for people like me. I didn't belong there."

She understood his sentiments. She hated London, and she had no desire to head back there any time soon.

"When I got back here, the gates were already closed. They haven't really opened since."

"Not even for Institute agents?"

He glanced at her, guilt rich in his eyes. "Not for ones like me. They closed my department the moment I got here."

That was no surprise. PCU was run by Wade Adams, a disenchanted Institute agent who saw past their propaganda. Adams took down the Reachers that broke ranks, men like Charlie who wouldn't settle with a life in hiding. He pulled Mark out of prison, offered him a job and an opportunity: punish Rachel for leaving him. Then it all fell apart. Adams was a man of integrity, intent on doing the right thing and not just following orders. When he was forced to pick a side, he picked Charlie as the lesser evil and died for his cause.

"You lost your job." She didn't even try to hide the relief in her voice.

It was premature. "Not exactly."

He brought the tea over, handing her the cup that wasn't chipped.

"I thought I might. Then, when they didn't fire me, I thought they were going to kill me. Sometimes I kind of wish they had. Instead, they gave me a new job."

"What kind of job?"

He gestured to the window pensively. "The unrest here, it's out of control. Worse than I've ever seen it. People are actually talking about civil war again. I don't know—after the things I've seen, it's possible. London's not relenting; the Union won't stop fighting. There's only one way this is going to go. London have set up a task force at the station, and the Institute made sure I got on it. We're supposed to shut down unauthorised Union activity, but you know what it's like here. We do what we want. Cause more trouble than we stop."

It was strange seeing him so enlightened. When he was a beat cop, he believed in the badge and what it stood for. It didn't even occur to him his colleagues were bigger crooks then the criminals they were butting heads with. She liked this change.

"So your job is riot control?"

"As far as the station are concerned. The Institute are less concerned with stopping the unrest. They wanted someone on the ground. I crack skulls with the rest of the team, and when their backs are turned I pass information on to the Union."

It was a dangerous position to be in. S'aven police were tight and loyal. Mark had already been convicted of the murder of his partner, and nobody at the station cared that he was innocent. If they found out he continued to be disloyal, he wouldn't need to worry about the Institute killing him: his colleagues would do it for them.

"You're a double agent."

"I think I'm a triple agent. It's not all bad. This way I can at least get innocent people out of the way of raids. Stop some people getting hurt."

"Mark, if anyone finds out…"

He wasn't cunning like Charlie. He wasn't self-preserving like Roxy. And he would never be ruthless like John. Mark was a good man in a very bad world, and from his latest vantage point he was going to get himself killed. She cursed herself for ever getting involved with him. She'd led him to the Institute, torn him from his simple, ignorant life. She was just like Charlie, drawing innocent people into the Reacher world without considering the consequences.

"It's okay. I know what I'm doing."

"How can you? Look, you need to get out of S'aven. Here." She fished out the money she'd intended to use for supplies. "Take this."

He pushed her hands back. "Rachel," he said sternly. "I'm okay. I can handle this."

"Of course you can't handle it. You're *you*. You're kind and honest and too good-natured for messing about in things like this."

He let out a sad laugh and placed his mug on the floor. "Things have changed. I've changed."

That was her fault too. Mark had been happy. Ignorant but happy.

"I'm sorry," she said, sinking back into the sofa, defeated and ashamed of herself.

"Don't be. There's nothing to be sorry about."

"Because of me you've lost everything."

"I never had anything, not really. You opened my eyes—and the view is shit, but I needed to see it. I'm grateful."

"Grateful? You went to a work camp because of me."

He sighed and regarded her thoughtfully. "Quit it. You're trying to provoke a reaction from me. Well, it's not going to work. Everything you did wrong, I've forgiven you for. And nothing will ever compare to what I did to you."

A shiver rolled up her spine. "That wasn't your fault. You didn't know what the Institute would do, what they were. And you did the right thing in the end. Thanks to you, I was rescued."

"That's not what I was talking about." His jaw clenched; his breathing deepened. He looked upwards and swallowed. "I mean about forcing you into a relationship. I'm so, so sorry, Rach. I didn't know. I thought you wanted to be with me. If I had known, I would have never made you..." He closed his eyes. "It's unforgivable."

"Mark, you never made me do anything."

He looked up at her incredulously. "Smith told me everything."

"Charlie?"

"He said you were too scared to leave me, that I was practically raping you."

"Charlie was talking bullshit. He does that a lot, probably to get a rise out of you. Mark, you know about my powers, what I can do. You couldn't force me to do anything I didn't want to. Sure, when we met I was scared. I thought that you might be like the other cops and that if I denied you, you'd look into what I really was. But those worries were over almost immediately."

"You wanted to be with me?"

She paused. She didn't want to lie to him, but she didn't want to hurt his feelings either. "I don't know. Back then I just wanted to stay alive, and being with you was my best shot. I know that makes me sound heartless. If it's any consolation, I was the one using you, not the other way around."

"You never loved me?"

"Not like you loved me. I don't think I'm capable of that kind of affection. I've spent so long running, thinking the world is going to end in the morning. Feelings like love don't come naturally to me." She touched his hand. "But I care for you. And if I had known you took the blame for Gary's murder, I would have come for you."

She drank her tea. It was exactly as she liked it. He hadn't forgotten.

"There's a lot about S'aven I hate, but I often think back to the nights off we'd get together, when we'd just shut out the world. It felt like it was only us two. That I wasn't being hunted. That we weren't poor. For the night, we could just be us. That was perfect. Sometimes I'd trade everything for another night like that."

"I still love you. I've never stopped loving you."

"Mark..."

"No, let me finish. It took me a while to realise it was unrequited, but I'm okay with that now. And I'm okay that you're with the brothers and not with me. You're safer with them than you ever will be with me."

Rachel was stunned. After everything, she deserved no more than his contempt. She cupped his face, grateful for his affection—and guilty. He leaned in to the touch; his breath quickened. She could sense his fear, his hope, his desire.

And she could no longer ignore her own. They were taking too big a risk being together. She should do them both a favour and leave.

But she didn't. Instead she closed the gap between them. The familiarity of his lips was all-consuming. Everything melted away: S'aven, Charlie, John, Roxy. Suddenly she was back in her old flat, taking advantage of a break between shifts. She was no longer a Reacher; the Institute was a distant nightmare. Kissing him was a physical response to her own attraction, not because she needed to get into his head or manipulate him but because she was human and she craved him.

When she pulled away, she was expecting his doe-eyed blank stare, but like the flat they were in, he too was no longer the same. He knew what she was, and he wasn't disgusted or afraid. After everything she had done to him, he still really did love her. She wanted to shake him and hit him until he saw how dangerous she was. But she didn't. It was so long since she had been touched like this, held like this.

"I really shouldn't be here," she whispered, more to herself than to him.

Mark moved away, sadness rich in his eyes. "You need to get back to them?"

"No, not immediately."

"You can stay if you want to."

She did want to. For a little while she wanted to pretend that the world outside was nothing. That all that mattered was her and Mark in their flat.

Before she could stop herself, she leaned forward and kissed him again. The contact caught them both by surprise. Mark pulled away, his eyes wide, almost fearful.

"I'm sorry. I shouldn't be doing this."

"You never have to apologise for kissing me." This time he moved forward. His fingers hovered over her cheek while he searched for signs of rejection. She could feel his anticipation, his hope, his lust. And she closed the gap between them.

The touch spread like electricity through her body. She knelt over him, hungry for skin, deepening her connection with him. His thoughts and feelings flowed uncontrollably into her. She saw their life together through his eyes. It was filled with joy and contentment. He never had any idea she was different, or unhappy, or afraid. He just loved her and revelled in their relationship. God, to be that ignorant. To be that happy. She pressed deeper, her powers penetrating him the more he surrendered to her. Then she came to the dark place, the bitterness, the isolation. Mark in a work camp too afraid to sleep. She felt his terror, the gaping hole she had made in his heart.

She pulled away from him, her body trembling on his lap. Tears rolled down her cheeks. Mark wiped them away, confused and hesitant. He worried she didn't really want him. The guilt quickly followed. She didn't want him to feel this way. Mark was one of the last good men out there; he deserved the life he thought he had. He deserved to be happy. She kissed him again, pulling at the button on his shirt.

It had been so long since she'd been this close to anyone. When they were together she had tried to keep her powers in check. But now Mark knew what she was capable of. She could be free. And as she liberated herself, she found herself walking in his memories, thinking his thoughts. She watched the town she loved being destroyed. She saw the injustices erupting through the streets. She wanted to protect everything, to make it better, and recognised she was only prolonging the inevitable. War would come, and she would face it because this was what she was. This was now all she was. But she was still afraid. She didn't want to die alone. She didn't want to die for nothing.

Rachel pressed her fingers against his temples and promised him she would make it better. *Stay with me*, she said. They could be together away from S'aven. It would all be alright. He just had to trust her.

13

Like Scarlet, S'aven's future was visibly flaking away. The town was infested with socialism, covered with putrid boils of left-minded revolutionaries. The only possible solution was cauterising the site, obliterating every trace of free-thinking and eradicating any chance of contamination. London should have acted long before it got to this stage, but she didn't. Her wealth and greed had been allowed to flourish without prudence, and now she sat, fat and useless, watching the downfall of British society on all levels. It was time for them both to die.

Scarlet drove at speed down the motorway. The winter exodus from the north had already started, but this time it was being counteracted by refugees trying to break away from the violence in the south. Something was coming; everyone could feel it, and nobody knew where to hide. There was a very real possibility she would be dead before S'aven. That didn't seem fair. She'd laid so many cracks in S'aven's brickwork over the years—she deserved to see it fall. She pressed her foot on the accelerator. Time was not on her side.

Her former partner had been based in S'aven for months. After his epic train of terror was derailed, Johnson had fallen from the Institute's esteem. They moved him to S'aven to punish him, although he wouldn't see it as such. Johnson was the last of the drone strain, obedient to the end and utterly useless at ingenuity. He got lucky with the rioting in the town. The unrest in S'aven and the London border closure could be manipulated to the Institute's advantage. Johnson had one chance to redeem himself. If he could gain a stronghold on both sides, if he could control the pieces, then the Institute would keep him. And Scarlet monitored his progress, using her contact in S'aven's struggling police force to feed back information.

Scarlet had considered checking in with Mark Bellamy before finding Johnson, but the eroding of her cells was becoming too noticeable. The greying pallor to her skin could be concealed with makeup, but she couldn't hide the way it clung desperately to her skull. Bellamy was an oblivious fool, but she suspected even he would notice a difference. It was best to touch base with Johnson and make sure he was aware of her situation and his new role in the event of her premature demise.

The Institute had closed most of their safe houses, but the one in S'aven remained while Johnson was in place. She parked a street away from the abandoned underground station and made her way on foot over the torn-up tarmac to a small boarded-over entrance at the bottom of a stairwell. On closer inspection the board was hinged. She pressed her fingers around the edge of it and pulled. The wood swung back, yanking a nail from her ring finger. She cursed but didn't stop. The road was empty and desolate, but there was no reason to assume she wasn't being watched.

Behind the board another door blocked her, sealed with the key-coded entrance. She punched in the key and slipped into a tight entrance hall, letting the door seal behind her. In front of her a panel on the wall demanded a fingerprint and retinal scan before she could proceed. She looked at her bloody hands. The skin on her fingers was already starting to crack and blister. She pressed her index against the pad and waited. Rejected. She tried again, stretching the skin back over the tip of her finger bone. Accepted. The retinal scan rolled over her eye, and the heavy-duty door hissed open.

She'd hoped to find Johnson inside, watching the world from the comfort of the little office, but the room was empty. A camping bed was pressed up against the wall, a sleeping bag neatly rolled up at the foot of it. Underneath, a black rucksack sat on top of a silver case. She had a similar kit in her car. She felt wetness against her palm and remembered her hand was still bleeding. Bandages and first-aid supplies were stored in the computer station at the heart of the room. She pulled the green box free, spraying droplets of blood over the keyboard and screen. When she found Johnson she would have to ask him to take the whole finger off before infection set in. For now a bandage hidden beneath a leather glove would have to suffice. At least it wasn't her trigger finger.

She wiped the blood away from the computer, booted up, and signed into Johnson's tracker. After John Smith's escape they were all fitted with them—located at the base of the skull, too close to the spine for safe removal.

Absently, she rubbed at the scar on the top of her neck and went to go and find her old partner.

Johnson was parked at the edge of Lennox Street. His vehicle was inconspicuous amongst the others parked up the road. The only oddity—easily overlooked by passers-by—was the window tinting that concealed the driver inside. Scarlet tapped the window with her gloved hand. The car unlocked. She pulled open the door and waited for Johnson to remove his laptop from the passenger seat, then slipped inside. The vehicle was littered with discarded protein containers and waste bags. Johnson was, as ever, unchanged. Still imposing, still neat, always shrewd. He looked at her, and a rare hint of surprise caught his eye. The decaying process was always a surprise. She could remember how swiftly it took her siblings.

"There's been a change," she said in explanation.

Johnson was a practical man. "Do you have an estimated expiry date?"

"Seven months. Khosh would like you to ensure that my body is returned to the Institute when it happens."

Johnson nodded. He was a man of little emotion, but Scarlet knew he held her in some regard. She had mentored him back in the days when they hoped he and his kin were more than uninventive drones. Their work together had squeezed out the barest drops of originality and saved him from the fate of his brothers. They were all programmed to serve the Institute until death, but to have one's time extended was something to be celebrated.

"It means I have seven months to find the Smith brothers."

Johnson's jaw twitched. His orders were S'aven based. It would take a lot of careful words to convince him to leave his post.

"Who are you watching?"

"A reporter, Li Starr. She's based up there." He pointed to the single illuminated window above a shuttered Chinese restaurant.

"The woman from the radio? I thought we were closing her down."

"She got Carson Mooney to do her show. The Institute would like his words broadcasted for the present."

Of course they would. Mooney made London nervous, and the louder he got, the more agitated the capital would become.

"How long have you been here?"

"Two days."

Scarlet didn't say anything, but she was disappointed in Johnson. He'd been given a target, and he'd fixated on it when he could be working another angle while Starr toed the line. As ever, his lack of imagination had made his existence redundant. "Has there been anything of interest to report?"

"Not yet."

"Have you got cameras up there?"

"She sweeps regularly. I've bugged her computer. It records enough without alerting her to the fact she's being recorded."

"What about direct contact?"

"No."

Scarlet sighed. Her sore finger began to throb, and she was already feeling bored. Maybe she should have gone to Bellamy instead. At least he was fun to play with.

Then Johnson surprised her. "Will it be painful?" he asked. Curiosity was a rarity for him.

"I believe so." She pressed her hands together and tried to imagine the ache spreading throughout her body.

"If you recover Smith, will they be able to prevent it?"

"Cell deterioration is irreversible. But the point is not to prolong my life. We are both failed experiments. I am confined by an ungenerous shelf life, you by a disassociation with humanity. Our time is expendable but not necessarily unproductive. Not if we spend what usefulness we have on perfecting the cause. If we capture Smith, then the next generation will be perfect. That's the mission. Above everything else."

Before she could go on, a shadow caught their attention. The figure was undoubtedly male, sauntering up the street with purpose. From Scarlet's vantage point she couldn't make out the face, but there was something about the swagger, something familiar.

"Any ideas who that is?"

Johnson handed her his sniper scope. She peered through the lens just as the figure checked the street. For a second he looked right at her, and she recognised him instantly. It was impossible not to smile.

"James Roxton," she said.

"Roxton? I recognise the name."

"He's an associate of the Smith brothers, has been for years. And more recently, he's been following them around the country. Last seen in Blackwater."

She looked again, making sure she wasn't imagining things.

"In fact, as far as I was aware, Blackwater was supposed to be his final resting place. Mark Bellamy had told me he was dead."

"He lied?"

"Apparently so."

Her anger at Bellamy's deception didn't even register with her. She was too preoccupied with possibilities. James Roxton was alive, and finally she felt luck might be on her side.

"I'll take him out now." Johnson reached for his gun case on the back seat.

"No. I want him alive. It wasn't until after I thought he was dead that I realised how useful he could be. This is a good sign. If he's here, it means the Smith brothers are too. We won't even have to wait for them." She settled back in the passenger seat, the weakness in her body irrelevant, and started to laugh.

"What's so funny?"

"After all this time, who'd have thought it would be so easy."

14

Safe Haven had belonged to Sarah. Like many women, Sarah's mother had fled the north, hoping the south would offer her sanctuary from the war and famine raging back home. And like many women, she learned the gates to London would only open to the extremely wealthy. Sarah's mother found herself on the streets, selling her body for a better life while squandering her opportunities on drugs to dampen her sorrows. It was a trend that dominated the population. S'aven was created by a society of devastated optimists. And driven by a new generation of disenfranchised survivalists.

Charlie and John spent their lives passing through, plucking meagre spoils like travelling foragers, never stopping long enough to connect with the town. In fact, Charlie was sure, if this town hadn't borne his wife he'd have no trouble watching it burn. But it had, and, like the in-laws he didn't get on with, he had some respect for the pavements that once carried Sarah's feet, for the buildings that watched as she negotiated her way to him. They turned a corner, coming across a ruined station that had once housed Father Darcy's nomadic church. The sight of it made Charlie stop mid-step, his breath catching in his throat. The road was part of old London, sacrificed when the border was erected. The state of the building—a casualty of another barrage of bombings—was a historic catastrophe, but the memory of its former glory was still pressed together between the gaps in the mortar.

Etched into the wall, marking what had been the entrance, was a lone cross. Charlie ran his fingers along the groove. Faith, like S'aven, belonged to Sarah, not Charlie. He struggled to believe any supreme being would intentionally create a creature like him solely to be hunted and abused in the kingdom of men. But Sarah believed. She believed he had divinity, that he was special. And Darcy believed too.

The tips of his fingers traced the cross, and his powers deepened the crevice. The government had tried to ban religion, but here it remained. They had tried to eradicate him, and yet here he stood, stronger than ever. He stared at the rubble around him, fallen brickwork sitting like headstones, and remembered the first time he laid eyes on Sarah. The curve of her face, the wonder in her eyes. Meeting her had changed him. She drew him to the light, and for so long he basked in it without truly seeing where it came from. And now he was in darkness, empty, and alone. She would tell him this despair was for a greater plan. She would tell him to have faith.

"Are you finished taking in the sights, or should I take your picture?" John was waiting for him at the end of the street.

Charlie hadn't even realised his brother had moved on without him. "Don't you remember what this used to be?"

John shrugged. "Crack den. Church. Consistent shithole. Am I missing something?"

"It's where I met Sarah, you arsehole. Do you remember? We came to see Darcy, and Sarah was here."

"You introduced us in a pub," John said.

"Oh, that's right. You were still sulking about what happened at the Grandchester and wouldn't get out of the car."

John's face hardened. "A bomb went off in my face. Forgive me for being pissed off about it."

"She was here, putting out these battered old Bibles for Darcy. Do you ever think what would have happened if we never met her?"

John wouldn't answer. He didn't have to. If Charlie hadn't met Sarah, she would probably still be alive. The truth hurt, but Sarah believed in destiny. She was convinced they had been brought together for a reason.

"We would have gone after the Institute. Probably ended up dead. We'd have never met Rachel. Or Roxy. What if meeting her was something that had to happen? That her knocking us off course was a good thing?"

John's eyebrow twitched in annoyance. "And her and Lilly dying was a good thing too?"

"Of course not," Charlie snapped. Losing his family was the worst thing that could ever happen to him, but he couldn't help but wonder if that was part of a bigger plan. He was no longer afraid of death, but he was also intent his survival would count for something. "But maybe their deaths were of greater importance than we realise. That their dying had purpose."

John was unimpressed. "I think you're talking out of your arsehole."

"All I'm saying is, this place could be significant."

"Then when you're famous, get them to put up a fucking plaque," John said and stormed away.

Charlie's leg brace hissed as he hurried after his brother. He caught him two streets down and had to pretend he wasn't breathless. "What's with you? We're days away from bringing the Institute down—you should be happy. I know it's not what we'd planned, but we were kids back then. We weren't thinking about the bigger picture. This is the way to do it properly. We draw them out of the shadows, expose the truth. Tell the world what Reachers are and what the Institute do to them."

"And this has nothing to do with you and your ego?" John stopped, standing outside a narrow alleyway cutting down to the canal. "The great Charlie Smith standing like some fucking overreaching messiah in front of everyone, that's not what you're aiming for here?"

"This isn't about me. This is the most effective way to end them for good, I promise you. Or are you so hell-bent on diving into a fight head first you don't even care if it's worth winning? Do you even want to bring them down, or are you just intent on letting them kill you?"

John's composure changed, and Charlie could no longer read him.

"Fuck you, Charlie. You think they could kill me? Is that it? Let the motherfuckers try. I survived them. I keep surviving them. Or is it you? Are you too much of a coward to meet them head-on? They killed your fucking family, and you're acting like it's all part of some shitting plan. Like they were meant to die."

Charlie grabbed John's arm before he could walk away. "That's not what I'm doing. But I don't want their deaths to be in vain. Sarah and Lilly died because of what I am. If I just give myself up and go back to that place, what does any of it achieve? We need to do better. We need to make a stand for all Reachers."

"I'm not a Reacher." John squared his shoulders.

"John."

"I'm not a Reacher, and you know what, I don't really give a shit about your kind or your cause. I want to watch the Institute burn. So you can take all the fame and attention you crave and leave me out of it. I'm not standing with you.

And I'll tell you something else: your family died because you contaminated them. You tried to make home, knowing you were being hunted. Sarah was screwed the moment you let her into your life. That's on you." John glanced at the alleyway and snorted. "When you're famous, they can put a plaque here too."

Charlie frowned, then remembered the nook and the anticlimactic night he'd lost his virginity. Maybe he was more tied to S'aven than he had thought. And maybe the idea of being S'aven's messiah appealed to him more than he would admit.

15

Rachel hovered in the doorway. She looked back at the sofa. Mark wasn't sleeping, just pretending for her benefit. He was making it easy for her to leave, and yet she still found herself being pulled back. But this life hadn't been enough when she lived it before. It certainly wouldn't be enough now. The road ahead was dark and unknown, but it was hers to take. *Stay with me.* Even thinking it was absurd. The others would never allow it. She wasn't even sure *she* would allow it. And yet she'd thought it, pushed it into Mark's head, for what? To torment him further? She'd already drawn him into this dangerous world; why did she insist on risking his life? Before she did anything else she'd regret, she stepped out into the corridor and closed the door, trying not to think about what would happen to Mark now.

Retracing her steps back down the stairwell, she could almost believe she was off for another long shift at the hospital. Night had claimed the skies, the noise in the town rising with the darkness. She could see the emergency room filling up, only now it was a mix of her memories and Mark's. Cold air hit her face as she stepped outside, and she paused for a moment to watch the purple haze consume the buildings in front of her. This was Mark's favourite time of day, the resting time before the next shift started.

She stuffed her hands into her pockets and hurried back to the industrial estate. Sirens blared behind her. She quickened her pace, hoping to make it back before Charlie and John. She'd have to tell them what happened and could already see the faces they would make. Mark was a cop, strictly off limits for a Reacher on the run. At least that was what they would think. But he was more than a cop. And he was one of the few people she knew for certain she could trust.

When she finally got to the garage, she found the door unlocked. She eased it open. The van inside was illuminated by a fading solar light, hanging precariously on the open side door. Roxy was underneath it, wrapped up in his sleeping bag, toying with his last pack of cigarettes and looking as sorry as the surrounding neighbourhood.

"The serious rationing has begun." He held out his hand, showing her the crumpled packet. "Half empty," he whimpered.

She tried to muster her most sympathetically dismissive smile. "How did it go with Starr?"

His face brightened. "I think it's safe to say I charmed the pants off her. She's putty in my hand as long as she gets a good story, which of course she will. I take it I'm the only one who got lucky?"

Heat flared in her cheeks. "Excuse me?"

"Well, you were on a supply run and you're suspiciously unladen with goodies. Where's the food, love?"

"Oh, right. There's nothing anywhere. The warehouses are empty, market's dead. We've probably got more supplies in the back of the van than what's left in this whole town."

Roxy regarded his packet mournfully.

"Where are the others?"

"On their way, I imagine."

A few minutes alone would work to her advantage. Roxy naturally backed her corner whenever she had to go up against the brothers. If she told him what happened with Mark, she could get him onside and let him fight it out with Charlie if it came to it. Roxy knew the score; he understood physical indiscretions in the heat of the moment. He'd listen to her without judgement and prop her up in her moment of self-doubt.

"Hey, I, eh, need to tell you something." She was nervous, and frustrated with herself because of it. She cleared her throat and tried again, more confidently this time. "Okay, so I think I may have done something really stupid."

"Join the club, darling. I smoked two of these already out of boredom."

"Yeah, well, I trump your cigarettes and raise you one future argument with Charlie and John." She couldn't meet Roxy's eye. "When I was out I ran into Mark."

He looked at her, his face blank and expectant. "You're saying it like I should know what you're talking about."

"My ex Mark. The cop that was supposed to kill you but didn't."

He frowned as he tried to remember, then clicked his fingers excitedly. "Oh, the pouty one."

She let the slight slide. "I went down to my old tower block. There was a guy there used to sell cigarettes, so I thought I'd try my luck. Cheer you up. Only Mark was there. In the tower, I mean. He's moved back. And he was just walking through the door like the old days."

Roxy shrugged. "Did you at least get the smokes?"

She shook her head. "I had to talk to him, Rox. So much has happened between us, and we never really talked. I followed him to his flat and… well, we ended up together."

"Together?" His eyes widened. "Wait, you… and him. You boffed that prat? Made the two-backed beast with a filthy copper? Oh darling, you do know there's no need to go slumming it, don't you? In desperate times my loins are at your disposal."

"I didn't set out to do it. He was just there, we were talking and, I don't know, things just happened. He was hurting, and all I wanted was to make it better. So I kissed him and then…"

"Then what?" The humour was gone from his face. He glared at her, accusation already brimming in his eyes.

She'd made another mistake. She'd forgotten all about what happened to Roxy and where the firm boundaries of his hedonism sat.

"My powers took over," she confessed. "One minute we're kissing, the next I'm in his head. Living his memories, feeling everything he felt."

"Did he know?"

"I'm not sure."

Roxy wouldn't look at her. His mouth twisted in distaste. When he did speak, he was cold and too serious. "Rachel, I love you, pet, but going into a person's head like that. It's not okay. I don't know, maybe if we're working a job, trying to find something to win the game, maybe that's justified. But for sex. For intimacy. It's not right."

She closed her eyes, furious with herself. She'd forgotten Roxy knew firsthand what a Reacher invasion felt like. It wasn't long ago that he was being led into a back alley in Blackwater, his mind at the mercy of a Reacher girl intent on stealing his secrets. The experience had shaken him up, and he'd never condone Rachel doing the same.

"It wasn't like what happened to you," she reassured him. "Mark's in love with me. He wanted to sleep with me, and—"

"And that gives you a right to mind rape him?"

Her mouth fell open, but she couldn't argue with him. He was right. Mark trusted her, which she knew for certain because she'd violated his thoughts. How would he feel if he knew? She'd wanted to lose herself, but she lost control instead… at his expense.

"Who did you mind rape?" John and Charlie were behind her, John's brow arched at optimal disapproval height.

She looked to Roxy, but he wasn't going to betray her. This was her bed; she had better own it.

"I, eh, I met Mark when I was out. He's living here now."

John's whole face tightened. And she'd thought Roxy's reaction was bad.

"Did you tell him why we're here?" Charlie asked pensively.

"Do you think I'm stupid?"

"I never used to," John said. "We've got hours before the Institute arrive. We need to bail."

"He won't call them," Rachel said.

"And you know that for fucking certain, do you?" John's temper flared.

"Oh, that at least she does know," Roxy quipped. "You'd better tell them before John totally loses his shit."

"I, eh, I know for certain because we had sex. And now I know everything. I got in his head; I know exactly what has happened to him and what he's planning on doing, what he's capable of. He won't betray me. And he won't betray any of you either. He hates the Institute."

Charlie rubbed his face wearily. "So no harm done."

Stay with me.

If the words had penetrated Mark's subconscious, he could come after her. A part of her was starting to hope he would. She needed more time with him to make up for all the mistakes she was making. His memories stirred in the back of her mind—thoughts and images, but mainly feelings. He was afraid. The Institute would eventually kill him, and he was powerless to stop them. Didn't that make him like them?

"I sort of asked him to come with us," she said.

"You did what?" Charlie grasped his hair and looked to his brother apprehensively. "No way."

Rachel wasn't scared of John. He could puff out his chest as much as he wanted; she would stand her ground. A flash of memory seared her: Mark holding his nerve in front of that Institute bitch. If Mark could be tough, Rachel could be tougher. "Too late. I put the idea in his head. He's coming with us."

"There's not enough room. We already have to put up with him," he said, pointing violently at Roxy.

"Hey, I'm a delight," Roxy said. "But Johnny does have a point, pet. It's getting awful cramped in the van. I can't see how we're going to squeeze another body in there without things getting awkwardly intimate."

Rachel stared them all down. "Then we'll get another van."

An argument was about to erupt. Then Charlie stepped between them all. He raised his hands, the long-suffering father at the end of a very long family holiday. "Right now we need to be focused on the border. We'll worry about who leaves with us when we actually leave. You got it?"

Rachel nodded. The mission had to come first. She caught John's eye and could see he felt the same. Anything could happen in the next few days; it was pointless getting irate unnecessarily.

"Good, because we've now got to see if opening the gates hands-free really is possible," Charlie said.

Roxy started to laugh. "A sensible man might have done that before stirring up the hopes of S'aven's most unfortunate."

"A sensible man wouldn't have suggested it in the first place," John grumbled.

Charlie ignored them. "Rachel, you're with me. While we're making miracles, Roxy, John, you two can run an errand for us."

"Sounds exciting," Roxy said.

"It really isn't," John replied.

"Hey, unless you've got a better idea, this is the quickest way to impress the Union." Charlie glared at his brother, challenging him to object. "Or is it you're worried you can't handle it? After your injuries and everything."

"Screw you," John spat. "I could do it in my sleep, and you fucking know it."

"Then quit complaining." He looked to Rachel more seriously. "We're going to have to assume we're compromised staying here."

"He didn't follow me," she told them.

"No, but someone could have been following him. There's a stretch of wasteland west of Clapham. We'll meet up there midnight tonight, find new digs after."

16

Mark had to get out of the flat. Seeing Rachel again had sent his head spinning, and he needed to be clear of the building he'd once shared with her. He stepped out into the open air, and a sheen of icy drizzle coated his face. He could still taste her on his lips. It was too much. Too good. Her offer reverberated around every thought. Teasing him. To go with her—was it even possible? Since she left, he'd wanted nothing more than to have her back, to be with her. In their two years apart his feelings for her had only grown stronger, and even the possibility of a future with her was clouding his better judgement. But it couldn't happen. The water numbed his cheeks, and his racing, frantic thoughts found order. He had work to do in S'aven, a mission of his own choosing, a cause he believed in. If he left with Rachel he'd have to abandon the freedom of his own thoughts, and if he did that she would never see him for who he truly was.

Reluctantly resolved, he moved away from the flats in an attempt to distance himself from her memory. He felt for a slip of paper in his pocket and reminded himself he had other responsibilities now. That afternoon another home had been raided. Eight of the residents had been shot dead, but two survived and were in custody. Mark had their names and what their interrogations had so far revealed. With new focus, he moved quickly to meet with one of the few men he trusted.

They met in their usual place by the canal, two dark shadows moving along opposing sides of the old bridge. Mooney stopped first and leaned against the railings, watching the garbage floating in the murky black water below. Mark walked past, slipping his paper into Mooney's open pocket. He would have continued over the bridge, but Mooney called him back.

"You used to work for the Institute, right?" he asked.

Mark stiffened. He kept his back to Mooney, not trusting his poker face. "That's right," he said cautiously. "I used to work for the Paranormal Crimes Unit before they closed it."

"So you know about Reachers?"

Now there was a difficult question to answer. "I guess you could say that."

"What's said about them, that they're terrorists, determined to kill us all. Is it true?"

Mark paused, trying to look for potential pitfalls in his answer. He turned, daring himself to face the Union leader. "Some are."

Mooney nodded, as though he had already anticipated the words. "But not all?"

"Not even most." Despite the risk of being seen, Mark moved closer and leaned against the opposite railings. Just two men enjoying the view. "Why'd you ask?"

"Two of them showed up at the meeting today. Brothers. Charlie and John Smith. You heard of them?"

After Rachel's visit he shouldn't have been surprised. "Our paths have crossed before. Did they tell you what they wanted?"

"Apparently they want to support the cause."

From what Mark knew about the Smith brothers, they had no real interest in local politics or revolution. The brothers were criminals, very skilled, ambitious men, out for what they could get. If they were involving themselves in the Union, then they were doing it for their own reasons. Mark just couldn't fathom what they could possibly be.

"Carson, if the Union is found to be affiliating itself with Reachers, the authorities will label you as terrorists. It doesn't matter what the Smiths intend or how they help you. Even talking to them is enough to create division between the Union and the law."

"There's already division. It's my people that refuse to recognise that, not yours." He fished out the paper from his pocket. "We're being arrested and murdered for the cause.

And yet we still profess our righteousness, as though anyone actually cares."

It was a good point. On paper there was still legitimacy, and publicly the Union was still lawful. But beneath the surface the government picked them off with ruthless precision. And it would be the government that would write the history of these events. They could as easily manufacture an alliance with Reachers without any real evidence.

A year ago Mark would have naïvely believed in justice. But not anymore. What he knew of the Smith brothers made him uneasy, but they wouldn't deliberately set out to ruin the Union. Not with Rachel backing them. And there was even the possibility, with their help, the Union's efforts could be successful.

"If Charlie Smith has offered to help the Union he'll have his own agenda, and it will have nothing to do with your cause. But that doesn't mean it won't benefit you."

"If you were me, would you take the help?"

Mark was tempted to answer honestly, to tell Mooney that if were he lucky enough to have something Charlie Smith wanted, he'd lock it away and never let him near it. But that helped no one. And he'd already resolved to leave his scorned feelings back in his flat.

"I would exercise caution and do what's in the interest of the Union. Whatever promises Charlie Smith makes, assurances he gives you, make sure they're on him, not on you. Keep distance and make sure you get what you want. They can't be trusted, but that doesn't mean they can't be used."

Mark made to move. They'd already been together for too long. He'd made it to the edge of the bridge when Mooney called out to him again.

"Things are moving quickly. When it comes, there won't be any discrimination on our part either. Coppers will be treated as coppers. I won't be able to stop it."

Mark nodded. He had never assumed the Union would grant him immunity. He also didn't expect the Institute would need him once the revolution started. More likely he'd be moved on to spy on something else. He hated the idea of being back under their absolute control. But it didn't have to be like that. Rachel's offer circulated again in his mind, and he cursed himself at his lack of resolve.

17

The first breach of S'aven's snow spilled from the sky, white flakes choking the dockyard. Night had failed to claim the heavy clouds, and they glowed mauve, reflecting the flickering lights from London in the distance. Several ships were docked in the harbour, unloading cargo into expansive warehouses lining the seafront. When the borders were open the roads were thick with traffic, transporting luxury goods to Londoners by special order. With the city on lockdown, the warehouses were bulging.

Roxy and John stood on the waste hill overlooking the dockyard. There were extra guards on duty, but they were distracted—or more likely eager opportunists, ready to claim London's spoils for payment. The dock security force tended to be foreign, coming over on their cargo ships from France or Spain to protect the warehouses while their goods were being transported across the border. With London closed, these men were being delayed, their cargo rotting.

A ship was approaching the dock. Roxy didn't know much about boats, except this seemed smaller than the others clinking about in the water. Through his binoculars he checked the name, then checked his watch. According to John the ship had exclusive cargo from Spain, destined to fill the homes of distinguished persons once the border opened again. It was a weekly visitor to the docks and once a secret ferry transporting Reachers in and out of the country. To the other side of their garbage mountain, a heavy-duty flatbed transporter was approaching, due to pick up the incoming load and transport it to one of the warehouses.

Roxy nudged John excitedly. "Right on time. Here's our ride," he said and tossed his cigarette aside.

John flashed him a warning look. "Do not fuck this up."

"What the bloody hell do you take me for, darling? I am a professional."

The last time they'd hijacked a vehicle, it had been carrying Rachel and the stakes were too high to contemplate messing up. This time there was room for a cock-up—or two— and the uncertainty of it made Roxy giddy with anticipation. He sauntered down the junk mountain, and his foot caught on a hoop of wrought metal. He slipped and skidded on a sheet of green slime, grappling for balance before falling on his ass. He didn't have to look back to know John was shaking his head in disappointment. The truck was still moving, unaware of his imminent, albeit clumsy, threat. He scrambled to his feet, hurrying down the rest of the waste mound and hitting the tarmac like a graceless elephant. The lights of the transporter struck him. He heard the brakes on the tyres and hurled himself toward the vehicle.

The transporter swerved, coming to an abrupt stop and blocking the road feet from where Roxy stood. Roxy started singing, his words slurred, his movements erratic. He waved at the driver and collapsed. The men in the vehicle gesticulated wildly at him, revving the van engine. It was a false threat. If they had the balls to run him over, they would have done so already. Eventually, the passenger door opened. Heavy footsteps waded in the deepening slush. Roxy clasped the gun concealed in his coat. He rolled over and beamed at the stranger, pointing his weapon proudly.

"Sorry, love, I'm afraid this is a robbery. Now, if you don't mind obliging, this will all be over in a jiffy and no one needs to get hurt."

Robberies on the dockyard went two ways. Everyone was killed, or everyone complied. This man had been hijacked before. He conceded and raised his hands in irritated surrender. There was no point dying for cargo that wasn't going anywhere anyway. Roxy tightened a plastic tie over the man's wrists and left him by the side of the road, shivering in the snow. Charlie had been very insistent about not killing anyone. Roxy wondered if dying of hypothermia would count. He stuffed his gun into his belt and made for the van. When he got in the passenger seat, John was already at the wheel.

"Where's the driver?"

A shadow thrashed in the bushes to the right of the vehicle.

John slammed the transporter into first and eased the handbrake up. They hit the road, mimicking the speed of the previous driver.

The transporter cabin smelt of fried food and cheap cigarettes. Roxy flipped open the glovebox hopefully and showered the floor with empty packets and used tickets. Nothing useful. It made him question again why they were going after a single boat when several warehouses were brimming with goods at the other end of the harbour. Alcohol, contraband and, most importantly, cigarettes were all within their reach. Whatever had taken Charlie's fancy had to be important.

Roxy rapped his fingers on the door, trying not to appear impatient and failing. "Are you going to tell me what the mystery cargo is?"

"No."

"Oh, come on. Is it gold? Please tell me we're stealing gold off a ship. You know, technically that would make us pirates."

"Stop talking."

"I'm serious. This is a whole career venture we haven't even considered yet. And let's face it, with what Charlie's planning, we are going to need to go to ground pretty quick. A voyage on the high seas would be ideal. We could be pirates, John. Just imagine. Me with a parrot, you with an eyepatch."

"You're going to need an eyepatch if you don't shut up."

John slowed the transporter as they approached the dock entrance. A warden stopped them, signalling for their papers. He seemed weary and disinterested. Roxy passed him a clipboard from the dash and tried to mimic the sombre state of the dockyard. A registered transporter, arriving on time, was no cause for interest. In seconds they were waved through.

"You know, Charlie could get a peg leg," Roxy whispered. Finally, the briefest flicker of amusement crossed John's face.

Their ship was already docked, its container poised and ready for transfer. Roxy suspected the secrecy of the cargo was to prevent temptation. Charlie knew his history—he'd been victim to a lot of it, and he knew Roxy had uncontrollably light fingers when it came to robberies. Whatever was in that sealed container had to be worth a fortune.

John backed the transporter to the loading bay and waved the ship's crew to start loading. He got out of the driver's cabin and swapped papers with what Roxy liked to imagine was an old, bearded sea captain. It seemed like he'd done this before, and Roxy wondered if John had picked up cargo for Father Darcy in the past. A rust-covered crane creaked into action, moving the container from the ship to the transporter with arthritic slowness.

"We'd be quicker moving the bastard thing ourselves," he said when John was finished.

"We're ahead of schedule, quit complaining. Charlie figured it would take at least an hour to hijack the vehicle and get us here."

"That's because your brother times everything by how quickly he moves. So now we've got it, what's inside?"

John smirked and said nothing. Diamonds, contraband, treasures from a distant land. Roxy's fingers tingled at the possibilities.

John drove with determination back to the rendezvous point, deflecting with increasing annoyance every guess Roxy could muster. Charlie had chosen a stretch of urban wasteland to park the transporter. The area was a desperate home for wanted men unable to fully leave S'aven. Normally they scurried like rats through piles of rubbish, making temporary houses from the discards of the urban town. But the ominous signs of winter had frightened all but the hardiest elsewhere, meaning, for a while, the transporter would be undisturbed.

John parked up and switched the engine off. "I'm going to check the cargo. Keep watch. The last thing we need is to be ambushed by some fuckwit tramp looking for an easy score."

Through the wing mirror, Roxy watched John disappear behind the vehicle. He couldn't just sit there without knowing what cargo would sway the people of S'aven into rising up against London. He wasn't going to steal it, he told himself. Just take a quick look. He plucked the keys from the ignition and slipped from the transporter, padding quietly after John.

The container was dark inside, illuminated by a single windup lamp hanging from the top of the box and the thin beam coming from John's torch. From the ground, Roxy could make out stacks of wooden crates but not what they contained. He quickly checked his surroundings and saw no one nearby. In a swift move he launched himself into the container and swung the door to prevent any prying eyes from taking an interest.

The container thundered as the door slammed shut.

"You fucking dickhead!" John shone his flashlight into Roxy's eyes. "That door doesn't open from the inside."

Roxy patted the metalwork, hoping to prove him wrong, then laughed sheepishly. "Oh, well, I'm sure Charlie and Rachel won't be long." He checked his watch. Charlie really did underestimate his timings. He offered John an apologetic smile. "Guess you might as well show me the loot. Not like I can run off with it now, is it?"

John stepped aside, and despite being trapped with a man who was quite clearly contemplating murdering him, Roxy was excited. He twitched his fingers and ran them over the nearest crate. The contents, Charlie had assured him, would change the world. Roxy pushed back the lid.

"What the bloody hell is this? Oranges. We're stealing oranges." Roxy let the lid drop to the floor. Piles of oranges were crammed inside. He checked another crate. And another.

They were all the same.

John leaned against the container, smug and amused. "Problem?"

"Yes. I'm a thief, not a sodding greengrocer. This is your brother's big plan. Buy the support of the Union with fruit? I was right all along. The stupid bugger has lost his marbles. Did you know about this? Of course you did; you're as bloody crazy as he is. Oranges? I'm going to go down in history as the arsehole who helped steal oranges."

"Could be worse," John said. "You could be *trapped in a container* with the arsehole who helped steal oranges."

18

The Reacher files were unlike anything Li had ever seen. She had been through them over and over, re-reading reports, examining pictures, each time noticing some new horror. The story she was writing would cement her career in history. It could change the world. The prospect, especially with the unrest around the capital churning up so near to her, was making her chest tighten in anticipation. But each time she closed her eyes, her mind would replay the image of the dead Reacher girl on the slab, and she would be overcome with an unease she couldn't explain. When she saw the body she felt a pang deep in her stomach, an unsettled combination of disgust, terror, and relief. She wasn't a Reacher, and this fate would not befall her. But how many of *them* had ended up in that place? She had to go public. Atrocities like these could not be ignored.

Her fingers were aching from a day of typing and note making. She rubbed her eyes and saw she was surrounded by discarded thoughts. Slips of scribbled paper carpeted her floor, trails gone cold or just too dark to risk venturing further into them so soon. She felt she should visit the laboratory in the last file, to see the dead girl for herself. This information was new, and for some reason that made her connect with it more than the other dead Reachers. But there was no time for trips across the country. For maximum impact her article had to be ready for whatever was coming, which meant she had to work faster.

The light above her flickered. Blackouts were becoming more regular. She suspected it was a deliberate attempt by London to weaken the Union's resolve, but that was an article for another day. She pushed harder, hammering the keys with a diatribe that was five edits away from being an acceptable piece of literature. Li had found it was best to let the words pour out of her and clean them up in the hours afterwards.

She finished her first draft and sat back in her chair with contemplative purpose. Then the power cut out. She had a portable generator already waiting, and in a few seconds she was back to her work, taking in the gravitas of the story with each word. This was good. So good it gave her goosebumps.

A sudden banging on the door downstairs made her jump. Her location wasn't a secret, but she rarely received unexpected guests, and in her experience if they were unexpected they were trouble. She checked her phone: nobody had tried to get in touch with her to set up a meeting. The banging persisted. Instinctively, she checked her weapon was in place, then shook her head. She wasn't going to open the door. Whoever it was could wait.

She turned back to her computer and the greatest story she had ever written.

The crash thundered up the staircase. It sounded like wood breaking, but it took the heavy footsteps bounding upwards before she registered it was her front door, her security that was in pieces. She reached behind her, heart racing, breath shortening. It was all happening too quickly. Her fingers fumbled. When she finally clasped the weapon, ready to blow holes in the intruder, he was already in front of her.

His cold, black eyes bore into hers, and she was frozen. He pulled the weapon from her hand and struck her hard across the face with it. She hit the floor, head spinning. Her fingers clasped the dirty carpet, and she blinked through the throbbing pain. She wanted to be sick but swallowed the rising bile and tried to filter out the ringing in her ears. *What the fuck was that?* Then it dawned on her: intruder, gun. She was in danger.

Li had reported through war zones. She'd interviewed killers. Exposed criminals. She didn't scare easily. And yet there was something about the man hovering over her that made her tremble. His body was a peculiar shape, his bones seeming to bulge unnaturally at the joints. His skin was monotone in colour. His eyes too dark. His lips too tight. And Li was suddenly reminded of the girl on the slab and how bereft of life her corpse clearly was. This man was the same, and his animation did nothing to dispel the ghoulishness of his nature.

A day earlier she would have reasoned this was just a man—a bad man perhaps— but no worse than those she had previously stared down. Now she knew there was more. And this man could be anything. Real fear choked her throat. Her bladder betrayed her, the wetness between her legs just enough to shame her and draw her back from absolute terror.

"Who are you? What do you want?" Her voice sounded weak, pathetic. This was it: the moment she died. She didn't want it like this. Not this brutal.

The intruder said nothing. His spiderlike legs stretched outwards. He moved closer to her desk and the story still open on her laptop. He picked the computer up, yanking it free from the generator. In one sharp twist, he launched the device at the staircase. Li flinched as it clattered down to the broken door. She pressed her hands deeper into the carpet, waiting to follow her work.

The intruder took a step closer to her. His breath was unnaturally odourless. "Where is it?" There was no tone to his voice. No emotion. No humanity.

Li's heart was thundering in her chest. She tried to take a bracing breath and nearly hyperventilated. The intruder just stared at her, his patience terrifying.

"The rest of your data. I know it's here. Where is it?"

Don't look. The chip James Roxton had given her was taped under the bed. She cursed herself for being so careless with it. As soon as she knew the value of it, she should have got it as far away from her as possible. But she didn't want the story to fall into the wrong hands. And London was sealed, the authorities tinkering behind the border, unable to reach her. Or so she'd thought.

The intruder stood over her. She shuddered under his shadow. He began to remove the leather glove from his right hand.

"Have you ever had a child, Ms Starr? No, you haven't. They say that women are better equipped at managing pain because they are naturally engineered to give birth. In my experience I'm inclined to agree. I've seen women endure far more than men. But not because they are capable of numbing themselves to pain—if anything, there is a sensitivity to their bodies that heightens the sensation. No, the women endure because they are built to survive sustained agony. While a man's body will give out with shock, a woman will suffer. Have you ever suffered, Ms Starr?"

Li was crying. She didn't want to be this weak in front of him, and yet she couldn't control herself. "You're... you're just trying to scare me."

"I'm not *trying* to scare you. You are scared. It's a very reasonable reaction to this situation. Fear is a survival instinct, and yet in so many cases it's the very thing that leads to a creature's demise."

"Are you going to kill me?"

"That depends entirely on your instincts. And your endurance."

He lifted her without effort, his fingers clenching her arms with astonishing strength. Li thought about kicking out, but she knew she could not overpower him and was too afraid to make him angry. He dumped her over the bed, her backside up in the air. She pressed her head into the bed sheets, her sobbing uncontrollable.

She felt his hand as it pushed aside her clothing, exposing her bare back to the coldness of the room. Then he struck her spine, and her whole body went limp. She dropped into the bed, unable to move, to even talk. But she could still feel the weight of him as he pressed his body over hers.

"I can make this permanent," he told her calmly. "In a single strike I can leave you like this forever. You will be paralysed, and I will keep you alive. I will keep you alive for as long as I like, and if I like I will hurt you. Violate you."

Tears pooled down her nose and into her mouth.

"Now, where is it?" He moved around the room, but his attention never left her.

She couldn't raise her head or even flex her fingers. She was so terrified she had lost all her earlier determination to publish her story. She wasn't even thinking about the chip. And yet he could read her. Something she did betrayed the location of the device, and he stopped right where it was hidden. He bent down, ran his spindly fingers under the bed frame, and plucked it free. He put it in his pocket and returned to her.

"From now on, you should be careful who you associate with, Ms Starr," he said.

Li closed her eyes. This was it. A not-death. A worse fate than anything she had ever conceived.

There was noise and then footsteps. And then nothing.

She waited, breathing as deeply as she could. But he was gone. She started crying again, louder this time. Her useless body stifled each sob, until suddenly she could move her fingers. Her feet followed and then her legs. She rolled and saw the damage done to her room. With effort, she grabbed her gun from the floor and positioned herself against the foot of the bed while the rest of her body recovered. When she was certain he was gone, she reached for her phone.

19

Father Darcy used to preach about building a Kingdom on Earth. A place where there was peace and acceptance, and Reachers could happily skip through cornfields without getting shot. And while he promised this dream, he smuggled Reachers around the country, keeping them out of the grasp of the Institute. Charlie used to wonder why, if this promised land was so achievable. Now he understood. The peace was attainable, but it had to be claimed, fought for. There had to be sacrifice.

He was prepared for this now. Before, his mind had been too preoccupied with violence and destruction. But that wouldn't destroy the Institute. They thrived on chaos and pain. What he needed was to show the world enlightenment, to highlight the possibility of this Kingdom, to prove it was achievable.

Sarah had believed in fate and destiny. She had faith and tolerated his lack of it, because along with her God, she believed in him and his abilities. Outside of grooming his ego, he never put too much thought into her devotion to his cause. But what if this was his purpose? What if a higher power had sent him here to restore the world? Who was he to deny this fate?

Snow fell from the smog-filled sky like granules of sand in an hourglass. The days were shortening, as was their usable time in S'aven. The border was celebrating its thirty-second year separating poverty and privilege. The concrete wall topped with barbed wire was standing strong, but it was not without some weaknesses. The main gates consisted of two lead-plated doors twenty feet high, operated by an electromagnetic locking system located on the London side of the boundary.

From the privacy of their van, Charlie inspected the obstacle. He knew the border was independently generated from the other side of the wall. He knew that the watch on the generator was sporadic and lax. Opening the gates from London's side would be relatively easy. But he'd lose the drama and ceremony, and he'd have to figure out how to get himself across a border that hadn't opened in weeks.

Since the curfew had been put in place, a small gathering of Union workers watched over the gates, taking shifts in case anything should occur that affected their jobs. Carson Mooney was not there that night, but those that were would no doubt feed information back to him. Charlie needed to inspect the border in secrecy, away from the guards and the prying eyes of the Union.

He clambered out of the van, his braced leg striking the pavement with determination. The cold penetrated the layer of stubble on his face, and he drew his coat tighter. The Union men and women were in threadbare coats, their lips blue. Charlie didn't have that kind of dedication. Rachel stretched out her hand towards him. He took it and waited for the familiar hum of her power to drift through him. Most people wouldn't feel her influence, but Charlie always detected it—like a warm glow calming his body. He nodded at her, and together they walked unseen towards the border.

The Union men and women waved their crude placards, the cold having snatched away their chanting days earlier. Charlie and Rachel wove through them, Rachel's powers rendering them invisible.

This is an outrage.

Rachel's words penetrated his skull, but they weren't meant for him. He heard them repeated by the protesters, mutterings sparking a fire. The small crowd rose up, suddenly shouting and waving their signs with vigour, attracting the attention of the border control keeping watch at the top of the wall. Charlie and Rachel slipped unnoticed through the mini riot and made their way to the very edge of the border.

London was protected first by a barbwire fence. Charlie clasped it with his free hand and closed his eyes. He could feel Rachel, her energy flowing through him, and then he felt the barrier. It was all connected. Metal to concrete, iron to steel to lead. He sensed the electrics binding it all together. Sweat started to form on his face. He concentrated harder, ignoring the violent pounding of his heart. Of Rachel's heart. The mechanics of the wall were complicated and vast, and his powers spread through them like blood, joining him with them.

His legs shook. The weight of the wall pressed against him. His chest tightened, and he braced himself against the fence, struggling to breathe. Then he discovered the mechanism that would release the gate catch. This was it: all he had to do was overload the system.

The victory was too brief. In his internal celebration he lost focus, his mind unravelling from the fence at a painful speed. He moaned and fell back onto Rachel, trying not to throw up over her.

"Are you okay?" she asked as she struggled to hold him upright.

"I think so," Charlie gasped and wiped the sheen of sweat from his forehead. "Maybe this was a bad idea."

He pushed himself up. There was no way he could give up now. "No. I was nearly there. I can do this."

Now he knew where to focus, it was easier. He let his power flow through a familiar channel, reaching the lock with purpose. But the strength required to release the mechanism was immense. His body started to buckle again under the strain. Rachel wrapped her arms around him, holding him up before he collapsed a second time. He was panting, his head throbbing violently. Rachel held him tighter, and something changed.

Her hands clutched his waist, the warmth from them growing stronger. He concentrated on it, drawing the heat through to his own hands. The surge unravelled. He shuddered and took control of the lock. He could release it. He could make it move.

"Charlie," Rachel pressed against him.

He opened his eyes and realised they were being watched. One of the guards in the overhead tower was staring down at them, rifle poised. Charlie turned his head into the curve of Rachel's neck. She feigned a laugh, loud enough for the guard to hear. He pressed his hand to her mouth and gave the guard a bashful grin. From that distance they would look like overexcited lovers unwilling to wait for privacy. Rachel pressed a kiss to Charlie's lips and pulled him away from the wall.

When they were at a safer distance, she wrapped her arms around him, keeping them moving back down the street. "Whatever you did stopped my powers," she said. "One minute I've got a barrier up, the next I'm trying to unlock one."

"I think I used your strength," Charlie said.

"You did what?"

When they got in the van, Charlie's body tingled with the residual adrenaline. He was excited. So excited he couldn't even think clearly.

"I can do it. I can open the gates, but I'm going to need your help."

"If I help you, I can't protect you," she said.

That didn't matter. When the time came he wanted everyone to see. He fell back in the passenger seat, exhausted and invigorated at the same time.

"Are you sure about this?" Rachel said as she started the van. "There'll be no cover, and we're just going to stand there, committing treason."

"John will cover us. Besides, they won't know what's happening until it's over."

She wasn't convinced.

"Sooner we do this, the sooner we're on the road."

He caught her grip tightening on the van steering wheel. John was already having doubts; he couldn't lose Rachel as well.

"So you and Mark," he said, moving the subject away before she had time to object. "That was unexpected."

"I didn't plan it."

He held up his hands in defence. "Hey, I'm hardly one to judge. And it's not like you guys don't have history. I just want you to be careful."

"Mark isn't a threat to us."

"I'm not talking about him screwing us over. I'm just saying you need to be clear what you're going to be getting him into. When the gates open we are going to have to go to ground quick. It won't just be the Institute after us either. It's going to be tough. If he's with us, he's going to have to handle the pace. And you're going to have to cope with the guilt if it all goes wrong."

She looked surprised. "You're saying he can come with us?"

"I'm not going to kick up a fuss."

"John is."

Charlie dismissed the concern. "John doesn't get it. He doesn't think like, well, like normal people. It's all about duty with him. He's never going to meet someone and settle down—that's just not in his nature, and he can't empathise with it. But he accepted Sarah, eventually. Anyway, it's not him I'm worried about."

She frowned.

"You must have noticed Roxy's thing for you."

"Don't be ridiculous."

"I'm not. I've known Roxy a very long time, and that man has never done anything for anyone without a self-interested motive behind it. He's been slumming it with us all year—it's obvious why."

She shook her head, not believing him. "We're friends, nothing more. That would be too weird."

He could have pressed the issue, but maybe it was better she was ignorant. There was no point in changing their dynamic at this crucial stage. "Just be careful, okay. The more you expose Mark to our world, the more you put him at risk. And us."

"Says the man who wants to tear down the border in full view of the authorities tomorrow."

The transporter was waiting for them in the wasteland, as Charlie had expected. Its contents would spark the first wave of enthusiasm for the Reacher cause. Protein, money, water—they were commodities the people of S'aven needed, especially now, but a container of such necessities would not excite them. He had to obtain something they would want, something they didn't think they could have, something that represented the unjust divide London flaunted.

"Something's not right." Rachel slowed their van.

Charlie looked more closely at the parked transit. She was right. He was expecting to see Roxy standing out in the open smoking one of his last cigarettes or John pacing because they were late. But there was no sign of either of them. The passenger door was wide open, a layer of snow coating both sides.

Charlie gestured for her to stop where they were. "Hide us," he said.

"It might be too late."

"And it might not." He drew his pistol from his coat. "Hide us."

They approached the transporter with caution, checking the driving compartment first. It was empty. No signs of a struggle. A noise came from inside the container, startling Charlie. He signalled to Rachel to cover him as he moved around the back. She stood at his side, her own gun raised, and nodded. He reached out, feeling for the locking mechanism in the door rather than risk getting too close and opening it manually. He twisted his wrists and the doors swung open violently, exposing the crates of oranges. And John.

Kissing Roxy.

20

Charlie's mouth fell open, but he couldn't speak. He couldn't even form a coherent thought. John kissing Roxy. Roxy, who he had hated for as long as they had worked together. He had too many questions and no idea where to start. They were supposed to be on a job, the biggest job of their lives. What the hell was John doing? Charlie was about to start with that, take the professional angle and ignore the awkwardness billowing between them all. Then he caught John's eye, and suddenly he was a teenager again, staring at a frightened lost boy who didn't know what to do.

John was afraid and uncertain and embarrassed, all the things Charlie had thought he'd outgrown. He stood frozen, vulnerable, and Charlie's heart sank. He was the big brother, the responsible one. He had vowed to take care of John, not scrutinise or judge him. And if John was afraid of what he would say, then Charlie had failed him. The air was thickening. It was up to Charlie to solve this, to make it alright.

He stared up at his brother, knowing he had to say something to move them forward and away from this moment.

"I can open the border," was all he could manage.

And the silence stretched on. John stayed motionless, a creature caught in the headlights in its final moments. Charlie realised he had no idea how to make this better. They weren't talkers, or huggers, or men who dabbled in emotions. What was he supposed to do?

Roxy looked between the brothers and then clapped his hands, forcing a showman's smile. "We're all set then," he said, edging closer to the open air and possible escape.

Charlie clapped his hands too, then frowned at the ridiculousness of the gesture. "I mean, yeah, we're all good. All set. We're all set. And it looks like you guys had a good night too. I mean the cargo. You got the cargo together. Which is great. Well done." He took a step back. "I need to… eh… go get something from the van."

He pivoted mechanically on his braced leg and slammed straight into Rachel. She gawped up at the container until he grabbed her arm and tugged her forcibly away. The van represented the last moments of his successful evening. He figured there was every chance, if he waited in there long enough, normality might return and this whole moment could be forgotten about. Unfortunately, Rachel had no intention of letting this one go.

"I'm not dreaming, am I? They were kissing? I mean, I had a dream like that once, but this all seems very real." Rachel stared back at the transporter when they got in the van. From where they were sat, the inside of the container was just out of view. "I thought they hated each other."

So did Charlie.

"Apparently not enough," he said.

Before he had time to reflect on what he thought about this, John leapt from the transporter. His eyes should have naturally fallen on the van and Charlie and Rachel inside, but he purposefully ignored them. In six determined strides he launched himself into the driver's seat of the transporter and slammed the door shut.

"I guess it's not me Roxy's been sticking around for," Rachel said.

Charlie glared at her. That couldn't be possible. Could it?

"Are you going to go and talk to John?" she whispered.

He had no intention of talking to anyone. "What would I even say to him?"

"I don't know, maybe ask him why he's been sucking face with his archnemesis." "Sucking face?"

"What if it was a prelude to something else? What if we were five minutes away from walking in on another dream I had?" She pressed her hand to her gasping mouth.

"You need to get your mind out of the gutter."

"Like you're not thinking about it. At least go and ask him what's going on."

Charlie shook his head before his thoughts got away from him. "Whatever happened is between them. It's nothing to do with us. We'll just wait here until they're ready to get on with the job."

As he spoke, Roxy clambered from the container. He dusted himself down and lifted his head towards the van. His eyes met Charlie's, and another awkward moment passed between them. Charlie swallowed. He had a horrible feeling that this wasn't going to go away easily. With cautious steps, Roxy walked around to the driver's side.

"What do you think he's saying?" Rachel asked.

"I don't know." He couldn't begin to comprehend what could possibly be said in a moment like this. Whatever it was, Roxy's own composure started to waver. He threw his hands in the air, shook his head, and marched away from the transporter.

"You seriously think this isn't any of our business? Charlie, we're about to pull off the biggest moment in Reacher history, and those two are preoccupied with a lovers' tiff."

Lovers? This was all getting to be too much. Of all the times this could happen, of all the jobs. Rachel was right. Whatever this was, it was threatening their mission. John and Roxy knew how important the job was. What were they thinking, complicating matters that had no business being complicated? Charlie had to do something. He could open the border—that was infinitely more important than anything that went on in the heat of the moment. He was resolved. He'd sort this.

He reached for the door. They needed to get the cargo to Mooney anyway. He'd make sure John was focused on the mission and nothing else.

"I'll speak to John," he told Rachel. "You speak to Roxy. I don't care what happened in that crate; I won't let Roxy fuck this up. Make sure he knows that."

Charlie slammed the door shut. Roxy made it to the van in time to be startled by the noise. He looked up and put his hands in his pockets.

"Everything okay?" Charlie asked.

Roxy lifted his head. "Everything is just dandy, Charlie love."

"We need to get this cargo out of here. Stay with Rachel until we get back."

"Sure thing," Roxy said, and went to open the back of the van.

Charlie let him be. Rachel was much better at dealing with Roxy. She'd have him straightened out. He needed to get to Mooney and convince a group of people who were terrified of Reachers that he could make all their dreams come true.

He hauled himself into the passenger seat of the transporter. The tension was already heavy and thick. John said nothing. He started the engine, clearly intending to drive the whole way in a brooding silence, but, as much as he wanted to, Charlie couldn't let him. When the time came, Charlie and Rachel's safety would be dependent on John. Charlie had to know his brother was focused on what was really important. He had to be able to trust him.

The transporter rolled forward, rumbling through the wasteland like a coming storm.

"So," Charlie started. "Are we going to talk about what just happened?"

"Nothing to talk about."

"I need to know whatever is going on isn't going to get in the way of what we're doing."

"It won't."

It was a natural place to stop. Charlie nearly allowed the conversation to die. But the tension was still too raw. "Okay. But what the hell was that?"

John's grip tightened on the steering wheel. "It was fucking stupid, and it won't happen again."

When they were teenagers, Charlie would boast about his meagre sexual conquests. He remembered proudly pointing out the alley where he'd managed to clumsily seduce a girl he'd met at the market—and clearly, all these years later, John still remembered it too. He could remember bragging about his relationship with Sarah. In part, he wanted to boost his stature in his brother's eyes, but also he felt responsible to educate John that there was more to the body than function. John was always so detached from other people. He showed no interest in forming relationships or even indulging in the occasional one-night stand. But as Charlie watched his brother drive, he couldn't help considering John's sexuality and potential virginity. It was naïve to think of John as some sexless being. Obviously he wasn't.

But that meant John had kept a part of himself hidden. And Charlie couldn't fathom why. If his brother had feelings for someone—even Roxy—he'd be thrilled. He wanted John to be happy, and the happiest time in Charlie's life had been when he was with Sarah. If his brother could find that kind of relationship, it would make all their hardships worthwhile.

"You know it doesn't matter if you like him—"

The look Charlie received was vicious, but he persisted. He'd fight through and find the real John beneath the hostility.

"What I mean is, if you have feelings for Roxy, that's cool. I'm cool with it. I support you."

"Don't do this," John growled.

"I just want you to be happy."

"Don't, Charlie."

"And if happiness is with Roxy, then that's great. Roxy's great."

John smacked the steering wheel. "He wouldn't shut up! That's all. I was trapped in there for hours, and the fucker wouldn't stop talking. He kept going on and on about the bloody oranges. I just wanted him to be quiet."

Charlie paused. His readiness to embrace this new development suddenly halted.

"Oh. So you don't... *like* him?"

"I've never liked him. I don't like him. I will never like him."

Charlie almost laughed in relief. His brother hadn't changed. Their situation hadn't changed. And now they could put this whole nonsense behind them. He settled back in the seat and tried to relax. They had their cargo, he could open the gates, and John wasn't keeping secrets. Soon the world would change, but he would be the one to change it—and he would be in control.

21

The wind pulled at Roxy's open coat in a vain attempt to draw him back to the container. Before Rachel could catch his eye, he put his head down, his hair whipping against his face as he walked towards the van. The transporter rattled into life and thundered past him. Roxy just kept moving: jaw tight, fists clenched, head fixed low. He got to the vacant driver's seat and continued walking.

In the wing mirror, Rachel caught him watching the transporter fade from view. He shook his head and reached for the door. Rachel heard the back of the van being opened, and curiosity got the better of her patience. She hopped out of the van and shoved her hands in her pockets before the cold got to her fingers. This winter was going to be brutal.

She found Roxy in the back of the van, one foot braced inside while he rummaged through their belongings. He tore through the bags furiously, shoving things that were his—and things that weren't—into a small duffel. Then he pulled open the sports bag they kept their cash in and paused. Rachel swallowed. She didn't want to see him do this.

"What are you doing?" she said.

He clasped a wad of notes. This money was supposed to see them safely back to the farm. This was their lifeline. She couldn't believe he'd just take it from them, not when the stakes were this high.

But he was taking it, and he seemed unremorseful too.

"What does it look like?" he grumbled.

"Well, it looks like you're trying to rob us. But I know you wouldn't do that, because as much as you are a light-fingered, untrustworthy bastard, you're not a murderer. And you know as well as I do that if we don't have that money we are going to get stranded here.

We'll die here."

It wasn't like he hadn't screwed them over before. She knew his history. He'd stolen from Charlie and John; he'd even sold her out in the past. Roxy had been a self-interested, opportunistic crook when they first met. But three years had passed, and a lot had happened to them all in that time. She'd seen him change. She was sure he'd changed. Roxy was her closest friend. Even in her darkest moments he could make her smile and see more than her own depression.

Now he wouldn't even look at her, his shoulders trembling with oppressed emotion. She could sense snippets of it with her powers: hurt, anger, despair. Tendrils of turmoil escaping from a tightly locked box. He was losing control of himself. He was panicking. The money stayed in his hand, hovering between his duffel and the bag it came from. His conscience won out and he dropped it, leaving it in the van for them.

She reached out to touch him and draw him back from this moment of madness, but before she could, he was throwing his bag over his shoulder and putting distance between them.

"Roxy, I don't understand. What the hell is going on?"

He kept his back to her, but his anguish was so strong it radiated from him in a heavy red aura around his head.

"Roxy, please talk to me." She pressed her hand to his shoulder, overcome with his hopelessness.

"I have to go." His voice was weak and quiet.

"Go where?"

"I don't know. I haven't thought that far ahead yet." He turned to her, his eyes rich with tears. He swallowed, gaining a second of composure. "Don't make this harder than it needs to be, love. You know I hate making a scene."

She touched his face, running her fingers through the scrub of beard on his cheek.

His eyes closed, and a single tear escaped. Rachel brushed it away. Roxy was never like this. He was never sad, and he certainly didn't cry.

"Okay, you need to tell me what has happened, because when I left everything was good. Is it because of John, because of what you guys were doing? Is it Charlie? The job? Is it me?"

"Leave it, pet."

"No. I won't leave it. You are my friend, and you are hurting. I need to understand. Why are you going?"

"It's not important."

"After everything we've been through together, that's the bullshit you're going to try to sell me. Fuck you. You owe us an explanation."

"I don't owe them shit."

"Maybe not. But you owe me one. You can't leave me here without answers. Please, why are you leaving?"

His face twisted as he battled with himself. She could see the conflict raging in him. Another tear escaped his eye, and he sighed at himself. "Because John wants me to go," he said in defeat.

"When do you ever do what John wants?"

He pressed his lips together.

"This because you kissed him?"

"I didn't kiss him. He kissed me, pet. And he wants me to leave so he can pretend that he didn't."

She couldn't make any sense of that logic. "He can pretend as much as he wants; we all saw it. And so what? What does it matter that he kissed you?" She planted a kiss of her own on his lips. "There. I've done it too. What's the big deal?"

She pulled away and realised that was the real question. Why would a meaningless kiss be an issue? Unless it wasn't a meaningless kiss. Unless this situation wasn't meaningless at all. When she looked at Roxy again she could suddenly see a difference in him. He was older, more tired. They were all weary from the months on the road, but this ran deeper. Without his flashy smiles and innuendoes, it was obvious. He was burdened and lost and defeated. And he had always been this way.

"I need you to tell me what's going on." She lowered him onto the back of the van and sat beside him, keeping her hand laced with his, shackling him to the conversation.

"The last person I told was dead two days later. It's probably best you just let me go and count your blessings."

"Bollocks. You tell me now. This is bigger than a random kiss in the heat of the moment, isn't it?"

"You could say that."

"Not the first kiss."

"No."

Rachel felt a chill run down her back. They'd been living on top of each other for months. How had she missed this? "When did it start?"

He stared at their linked hands and chewed on his lips. She could feel the secret battling inside him. *Tell me.*

"Charlie told you about the Grandchester, right? Well, what he didn't tell you, what he doesn't know, is it wasn't John who set off the bomb. I was raiding the safe, had my fingers on this priceless sodding computer chip, when he got to the room and I tripped some bloody booby trap and boom. We both woke up trapped—and together. He took the chip, and he made sure we both got out alive."

"Charlie doesn't know?"

Roxy shook his head.

"So you got out and...?"

"And there was chemistry. Very real, mutual and explosive chemistry. I couldn't just let him disappear, so I picked his pocket, took the chip, knowing he'd come after me."

"Which he did?"

"I made it very easy for him. Breadcrumbs as big as your fist to follow. He found me. One thing led to another. And in the morning, we very reluctantly said our goodbyes."

"No way." Rachel's hand pressed against her mouth to keep herself from bombarding him with questions.

He seemed to appreciate her restraint. "We honestly didn't think we'd ever see each other again. Oh, you should have seen his face when I showed up on Sarah's arm three months later. He was bloody livid."

"Livid?"

"You know what a control freak he is. He didn't want Charlie knowing that we knew each other. Told me I was to keep my big mouth shut and forget it ever happened."

That sounded more like John. "I take it you ignored him."

"Actually, back then I was more reasonable. I did exactly as I was asked. It was John that couldn't forget it. He came to me after our first job, and he's the one that kept coming back. He's the one that starts it. I'm just too weak to listen to common sense and call it quits."

"How long have you guys been...?"

"Shagging? Ten years, off and on. Probably more off than on." Roxy straightened, as though telling her had released some of the weight he was carrying. "Maybe it's more than that. I think it's more. Sometimes I think he does too. But then something happens and he reminds me it's nothing. That I'm nothing."

She was nearly afraid to ask. "What did he say to you tonight?"

He didn't want to tell her, she suspected, because it was still very raw. "I asked him how I could make it better." He swallowed. "And he… he told me to leave. I asked what that meant for us, and he said there was no us. There's never been an us. It's all in my *fucking* head. He's very eloquent when he's pissed off."

"He had no right to say that to you."

Roxy waved her comment away. "It's my fault. He's always been like this. And I need to stop deluding myself that it's ever going to be different."

"You've been staying with us to be close to him."

"I am quite the pathetic sap, aren't I?"

She would never see him as pathetic. It wasn't his fault he'd fallen for an insensitive, heartless arsehole. If anyone should get out of town it should be John, but even as she thought it, she knew that Charlie and John came as a set, and she would have to leave them if she took Roxy's side.

This time it was her tears interrupting them. "I'm going to kill him. He has no right to treat you this way. Stay, and I'll help sort it all out. I'll make him see what a wanker he is."

He patted her hand. The gesture was so distant it made her cringe.

"I can't, pet. I'm too old for this nonsense. And John Smith is never going to change. If I stay, he will get me killed."

The idea of struggling through each day without him made her stomach lurch. Roxy was the light in the darkness, the smile at the end of sadness. He kept her going, giving meaning to the hardship they were constantly under. She loved him, and losing him would be unbearable.

"I need a cigarette," she said.

He pulled one of six from his last packet and lit it for her. She wasn't a big smoker, but when her head was spinning it was one of the few things that could calm her down. She drew a deep breath and exhaled a plume of smoke. Instantly, the whirlwind of emotions settled into a steady breeze.

"I don't believe it. You've kept this a secret for ten years. I didn't think you had a discreet bone in your body."

She offered him a drag, but he refused.

"Just the one, it would seem."

"Are you going to at least wait until they come back?"

"No. Best to go now, while I'm thinking clearly. Besides, if I wait, Charlie will start crying, then I'll start crying…" He smirked and rose.

"I love you, you know," she said.

"I know. And I love you too, darling. I'd ask you to come with me if I thought you'd ever leave them." He kissed the top of her head.

"Where are you going to go?"

"I'll start with Thailand, track down Mother and play at being heartbroken for a while. Find a rebound or two. Drink until my liver starts to ache. Then who knows. I could even—"

His phone started ringing.

"So much for my grand exit." He looked at his screen and frowned. "It's Li." Rachel wiped her face as he answered.

"Li— Alright, alright. Calm down, darling… It's okay. Don't panic. I'll be right over. Just sit tight. I won't be long."

He hung up and rolled his eyes.

"Someone hit Li's place. Shook her up and swiped all the files we gave her. The story is gone." He threw his bag back into the van. "Looks like you've got the pleasure of my company for a little longer. We better get over there."

"Come on, I'll drive."

22

With the border closed, haulage had effectively ceased in S'aven. A sudden unexpected vehicle bounding down the road was already drawing attention. Charlie wanted the Union to take notice, but he was also conscious every moment in the open was a risk. It was imperative they move fast, not just with the drop-off but with opening the border too. If London suspected there was going to be trouble, they would strike first. And if the Institute discovered he was in town, the mission would be a total bust.

John seemed to share his sentiments. He pressed down on the gas, and the truck surged through a red light.

"Slow down," Charlie warned. "We don't want to seem like we're on the run."

John gave him a look but eased on the brake regardless. At a more respectful pace they tore through town, still catching the eye of every passing bystander. Charlie checked his watch. The countdown had begun.

The Union meeting was in the same bank as the previous gathering, although the crowd seemed to have doubled in size. Men and women spilled out onto the street, their faces more desperate, their panic more obvious. John slowed the vehicle, allowing them opportunity to gawp and get out of the way. He pulled up and the truck hissed, shushing the crowd into a stunned, confused silence. A ripple surged through the bank, drawing out those still in the building on a current of curiosity.

Charlie scanned the faces, trying to find Mooney amid the gaunt and the grey. "I don't want to take any chances tonight," he said to John. "Hang back and keep an eye on things. We don't know who's out there."

He made to open the door and paused at the number outside awaiting him. He'd never suffered stage fright before, but then he'd never faced an audience this big either. There was no turning back: if he couldn't stand his ground now, how would he be able to open the border with them all watching? He reached for the handle, and his fingers fumbled on the cold metal.

Red-faced, he glanced over his shoulder, succumbing to the nerves, and spotted Carson Mooney weaving his way through the throng. The Union leader appeared taller than the others as they parted for him. He approached the transit coolly. His ease was infectious, and Charlie felt himself relax despite the crowd's scrutiny. He took a breath and leapt from the vehicle to meet Mooney.

"Mr Smith, I didn't expect you back so soon." Mooney held out his hand. Charlie took it as a good sign.

"I think we can all appreciate time isn't on our side. We've come to make a donation." Charlie gestured to the truck and led Mooney around the back. Like obedient sheep, the rest of the Union followed.

Charlie pulled back the door to the container, the contents concealed in the darkness.

He climbed inside and offered his hand to Mooney. The Union man's reaction was crucial. Outside his people were starving, and all Charlie was offering was a container full of oranges. On the surface this was a lousy donation. But if Mooney could look past the practical disappointment and be inspired, tonight would be a success.

He watched the Union man take in the cargo, his face stony and guarded.

"This belongs to London," Charlie explained. "You're starving, and they are still shipping in food and letting it rot in the dockside warehouses."

Mooney picked up an orange and clasped it to his nose, savouring the scent. "Do I even want to know what these cost you?"

"Nobody died, if that's what you mean. Two delivery men with sore heads and egos in the morning. That's all. But this is just to show your people what is waiting for them. This is nothing compared to what I can really offer them."

Mooney turned to Charlie, the whites of his eyes glowing in the darkness.

"I can open the border, and all the benefits of London will belong to your people. Trucks like these and more can be theirs."

"If the border falls, there will be war."

Charlie appreciated his hesitation. Only a reckless leader would consider war an easy option, even when it was the only option.

"There's already a fight coming. It's inevitable. But as things stand, London thinks it has the upper hand. As long as they're behind their wall, they will strike against S'aven without conscience. What are they going to do when they realise they're not protected anymore? You can either surrender, let winter claim what's left of your people, or make a stand and try to stop them from shutting you out of the city and cutting off your lifelines again. It is time, we both know that."

Mooney lowered his head. "You want to help us… what would you be asking for in return?"

"Just the acceptance of my kind. We're tired of running, and we need a safe haven of our own—a society that will embrace us, not kill us."

Mooney gestured to the crowd outside. "They have their own minds, but if this sways them, if they believe in you, I'll back you," he said. "I'll back all Reachers."

Charlie flexed his fingers and suppressed his nerves. This was it. He grabbed a crate and made his way out towards the crowd, his leg brace clunking hard on the bottom of the container. The people awaiting him were curious, Mooney's welcome buying their patience, but what would they do when they understood who he was? What he was? Charlie put the crate down at the edge of the container. He saw eyes widen at the sight of the fruit. There was excitement, anticipation; it crackled in the air like electricity. Charlie knew the next moment was crucial, and he had no idea how it would go down.

He straightened his back, concentrating on the power running through his body. He raised his hand. One by one the oranges rose with it. Immediately, he could feel the tension tighten in the street. The people were frightened. Decades of propaganda had warned them about this moment. *Remain vigilant.* They were ready to run, to turn against him. Then Mooney stood behind Charlie, holding their attention like they were terrified rabbits on an open road.

"I've seen many of you side by side, staring down the border patrol as they trained their weapons on you. I've seen you defiant. Brave. And yet now you're so quick to run. Let me ask you, where do you run to? Where are you going? To ramshackle homes, to dying children, to hopelessness? All to get away from this man? Then what?"

Mooney climbed down from the container and stood among his people, an orange in his hand. Charlie let the other oranges fall back into the crate. He was at Mooney's mercy.

"Now, here's another question. What makes you run from him? When your own government points weapons at you, why would you turn away from a man offering his help? I'll tell you why. Because that's what London wants. They want you to be afraid. They want you to run from men like him, from Reachers, to hate them. For years we've all heard the warnings. Kept watch. At whose bequest? London's. And why? Could it be because this man and those like him have the power to help us? Could it be that if we were to unite with Reachers, if we accepted their help, we would be a real threat to the capital?"

The idea was spreading like wildfire through the crowd. Charlie could see eyes sparking with possibilities. He could see hunger and excitement. He'd imagined himself the driving force of this rebellion, but he was merely a catalyst. Suddenly he felt small in comparison to the Union leader. Sure, he could open the border, but he would never be able to lead these people through it. He would not be their messiah.

Mooney tossed his orange to a woman Charlie's age at the front of the crowd. Just like he had done, she pressed the fruit to her nose and inhaled deeply, those at her side licking at their lips in anticipation.

"Don't we deserve the same as those across the border?" Mooney tossed another orange. "Reachers, workers, we are all slaves to their whimsy. Divided. Powerless. What hope do we have? What lies in our future but suffering?"

Charlie took the opportunity to grab another crate, and another. Each one added more fuel to the crowd's enthusiasm. He turned and found others had joined him in the container. Men and women—who once would have been his enemies—now shared the work, passing out the spoils in celebration. He waited until their rhythm surpassed his own and left them to dispense the rest without him. He jumped out only to have Mooney grab his arm.

"Looks like you've made an impact, Mr Smith," he said.

"With some help. Thank you. For what you said."

"It's the truth. That's what they deserve. And that's what I ask from you. Can you really make good on your promise and open the border?"

"I can. But the longer we wait, the more chance of London hearing about our alliance and coming for us."

Mooney nodded. "We've got a demonstration march tomorrow. The crowd will be the largest yet."

"All those people, might be worth giving them a show," Charlie said as the last orange disappeared.

23

Rachel parked the van a street down from Li Starr's bedsit and got out to check the street. She'd always considered this part of S'aven the glamorous side of the shantytown, an area an overworked and underpaid doctor rarely visited. The remnants of the former glory days of S'aven's strip were just about visible in the crudely written signs boasting cheap drinks and even cheaper women. This had been Roxy's kingdom. His mother's club was the highlight of the strip, and the surrounding buildings bolstered his realm with an array of dive bars, gambling houses, and opium dens.

Now the strip was a morgue, each club a corpse. She closed her eyes, feeling around for prying eyes, stray thoughts. She sensed nothing close by, but only fools took unnecessary risks. When she returned to Roxy in the van, she pulled open the passenger door and offered him her hand.

"Ready?" she said.

"Are you that afraid I'm going to do a runner?"

She was, but she wasn't going to tell him that. "I'm thinking that if your journalist was attacked then someone might be watching her place, and it would be a good idea if they didn't see us coming."

Roxy's face softened into his usual smirk. "Fair point. Lead the way then, darling."

He took her hand in his and hopped out, easing the door closed gently. Rachel's powers naturally concealed them as they moved out into the open. There had once been a healthy nightlife beaming from the bars lining the pavements. Now it was all in darkness. A cold breeze ran up the road, and Rachel shivered, moving closer to Roxy for warmth and to keep a firm grip on him—as though that alone would compel him to stay.

They made to cross the street, and Rachel stopped. She scanned the few parked cars, looking for signs of life. Something felt off. She searched again, finding nothing but sinister shadows and paranoia. Her breath quickened in her chest. They shouldn't be here.

"What is it, pet?"

"I don't know." Her feet made a rebellious step backwards, pulling Roxy with her. "Maybe we should wait for Charlie and John to get back, and we can all do this together."

Roxy's jaw tightened. "How's about I go over; you can cover me from here. If I get into any trouble, you can come and rescue me."

He made to break free of her protection, but she couldn't allow it. She gripped his hand tighter.

"Pet, it's now or never."

"We'll go together. Just keep your eyes open. This whole setup makes me uneasy."

Her powers allowed her and those in contact with her to go unnoticed. It was a useful skill, but not infallible. If someone was looking for her, someone who knew about her abilities, she wasn't sure she'd be able to manipulate their attention enough. And the moment her thoughts started to waver, she felt her powers weaken.

We're not here. She mouthed the sentiment to make it stronger.

Then they started walking with renewed purpose.

Rachel was so engrossed in keeping them hidden, she was surprised when Roxy jostled her arm. They were standing outside a dirty brick building. In front of her was the remains of a front door, shards of wood and plastic littering the stairs beyond. Whoever had done this had used tremendous, terrible force. Rachel glanced at Roxy. They were thinking the same thing: it was a professional hit.

Roxy's composure changed. He took the small snubnose from his pocket. "Stay down here," he whispered. "I'll check it's safe."

Rachel stepped away from the door. She tried to scan the area again, and the sudden fear that struck her made her gasp. Roxy was already climbing the stairs.

"Li, love! It's me, I'm coming up now. Please don't shoot me."

Rachel hurried up after him, covering the rear whilst trying not to fall up the stairs. There was movement above her. Then she saw a woman hovering over them. There was a gun in her hand and determination on her face. Until she saw Roxy. Then her whole persona crumbled. She fell into him as soon as he reached the top step and embraced him desperately, sobbing hard into his shoulder. Rachel hovered uncertainly in the middle of the staircase, staring up at Li Starr in her moment of weakness. Their eyes met and Li straightened. She was a strong woman, and she wasn't about to show Rachel her vulnerable side.

Roxy noticed the change in her. He glanced at Rachel and beckoned her forward. "This is a very good friend of mine. She's here to help."

Li gave her a curt nod and turned her attention back to Roxy. "He took the files you gave me and the notes I was working on. Everything."

Roxy patted her hand. "Never mind that, pet. Are you okay?" He led her deeper into the bedsit, encouraging her to sit on the chair by her bed. "Are you hurt? Rachel is a doctor, best in town—she'd be happy to check you over. I can pop out if you need, give you a bit of privacy."

Li shook her head. "I'm fine. Just spooked, that's all. The guy, he… well, he wasn't your normal type of thug."

"Do you have any idea who he was?"

"No. But he knew what I had. He even figured out where I'd hid it. And he…" Li took a breath to steady her nerves. "He was scary, Roxy. Really fucking scary."

Rachel couldn't even begin to imagine what type of man would frighten Li Starr. Roxy glanced at her, sharing her sentiments.

"He's probably bugged this place."

"That's what I thought, but I can't find anything other than cockroaches. I figure it was in my laptop. Which he took." She rubbed her face. "I'm sorry. It had everything on it. All the evidence. My story. If you can get it to me again, then I can start from scratch, but if they're still watching me…"

Roxy swore under his breath. "Then they'll just come back. Or worse, they'll suppress the story some other way. No, we need to move quickly with maximum impact. We need people on the side of Reachers for what comes next."

"I've got a broadcast scheduled in an hour. There's a Union march tomorrow. I've got some prerecords with protesters I was going to use, but I could scrap it and go live with what you told me. Of course, without corroborating evidence, it's just me trying to convince the world I've not totally lost my mind."

"What if I could give you a witness?" Roxy said. "An interview with a real-life Reacher?"

Li's eyes widened incredulously, until Roxy gestured to Rachel.

"Roxy," Rachel warned. "This isn't a good idea."

He ignored her. "The rest of the truth can come later. What's important is impact. Rachel has been on the run since she was a kid. She's seen everything in those files, and she's lived a lot worse. What if you interviewed her and she told you exactly what it's like being a Reacher and what the government are doing?"

"People would listen," Li said. "No Reacher has ever voluntarily come forward. People would want to know what she had to say. Whether they'd believe her or not is another matter."

"They'll believe her. She's built from integrity and righteousness."

Rachel felt panicked again. This was moving too fast. There was no way she could broadcast herself to the rest of the country. She was a creature of the shadows, not something to be thrown into the limelight for people to scrutinise. And when she screwed up, when she said the wrong thing, she risked the success of their mission. She risked the future of all Reachers.

"Roxy, I can't do this," she said. And that was before she got on to what Charlie and John would think. This couldn't happen.

Roxy left Li's side and cupped Rachel's face. "Nonsense, pet, you were made for this." He pushed her hair back behind her ears and pressed a reassuring kiss on top of her head. "Tell the world your story. Tell them about saving patients in the hospital, about your sister. Tell them about the Institute capturing you, about what you saw in that laboratory. You are the epitome of a good Reacher. And this is radio. They won't see your face. You can still hide in plain sight. But the world deserves to know your story."

Rachel shook her head.

"You can do this," he assured her. "You can, because we need it done. If there's no story, we've just got Charlie—and we all know what happens when he's left to his own devices."

"Charlie would not like this, and you know it."

Roxy pursed his lips and rolled his eyes. "Then I'll stick around until they get back and take the blame for it," he said.

"Seriously? You'll stay if I do this?"

"I'll stay for as long as you need me."

Her decision was made. "Fine. Let's do it."

The recording room was small and blackened with damp. A table in the corner housed a crude transmitter. It reminded Rachel of the archaic equipment they relied upon in S'aven's busiest hospital. She sat opposite it on a creaky stool and felt compelled to sit as still as possible. Li sat beside her, composed and professional, restored by the familiarity of her workstation. She adjusted the microphone for Rachel and handed her a set of headphones. Rachel took them and watched them rattle in her quivering hands.

"Are you ready?"

"Not really." She looked to the doorway. Roxy leaned against it and gave her an encouraging smile. If doing this meant he'd stay, it would be worth it. At least that was what she was telling herself.

"Good evening, Britain and beyond. For the next hour you'll be listening to me, Li Starr, and today I'm sharing the airwaves with an unexpected guest. So let's get the introductions out of the way." Li nodded at Rachel to speak.

Rachel swallowed and moved closer to the microphone. "I'm, eh... I'm." The words clogged in her throat.

"Take your time," Li mouthed.

"Go on, pet. Just pretend you're talking to me," Roxy whispered.

She tried again. "My name is Rachel. I was born in Red Forest. And I'm a telepathic Reacher."

24

Roxy watched as Rachel unravelled her story in that tiny room and felt a pang of guilt. Despite everything she had suffered—the decimation of her family, the trauma of working in healthcare, the constant persecution—there had been no break in her character. She was so remarkably strong and constant. Even though she preferred the shadows, she was pouring out her life because he had asked her to. Because it helped their cause. Rachel truly was something special, and she deserved this moment—even if she didn't appreciate it. She glanced up at him as she spoke about her sister, about meeting Charlie and what she learned of his family. The scene felt groundbreaking, and a part of him was proud he'd played some part in making it happen. But the more she spoke, the more resolved he was that his involvement in what would unfold was over. And although it broke his heart to part with her, it was time to go.

He took out his cigarettes and waved them at her. She smiled, comfortable now she'd settled into her story. Then she turned back to Li and changing the world. He waited, taking it all in for one last moment. Then he left. The stairs creaked as he descended. He wondered if the noise would disturb the recording. When he got to the bottom he looked up, expecting to see Rachel, her face full of knowing and disappointment. But the landing was empty; his getaway was clear. He placed the cigarettes on the bottom step. She would find them when she was finished, and she would know what it meant. Goodbye Roxy style. Although now he thought about it, his departure would usually be tainted with lashing out somehow at John.

But doing that would be repeating a cycle, and this was about breaking a bad habit, not continuing one.

I don't want you around. How many times had he heard that in the past decade, and yet this last time seemed to hurt the most. Just like his brother, John was a narcissist, and Roxy was not going to be a casualty like Sarah was. Roxy's mother had warned him where this relationship would end. It was time he listened to her. John had proven time and time again he was more than capable of living his life without Roxy. It was time for Roxy to do the same.

He stepped out into the cold night air. A couple of months in the Thai sun would suit him, and if he moved quickly he'd be able to get there and drown his sorrows before any real regret set in. Roxy was pragmatic; he didn't need to wallow in a desperate situation if there was an alternative. To live without John Smith was possible. To live with him was never going to happen.

He was sorry not to see the job through, though. As frustrating as Charlie could be, he was still brilliant when it came to getting what he wanted, and Roxy would have loved to rubberneck in the aftermath of the border being torn down. Maybe he'd come back in a couple of months to see the damage. He dismissed the thought as soon as it sparked. Distance was the only chance of survival. Put several countries between them and he might, just might, rehabilitate himself.

S'aven had already changed too much anyway. This was no longer his town, and it wouldn't be long before he outstayed his welcome. Best to move on before he got caught up in his usual trouble.

He crossed the road quickly and glanced to the alleyway on his left, checking for any opportunistic thieves. Instead something else caught his attention. In the dark gloom, there was a white blemish. A bare leg twisted against the pavement. It wasn't the first body to wind up in that alleyway, and it wouldn't be the last. Roxy was about to move on, but the leg moved. And the movement was accompanied by whimpering. It wasn't the first injured girl to be dumped in the alleyway either.

"You alright, love?" he asked. He checked the surrounding street. It was empty, the wind kicking up litter like urban tumbleweeds. The woman's sobbing ceased. Her leg slipped behind the dumpster. She was trying to hide from him—not surprising, if she'd been attacked.

Roxy moved forward slowly, keeping his hands visible. He saw the woman's thighs, the hem of her dress. She was lying face down, shivering, her red hair over her face. Her skin was unnaturally pale and raw. Roxy knelt down beside her, careful not to touch her and cause her further distress.

"It's alright, pet. I'm not going to hurt you. You're going to be okay."

He started to remove his jacket to cover her up, and that's when he felt it. The cold barrel pressed into the back of his head.

No coming back from that shot.

He raised his hands. There was no need for this to go badly. This wasn't the first mugging the alleyway had seen.

"Wallet is in the jacket pocket, mate, help yourself. No reason to waste bullets tonight."

The gunman did nothing. Roxy heard laughing and looked down at the woman. She turned to him, flicking her auburn hair from her face, exposing a creature he was all too familiar with.

Roxy could talk himself out of anything. But not this. He opened his mouth, and bile rose in the back of his throat. She got to her feet, the vulnerability in her pale body gone. How could he ever have thought she was helpless? Roxy heard footsteps in the alleyway behind him, a vehicle coming up the road.

Ambushed.

Fuck.

"James Roxton," she said, her venomous tongue rolling his name around like a taunt. "It would appear you're a hard man to kill."

He wanted to bite back at her. To tell her she could go to hell. But the words clogged in his mouth. This woman had brutally murdered his best friend. She hunted the man he loved. If he could kill her he would. He would find a knife and slice it into her flesh just like she had done to Sarah.

Scarlet gestured that he should rise, and when he did, she pushed herself dangerously close to him. If he clasped her tightly he could strangle her. Would he be able to kill her before the bullet struck? It was worth a try. She anticipated his actions and stepped out of his reach.

"The infamous James Roxton. Alive and kicking, who'd have thought it? Do you know, I don't even think I can put into words how pleased I am to see you."

Roxy's jaw tightened.

"Firstly, let me apologise. You see, I thought you were just some Reacher groupie, following those brothers around because you had nothing better to do. If I had known, I'd never have tried to kill you."

He didn't like where this was going.

"You remember the Reacher girl, the Rachel wannabe. She was working for me. Trying to keep herself alive by siding with the enemy—didn't work out well for her, did it?"

A chill rattled up his back. This was not good.

"I forget her name now. I suppose it doesn't matter. What is important is what she did. Do you remember? She told me everything, how she led you outside. Took you into a back alley—not unlike this one, I bet. Then, while she was on her knees for you, she slipped inside your head. You'd created a wall in there. I remember her telling me how hard it was to break you. But there was a recent memory, something you hadn't suppressed yet. A secret you couldn't successfully hide from her."

He was going to be sick.

"You can imagine my surprise, can't you? John Smith, our perfect little soldier, engaged in a secret affair with some washed-up gambler with crooked teeth."

Roxy sucked in the acidic air around him. This was his fault. He'd screwed up, just like John always thought he would. And now the Institute had him. Now they would use him as bait to draw John out into the open. No, Roxy wouldn't let that happen. Whatever it took, he wouldn't let them take John away.

Scarlet was smirking like she had won already. "I'm curious, how rational do you think he'll be when he comes for you? He was very calculating and calm when we had Rachel. Do you think he'll be the same with you?"

"He won't come after me," Roxy said, his words lacking in conviction.

"Don't be so humble. Of course he'll come for you. Just like his brother came for that little wifey of his."

If he was dead, there would be no bait. He was already leaving; he'd made it clear his time in S'aven was over. If he disappeared, the others would assume he was keeping his distance. They wouldn't look for him. They wouldn't come for him. How long was he really going to last in this world anyway? Wouldn't it be better to go out like this? To die saving John?

He straightened his back and stared at the Institute bitch. She'd killed Sarah. She could kill him too for all he cared. But she wouldn't get John. Not while he was breathing.

"Go fuck yourself," he said and leapt at her.

Pain struck his spine. His legs buckled, betraying him, and he hit the filthy street hard. When he tried to move, a cold numbness ran up his body. Shadows lapped at his body, and he welcomed them. *Let it be like this*, he thought. And he closed his eyes and thought of John.

25

Rachel slumped in her stool, exhausted. She felt the echo of her story around her, a story she hadn't even realised she'd been harbouring. It was a lifetime almost forgotten, but each step she had taken had led her to this moment, to being in this room, stripping herself bare. She wrapped her arms around herself, feeling a mixture of vulnerability and liberation.

Li switched off the tape recorder, and it made her jump. She had become lost in her own story, forgetting there was an audience listening. Her heart started to sink when she realised she'd lost control of her filter. Her mind raced to remember what she had said. She had told them about wading through a civil war with her sister and father. She had told them about arriving in S'aven and meeting Father Darcy. Living in the convent; she'd mentioned that too. And then there was the hospital. Did she tell them about Charlie and John? Oh God, she did. And she'd talked about her powers. She told them about treating patients in S'aven, helping them with their pain and addictions. Would they be receptive to that? Or would they see it as a violation? Would they believe any of it at all? And if they did, what would they do?

"Was everything you said true?" Li asked.

"As much as I remember it. It was a long time ago," Rachel replied.

"Fuck." Li shook her head in disbelief. "The files, that was big. But your story. I don't know how to explain it."

"I know. It's not exactly what you were hoping for."

"Are you kidding? This is the most sensational piece I've ever broken."

"But it's just a story, without proof—"

"People don't take facts to their hearts. Those files, they were abstract, and people would view them with emotional distance. What you've just said, how you've said it... fuck, Rachel, you're going to be famous."

Famous? That was the last thing she wanted. She told her story because they needed it to bring down the Institute. She didn't want to be associated with it outside of the recording room. She swallowed a growing lump in her throat. If this was the wrong decision, everything they'd worked towards could be destroyed.

"Where is it aired?"

"Radio mainly. But I've got a guy across the border who records the broadcast and puts it up online. In about an hour you'll go viral."

"Shit." She put her head in her hands.

Charlie was going to go ballistic when he found out. Maybe she could just blame it on Roxy. It was his idea, after all. She looked to the doorway. It was empty. The last time she had looked at him he was going for a smoke, but that must have been an hour ago. She went out onto the landing and called after him. There was no response.

"Something wrong?" Li asked.

Rachel moved down the stairs and stopped. A single packet of cigarettes awaited her at the bottom. She picked it up. It was half empty. His last pack. He'd left it there, knowing she'd find it. Knowing she'd know what it meant.

"Shit. Shit. Shit." It was pointless, but she ran outside anyway. The streets were empty. He was gone.

"What is it?" Li said, bounding down the stairs after her.

"Roxy's gone."

She crushed the packet in her hand, furious with him. He had promised her he would stay. She'd just exposed herself to the world at his behest, and he'd bailed before they could deal with the consequences. This was just like him.

But as quickly as the anger came, it disappeared. She knew, deep down, Roxy leaving had nothing to do with her. Beneath the bravado and nonchalance, he was hurting, and being forced to work with John would have made the pain unbearable. For his own sanity, he had to get away. She couldn't be angry at him for that.

"This thing is going to blow up any minute. I'm going to go to ground for a few days, find somewhere safe to start up again. Are you going to be okay on your own?" Li asked.

Rachel wasn't alone. She'd have to return to Charlie and explain what she'd done. Then she'd look John Smith in the eye and tell him that Roxy had left. And it was all his fault.

"I'll be fine," she said.

"Listen, people are going to be crying out for more. We could do a deal, exclusivity for big money—the border may be closed, but I still have some rich contacts in London."

Rachel shook her head. "I can't."

"What about the files? Can I get another copy of them?" She fished out a card with an email on it.

"We'll do our best. Good luck with your story. I've got to go."

26

Morning settled on the town, and Charlie's adrenaline was starting to wane. His mind was a hive of thoughts and ambition, but his exhausted body was taking priority. He yawned and stretched the ache in his back. In less than twenty-four hours he was going to change the world, but first he needed to rest.

He reached for the radio in the transit and turned through the static. There were a few stations still broadcasting, along with the occasional pirate transmission. Radio was less censored than TV or newspapers. London, with all her exposure to modern technology, had largely abandoned analog broadcasting and was slow to close the outspoken stations still transmitting. And all the stations seemed to compete for the morning air time when audiences were bigger and more inclined to pay attention. Charlie turned the dial and found a dead silence. He paused. Then the speakers blared into life.

"*It was just after Christmas when I made it back to S'aven. Sister Eda had got me a place to stay. And a job. All I needed was my sister. But I was too late. Izzy died before I could find her.*"

Charlie felt a chill running down his spine. He knew that voice.

"*I remember stepping outside and I knew she was gone. We were connected—all the years apart, all the distance, we still could sense each other. I could feel when she was in trouble, and then I felt the emptiness when she was murdered. It was like a part of me was gone.*"

"What happened to her?"

"*I had no idea. It wasn't until years later that I found out. Getting me out of S'aven and to the convent cost a lot. To save me, Izzy had to stay in S'aven. A man called Frank Morris bought her.*"

"The gangster?"

"Apparently. He forced her to work for him. To use her powers to steal secrets from his enemies. She was a child when she went to live with him. And she was sitting at his table when he was assassinated. She died with him."

"What the fuck is she doing?" John growled.

Internally, Charlie was screaming the same question.

They heard Li's voice next. *"What did you do after you knew she was dead?"*

"The only thing I could do. I went to work. I had a double shift at the hospital and worked until I couldn't feel my feet. And I did that until the hole in my chest stopped surprising me."

There was a brutal honesty to Rachel's words. She continued to talk, to tell Li about hiding herself in a town of pain and suffering. She spoke about her fears of being discovered, and confessed to using her powers to treat some of her patients.

"Sometimes people got angry; drunks, addicts. And I could make them calmer. I could stop them from hurting themselves or others."

Charlie remembered when he'd first seen her, staring down an addict with a temper. Medical staff took a lot of shit from S'aven, but they earned a lot of respect too. A Reacher, using her powers to help them—would they hate her for what she was or marvel at what she could do?

"A lot of the time it was just stopping them from suffering. I remember when Kingston burnt down and we were flooded with burns victims. In two hours we ran out of morphine, and we called, begged, London to let us have supplies. The border was closed, like it is now, and they wouldn't let anything through. God, the pain those patients were in. Some of them had third-degree burns all over their bodies, and there was no way they'd survive the week. There was so little the other doctors could do to help. But I could. I didn't even think about it at the time. I just moved through the rooms and the wards and touched those I could. The respite they got was probably only superficial, but I like to think it helped. It was only afterwards, when I was on my own, that I realised how dangerous it was to use my powers so brazenly. I was terrified one of the patients I had touched would report me—or one of my colleagues. That night I thought about running."

"But you didn't."

"No. I didn't until two years later. I was in the hospital—I was always in the hospital—when a man approached me. He was a Reacher, and he'd been hired to find me. He told me to run. He said if he could find me, others wouldn't be far behind. And so I ran. I left S'aven with him, and we've been running ever since."

"Running from what?"

"*From people wanting to use my powers for their own greed. And mostly from the Institute. I've seen what they will do to me if they find me. I've seen files of countless Reachers cut open in operating theatres. And I've seen the evil of that place in the eyes of my friend. Charlie was captured by the Institute, and he grew up in their laboratories. They cut on him, tortured him. All kinds of things. He was just a boy.*"

"But he escaped?"

"*I don't think he ever truly escaped. He got out of the facility, but eventually they found him, and they murdered his family as punishment. As Reachers this is our choice: we can run, or we can be captured. And as much as I can bring peace to others, there will never be peace for me.*"

A chill pinged through the nerves in Charlie's spine. It was eerie hearing his history through the speakers. Rachel had said his name, and it would not take long for people in S'aven to connect his story with his sudden appearance in town. He couldn't understand why she would do this. Now the world would know where he came from. They would see him at the border as a man who had lost his family, not a Reacher with immense power.

"She wouldn't do this on her own," John said. "What if they've got her again? Fuck, Charlie. If they've got her—"

"The Institute wouldn't have her broadcasting negative press about them."

That didn't mean she was operating under her own volition either. John was right. Rachel wouldn't do this unless she was being forced to. Charlie drew in a deep breath, hoping it would calm him. It didn't.

The transporter rolled through S'aven. They were supposed to take a winding route back to the dump site, but John changed course, taking the quickest road back. He pressed his foot on the accelerator, pushing the vehicle until it groaned with the strain. After a hard right the tyres struck frozen dirt, forcing John to slow down. Seconds later the buildings abruptly parted, giving way to the large open stretch of wasteland.

Charlie braced himself against the dashboard as they hit the dirt track. Their headlights lit up their lane in the road ahead, while the night concealed the land around them. The terrain was mainly open and exposed in daylight, but in darkness it was a perfect hunting ground. John slammed the transit into third and gestured to a light ahead.

Orange flames flickered at the sky, illuminating the side of a familiar vehicle. At least the van was here. It meant someone had made it back. Light meant life, he reminded himself.

"Slow down," he told John.

He raised his hands, trying to feel for weapons concealed in the blackness. Nothing. When he looked up, he saw a shadow cross their headlights. It was Rachel.

A relieved laugh escaped his lips as John pulled up the transporter.

He pushed open his door and leapt from the cabin. His braced leg struck the frozen earth and buckled. The momentum made him stumble, and he hit the dirt, falling on his knees. In all the drama, he'd forgotten he was no longer the young, fit man from Rachel's story. On the ground he winced at the burning in his thigh, knowing it was just an omen of pain to come.

Rachel was already at his side. She hooked her arms under his and raised him up. He grabbed her, revelling in the Reacher buzz she ignited in him. She squeezed him tighter, reminding him things were still very wrong. Gently, he eased her back, trying to see her face against the shadows. There was a redness to her eyes. Had she been crying? There was anger too, pressed between her lips. "Are you hurt?"

She shook her head.

"Okay, then why were you on the radio?"

She swallowed and released a little of the anger. "You heard it already?"

"Me and thousands of others."

She backed away from him. "I was hoping I'd get a chance to warn you first."

"Warn me that you were about to expose my whole fucked-up childhood to the world? Rachel, what the hell were you thinking, saying all that stuff?"

"Look, after you left we got a call from Li Starr. Someone broke into her place—they took her computer, all the files we gave her. They really shook her up, and she did not seem like a woman who was easily scared."

"Someone robbed her?" This was just typical; he was here to help S'aven, and the town repaid him with thievery.

"No. Someone went after the files. That's all they took. They left her money, her recording stuff."

John rounded the transporter. "They knew about the files?"

Charlie saw the anger reignite in Rachel's face. She folded her arms and stared at him as though he were missing something vital. But none of this made sense. Until a day ago, they didn't even know Li Starr and had no intentions of surrendering their information to a stranger. If someone went after the files they had given her, she had to be under surveillance.

"Does she know who it was?"

"No. All we know is he took everything she had, and the story without the evidence is just a conspiracy theory. You wanted something that would make an impact here. Roxy thought the interview was our best shot."

"I should have fucking known," John snarled.

Charlie's stomach lurched. He thought back to their conversation in the van. Roxy had been the one to spark the idea to go public. Had he offered more than a spark? He was a skilled manipulator when he wanted to be. And he did say Li had already offered him money for a story. All these months slumming it with them obviously came at a cost. Charlie understood now why Rachel was upset. They'd all been deceived. Again.

"Where is he?"

The van was too quiet. It could only mean one thing.

Rachel closed her eyes. "He's gone," she said softly.

This had hurt her. Charlie understood; Roxy was supposed to be their friend. They thought—this time—they could trust him.

"He left when I was recording with Penny. He's probably already on his way to Thailand by now."

The money. Charlie launched himself at the van. He pulled open the back, almost falling inside. Their bags had been emptied and rifled. His heart started racing. He felt about frantically, trying to find their money. Then his hands fell on a familiar strap. There was weight to the bag, but Charlie wasn't easily fooled. John was at his side, ready to witness another epic Roxy betrayal.

He opened the bag and frowned. The money was still there.

"I don't understand. It's all here."

John snatched the bag from him. He tossed several wads of notes into the van, looking for fakes and finding nothing.

"Starr must have paid him," John said.

"It must have been a shitload if he left us with this." He wondered how much Roxy valued their friendship. Maybe his relationship with the brothers was rocky, but Rachel at least was worth more than this. They were supposed to be close. Was this because of what she did with Mark? Charlie glanced over at her to see if she had already reached this conclusion.

"She didn't pay him anything. He was already planning on leaving when Li called him. He only took me to her place to try and help."

"Why was he leaving?"

"Ask him." She glared at John.

Charlie's head was starting to hurt.

"Tell him," she demanded. "Tell him that you told Roxy he had to leave. Tell him why you told him."

He turned to his brother, expecting John to be as befuddled as he was. But he wasn't.

John squared his shoulders, looking ready to fight it out.

"Hey," he reasoned. "It's not John's fault."

Rachel started to laugh, fresh tears forming in her eyes. "You tell him now, or I will."

John stood his ground, staring her down with equal intensity. "You're talking shit."

"You manipulated him. Gaslighted him. You didn't deserve him. You don't deserve anyone. Fuck you, John. Fuck you, you pathetic son of a bitch."

Charlie made to step forward and protect his brother, but John pushed past him.

"You're a coward, John Smith," Rachel called as he fled into the wasteland, never once looking back.

Charlie gawped at the nothingness his brother was hiding in until Rachel thumped him hard in the arm.

"Ow! What was that for?"

"Go ask your brother."

He caught her before she too could storm away. "Hey, in case you hadn't noticed, we are in the middle of a job here. We don't have time to piss about with this drama. What the hell is going on?"

She threw one last hate-filled look over the wasteland. "Roxy left because of John."

Charlie was about to roll his eyes and condemn Roxy again, but the severity in Rachel's face stopped him. He was missing something.

"Your brother has been lying to you. Him and Roxy have been fooling around for years."

"Don't be ridiculous."

"Charlie." She held his arm now, firm but comforting. This was her doctor move, steadying her patient before she delivered some earth-shattering news. "You know I'm telling the truth. All this time they've been having this toxic secret relationship. John controls it all; he messes with Roxy's head. It's wrong, Charlie. What he did to Roxy is out of line."

John had lied to him. He'd sat in the transporter and lied to him so freely Charlie didn't even pick up on it. He was supposed to be able to trust his brother. But then he remembered he'd kept his own secrets. He'd had his secret drug habit. It shouldn't have surprised him John kept his personal demons hidden. It shouldn't bother him, but it did.

"Did Roxy set you up to hurt John?"

"He didn't set me up. He saved the day, Charlie. I know it's not ideal, but we needed something to inspire S'aven into getting behind you. Roxy made the suggestion because he wanted to help. And he's right. It will help."

Rachel's voice was filled with calm conviction, just like on the radio. Maybe it was the hospital training or maybe an unexplored aspect of her powers. Whatever it was, people responded to her. Rachel had integrity. While he languished in grief and self-loathing, she continued, strong and defiant. Her story was one people would understand. She was a Reacher they could relate to. Roxy was right. Her interview was exactly what they needed.

"You're sure he's gone?"

"I'm sure. I tried calling. Nothing. He doesn't want to be found."

"Tonight of all nights."

"Don't blame Roxy," Rachel warned.

Charlie looked out to the path his brother had taken. "I don't."

"You need to talk to him."

"I know. But not now."

"You can't just pretend nothing's wrong."

"I'm not," he snapped. "But I've just committed myself to doing something I'm not even sure I can do. I will deal with him after I've got the job done."

She stood stony and unreadable.

"I need you with me, Rach. With just the three of us, things are going to be even harder. Please. This is bigger than us. It's bigger than them."

She nodded. "Fine. But afterwards, you talk to him, or I will."

Charlie put his arms around her and closed his eyes. He was suddenly so very tired. His head was pounding, his thoughts spiralling. First he would open the border, then he would smack some sense into his brother.

27

The squad room was silent. It was the third playing of Rachel's interview, and still nobody had said anything. Mark's colleagues were transfixed. He was transfixed. Rachel's composure, her honesty drew him in like a new disciple. The recording had hit the station two hours earlier. It was already circulating on the mainstream TV and radio news. He listened again to her describe fleeing Red Forest. He could imagine her holding her sister's hand as they trudged through the snow, her father's blood still on her clothes. He heard about her time in the convent and struggled to imagine her mingling with nuns. Then she spoke about her time in S'aven, of blending in, of trying to make a home in this world. He wasn't mentioned, but he knew his place in that part of her life. He was beginning to understand his place in the rest of it too.

Rachel's story meant a lot of things, and as the recording was played on repeat the men in the room were trying to figure out what. If it was just her account, they could have downplayed it as a hoax. But more had happened that night. Those watching the Union had witnessed another Reacher appearance. Two male Reachers addressing the Union rebels, Carson Mooney at their side. Mark could guess who the men were, but the rest of his squad were at a loss for answers. They were frightened by what this all meant. And they were already underestimating the danger they were about to face.

Mark's squad leader switched off the recording. "Our focus today is the riot. The country will be watching. One wrong move and the Unioners are ours. You hold the line. You wait for them to cross. And then we hit them."

"But what about the Reachers?"

The squad leader shooed away the question with his hand. "That's tomorrow's problem."

Mark watched them from the back of the room. Their confidence would be their downfall. He wondered what they would do if they knew the truth. They'd heard Rachel's account; he could see some of it had penetrated their thick heads, and yet in the same instant it was disregarded. These people were purposely shutting their eyes. This country was determined in her ignorance. But not for much longer.

The door to the meeting room was pushed open. The interruption was unexpected, and Mark's squad leader scowled at the woman stepping through. Her face was grey and sunken, so much so that the squad leader didn't recognise her. He glared at her impertinence, but she glared back, harder, more furious. Instantly he buckled, knowing he was no match for an Institute agent. No one was a match for her. Agent Scarlet Stone was a different breed of danger. Even sporting the marks of a losing fight, she still commanded their utmost respect and fear.

She addressed his team but looked directly at Mark. On paper he was her man, her spy, her pawn in this complex game. In reality, being in her company terrified him. She had to be here because of Rachel.

"You'd be wise, gentlemen, to not dismiss this Reacher threat. As meek as this woman may sound, I can assure you, she is capable of committing great evil."

Mark said nothing.

"And if you think her appearance in S'aven at this time is a coincidence, I'll not mourn your inevitable deaths." She threw a vicious glance at the squad leader. "You will protect the border at all costs. Do you understand?"

If they questioned her demands, none of them dared show it. She was known in the station as an agent, but few were aware of exactly where she came from—and even fewer understood what she was capable of. Scarlet's authority overruled every officer in the building, and anyone who had challenged her in the past was now conspicuous by their absence. She gestured to the door and the men began to file out, eager to be away from the trouble she brought. Mark made to leave with them. He was undercover, and as far as his team knew, he'd never even spoken to Scarlet before. If he was to be useful here, he had to keep up the act. He got to the door, his team still loitering within earshot in the corridor.

"Bellamy," Scarlet said.

The sound of her voice echoed down the halls. He saw his teammates' interest piqued, their attention now fully on him.

"Come with me."

Leaving with her would be an admission to the whole station that he was more than a bad cop. There would be no going back from this. He realised his time here was over, but it didn't bring the relief he'd been hoping for. Scarlet took the lead, and he started to dread what new hell she was leading him to.

"Your girlfriend has been busy," she said. "It's quite a story she's spinning."

Mark pressed his lips together. He didn't doubt a single word of Rachel's story. She was no actor or con artist; the pain in her voice was genuine and contagious.

"Where is she?"

"I don't know."

"She hasn't made contact with you?"

He wasn't an actor or a con artist either, but he would be. For Rachel's safety, he'd get on stage and give the performance of his life. "I didn't even realise she was in S'aven until I heard her voice."

"I see all of this is a surprise then. It's funny, Mark, you don't look surprised."

Hold your nerve. "When I met with Mooney last, he mentioned Reachers. He asked if they could be trusted. I thought he was just trying to scope me out. But after hearing… well, it all makes sense now."

He could feel her gaze intensify, peeling back his words to uncover his lies. The tension between them was growing. He was on borrowed time; he could sense it.

"I want to show you something," she said.

"I'm supposed to be gearing up with the others."

"Don't be foolish, Mark. They won't have you working with them now."

She marched through the station as though it were hers. Mark supposed in many ways it was. She could control everything here. She could destroy everything if the mood took her. He followed at her side, seeing his former colleagues' suspicious looks. He experienced an uncomfortable sense of déjà vu. The last time this happened he'd been wrongly arrested for murder. He wondered what charges would be drummed up this time.

The corridors started to wind downwards. They seemed to be heading towards a series of interview rooms on the third floor.

"Remember back in Blackwater, there was a Reacher girl who kept Doctor Curtis from losing control and causing trouble for us?"

Mark remembered. The girl, Maria, was like Rachel, only weaker. She could read minds, commit simple manipulations. She had lured Rachel and James Roxton to a secluded cottage, ready for the Institute to swoop down and capture them. Mark had facilitated the whole thing. He'd been so naïve back then.

"She's dead now," Scarlet said dismissively. "The Smith brothers killed her shortly after we left. Bullet in the back of the head. One of their own—now that was a surprise. But her death is largely insignificant, much like her existence. Except for one thing." They rounded a corner into a corridor with four numbered doors.

"You see, before we left, I was preparing to transport her to the Institute. But she convinced me to let her stay; she promised me she could be useful. You see, she could steal secrets—not to the extent of your Rachel, but she could skim the surface of the conscious mind. She used those powers on James Roxton. Do you remember him?"

Mark swallowed. For a long time he'd despised Roxton. That man had stood in Mark's home and pretended he was a government official. He'd offered Mark a fake job, lured him into a fake stake-out. And then he'd stolen Rachel away. For a long time, Mark had fantasized about killing the bastard. But when it came to it, that night in the fields surrounding the cottage, he'd pointed a gun at Roxton's head and the hate had started to weaken.

"Maria managed to get him alone. She infiltrated his mind—and it would have been a fruitless effort if it wasn't for a recent, unresolved incident playing on his memory. It was a moment captured a day earlier on his way out of S'aven. An intimate moment that he was trying to reconcile and evaluate. A relationship about to be rekindled."

Mark froze. He thought about Rachel, and he readied himself for the news she was with Roxy. It would hurt, but he could live with it. As long as Rachel was free, he'd be satisfied.

She led him into the viewing room. It was dark, stinking of cigarette smoke.

"Of course, the silly girl waited until after I ordered Roxton's death. And you'll remember that, won't you, given I ordered *you* to kill him."

She flicked on the lights, and Mark jumped. Beyond the window a familiar man was slumped in a chair, his hands cuffed behind his back. His hair was matted with blood and grime, covering a purple, swollen face. Roxton lifted his head, groaning at the effort.

Mark knew this was it. This was the moment she would kill him. In front of them was proof of Mark's treachery. He was done for.

"But look, Mr Roxton isn't dead. He's made a miraculous recovery. And it's very lucky. Lucky for me because I now have an unbeatable hand to end the game with. And lucky for you because you failing in your duty has benefited me."

He didn't know what to say. He stood motionless, staring at the prisoner, wishing they could trade places.

"It still doesn't make up for the fact that you lied to me, Mark. You did lie, didn't you? You told me he was dead when he wasn't. Why did you do that?"

Mark had been waiting for this moment. He'd rehearsed it over and over so it would come naturally. Now it was here, the words clogged in his throat. He felt sick. "I've never... I've never killed anyone before. I tried, but I just couldn't do it. So I lied. I didn't want you to think I was weak."

He couldn't tell whether she believed him or not. Increasingly he was starting to suspect she was toying with him, and the more he played the fool, the more she dragged this out.

"That's what I assumed," she said finally. "And like I said. It's lucky that this has happened in a way that has benefitted us both. So we'll forget that you lied. We'll just make sure it never happens again."

Mark nodded, afraid of doing anything else.

"Now, aren't you just dying to know?"

"Know what?" he croaked.

"Who James Roxton was sleeping with?"

She was trying to torment him. She knew he still loved Rachel, and hearing Rachel was with someone else would be the start of her punishment. He was the mouse in the room, she a ferocious feline letting him go only to swipe at him again. He straightened his back and braced himself for the blow.

"John Smith," she said, grinning.

He was too shocked to say anything. Instead he stared at the man behind the glass, Rachel's friend, and felt a new compassion for him. Did Rachel know? He took a shaky breath, trying to disguise his relief from Scarlet. If he could get away, if he could scurry into a hole she couldn't reach through, he could make it back to Rachel. He would make it back to her.

"I want you on the streets today. We know the brothers are working with Mooney. Go to the march, find their location, and contact me. Do you understand? I want to know where they are immediately."

He couldn't believe his luck. She was going to let him go, and as soon as he made it out, he wouldn't be coming back. He stood taller. "Of course, ma'am."

"Well, what are you waiting for?"

Mark bolted for the door before she changed her mind.

28

A pale sun cut through the late morning smog, illuminating the streets like fool's gold. An unusual stillness had settled on S'aven. Roads were open and empty. Homes were closed and silent. An acrid bitterness permeated the air, the bilious aftertaste from years of sickness. Rachel stood on the charred roof of Lulu's old club, watching the border wall and the static shadow-covered guards perched in readiness.

Her fingers wove patterns in the air, as she extended her awareness to those blocking the road into London. Fear. The town radiated with it. She could sense the border patrol, fixed in position with nothing but terror at their backs. A stronger fear buffeted the rest of the town. Fear from those trapped in S'aven, starving, dying. Fear that this would be another hopeless stand, that nothing would get better.

But Rachel wasn't afraid. She looked at Charlie as the tension in town tightened. It was time.

Leaving John in his vantage point up high, they clambered down the ruined building. She held out her hand for Charlie, supporting him as he crossed out into the open street. Rachel could hear her heart in her ears. A steady pounding, adrenaline pushing it faster. The noise grew louder as her heartbeat was accompanied by a thunderous drumming. Feet on concrete. Hundreds and thousands of feet.

The nearer they came, the louder their thoughts. So many were hurting and grieving. She felt their pull, their desperation, and nearly lost herself in it. But then she heard her own story, her words remembered, driving these people forward. They knew her history, and it had touched them. They were marching for their own futures and for hers and for Reachers everywhere. She closed her eyes, drawing on her own faith in Charlie and propelling it across the crowd. They could do this. They *would* do this.

Charlie gestured to a face in the mass of people. Carson Mooney walked empty-handed with his people. He caught sight of Charlie and Rachel but pushed on without ceremony. Rachel took Charlie's hand again and allowed them to be swallowed into the march.

They came to a crossroad, and there was hesitation. But instead of a police ambush, more protesters joined them, flooding their numbers from two directions until the streets were crammed.

"There was me worrying we wouldn't draw a crowd," Rachel whispered.

"It's a lot of people to impress," Charlie said.

Rachel gave him an encouraging smile. "You can do this. I have faith."

Mooney gravitated towards them through the throng. He held the hand of a young girl, her face as determined as his. Then Rachel noticed more children, their emaciated bodies trudging at their parents' sides. All of S'aven had come for this. The young, the old, the sick, the dying. She caught Mooney's eye and knew instantly what he was thinking. If Charlie failed, there would be no tomorrow for any of them.

Clouds misted over the sun, shrouding them in a sudden, ominous darkness. The border was lost in the smog, then in twenty feet the sky cleared and the wall was exposed. The shadows watching them from up high started moving. As long as the wall was up, they were safe, but nobody had ever seen numbers this strong before.

"Showtime," Charlie said, tightening his grip on her. "You ready?"

"Always."

Rachel concentrated on her own powers, channelling them into their connected hands. She felt a sudden nakedness as she was stripped of her own abilities, but she refused to falter. Charlie raised his free arm, his wrist twisting in the air. His eyes closed as he started to reach for the mechanics of the gate. Rachel could feel his actions as though they were her own. Through him she could move things with her mind; together they were unstoppable.

A shot snapped from the top of the border wall. A man fell at Rachel's feet. The power wavered for a moment while she was distracted. Another shot, another body. They couldn't afford to dawdle. She looked up and saw the shooter in the watchtower fall, his body crashing into the police blockade beneath him. John had their backs.

"You can do this," she whispered over and over. "You can do this. You can do this."

She felt a give in his body. Her own fingers flexed. When she looked, the gate was opening. The metal blockade creaked with the effort. But it was working. The concrete barrier that separated the rich from the poor was breaching. Light blossomed in the gap, shining on the dirty faces of the desperate. A gasp rolled through the street.

Charlie squared his legs. She took hold of him, pressing into his back, crossing her hands over his chest. He raised both arms, and the gates moved faster. He was doing it. He was actually opening the border. Rachel squeezed her eyes shut, holding him tighter and tighter. His body was shaking, his legs threatening to give way. *No pain, no pain, no pain.* She pushed every bit of will she could muster into him to keep him upright. To keep him working. And then she felt him fall forward. A bright, glaring sun blinded her. The gate in front of them was gone. The border was open.

She dropped to her knees with him as the crowd took in what had just happened. Charlie was sweating and breathless.

"You did it," she whispered proudly.

"You sure?"

"It's open."

"Thank God. I don't think I could do that again if I tried." With her help he pulled himself up.

There was a change in the people around them. The border was open, the impossible had been accomplished, and everything had changed. Rachel was momentarily overwhelmed with their fury and panic. *What now? Storm the border? Kill the fuckers?* She stared at the unprotected capital and the wailing mob hurtling towards it. If they crossed over, war would begin.

Rachel couldn't let that happen. She snatched Charlie's hand and in turn his power. She felt her arms radiating with strength and closed her eyes. Her mind reached out to the hive mind of the mob.

"Walk away," she said. "Walk away now."

The idea settled slowly on the faces around her. Then it spread. The delirium was over. They had won; there was no need for more bloodshed. Those with children were the first to leave. They turned their back on London, ready to return to their squalid houses, to their desperate lives. But they would do so stronger than ever, because now there was no divide. Now they'd shown that everything could be open to them and they would take it if they wanted to take it. London held no power over them anymore.

The tide moved and Rachel moved with it, backing away from the centre and flowing out to the wastelands of the urban landscape. Charlie let go of her to shake the hands of those passing by, and immediately they were separated. She watched him walking alongside Carson Mooney and decided to hang back. The impression he made with these people would affect all Reachers to come. And she was more than happy to disappear from their memories.

The mood in town had already changed. She could feel hope and faith sparking from enlightened minds. For the first time in their lives they had power, and, for this day at least, it was unblemished by traditional S'aven corruption. It was hard not to smile or join in the victory. Rachel wondered if this was what she was supposed to be: a liberator, a Reacher warrior for the oppressed. Could her traumatic history be for this moment? Was it worth it?

Before she could bask in the possibility of a future fulfilled, she caught sight of John weaving towards her and her mood instantly soured. He was unaffected by what had happened. She wondered if anything ever penetrated his soulless demeanour. Roxy certainly didn't.

"Charlie's with Mooney," Rachel said sternly, hoping he would leave her and go after his brother.

He didn't. "I know."

"I don't need a babysitter."

"He wanted us to pass under the radar."

John meant that Charlie wanted her to hide them. She pulled up the hood of her jacket and carried on walking. "Then pass under the radar and leave me alone."

The streets were clearing. She could make Charlie out up ahead. She stormed after him. Commercial buildings morphed into domestic shacks, and then they were heading over the canal towards a block of flats.

"You're being fucking ridiculous," John said when he caught up with her again.

"No. You are. You think you can just act like you've done nothing wrong?"

"You don't even know what you're talking about."

She stopped in her tracks and pushed him back. "I know that you've been using Roxy for years. Leading him on. Making him follow you around like a lost puppy. I know you got in his head, messed him up like some fucking sexual predator. And I know that you have been lying to us all."

John's glare was dangerous. Rachel was transported back to the first time she encountered him, remembering just how terrifying he could be when he tried. Or maybe he wasn't trying. Maybe this was who he really was, an Institute body imitating a rational man. The possibility was chilling. John had a temper; he was volatile, uncompromising, irrationally particular. He could be scary, distant, unapproachable. But he was also consistent. She could count on him to always be where he was needed, to have her back, to keep his word. She'd thought she understood him, thought she knew him.

How many nights had they sat under the stars, saying nothing, just adapting to the tranquillity of the night? He'd always sit a watch out with her when she was tired, and when it was cold he'd leave her a hot cup of tea before disappearing to bed. How could that same man have been screwing with Roxy at the same time?

She tried desperately to work him out.

"You don't understand," he said, his voice unusually soft.

"Then explain it to me. Why be so cruel to him?"

"Because I had to."

She started to scoff, and the breath caught in her throat. She thought about his words, about him and all they had been through. And she understood.

"John, I—"

"Rachel!"

Mark was running up the steps towards them. His feet hit the pavement, and he stopped. At first Rachel thought he was afraid. But it was something else. His eyes met hers, and she knew something was wrong. His lips trembled, holding in a difficult truth. Then his attention shifted. He was looking at John, his face a contortion of sympathy and terror. Rachel felt her stomach lurch. She didn't need the words. She didn't even need her powers. The worst thing in the world had happened. She felt sick. But it was nothing compared to how John was feeling.

29

History ran circles around them, and it felt like, no matter how far forward they had come, they would always return to the same inevitable moment. Now they were standing in it— new location, new people, but still the same déjà vu—Charlie chastised himself for not seeing it coming. He was a pig-headed optimist, led astray by his own ambition and success. But even if he had been more aware of the futility of his existence, would things be different? John had always said this would happen, that they were not entitled to happiness or love. His whole life he'd been waiting for things to go south.

Mooney's flat became eerily quiet. The Union men had flocked back there to celebrate their first Reacher victory; now they were going to be exposed to the darkness that followed the Smith brothers. The Union leader raised his hands, drawing the others' attention away from the Reachers they had allied themselves with.

"We need to move quickly, make sure we keep the gates open. Get word out that no one goes across the border. I want bodies assembled. It's important we show London we remain strong and together. We'll march to the wall again at first light. Spread the word. S'aven is united."

He ushered his people through his front door, one by one by one, to finish the fight Charlie had started.

Charlie watched them go, more grains of sand slipping through the hourglass. The flat emptied but seemed smaller because of it. The air was thin, his breath becoming laboured. He turned back to the Institute agent—was he still an agent?—and tried to see through the lie. But Bellamy was as transparent as glass. He was afraid and panicked and hopeful. He stood with uncertainty, his eyes darting frantically between John and Rachel.

"She let you leave? Even though she knew you lied to her about killing him, she let you leave?" Charlie asked.

How Bellamy had ever kept anything a secret from the Institute was a mystery to Charlie. The man's mouth flapped open like a suffocating fish bewildered by the sudden hazardous environment he'd found himself in. It clearly hadn't even occurred to him that the Institute was still manipulating him.

"She said that Roxton being alive was a good thing. That not killing him had worked in her favour."

His naiveté was infuriating. Scarlet would only keep him alive if he was useful to her.

"She told me to come to the protest and find you, then report back on your location."

Rachel shook her head. "What she wanted you to do was track us down and tell us everything. She wants us to go running in after Roxy."

"And when we do, she'll hit us with everything she has." Charlie closed his eyes, trying to anticipate exactly what would await them. Scarlet would be at least one step ahead. The territory was hers; she had a police force at her command. And she knew they would be coming. Willingly walking into her game was admitting defeat.

Mooney's door opened again. Charlie looked up in time to see his brother leaving. John slammed the door closed on them all.

Rachel stood at Charlie's side. "I thought he'd be throwing things by now. That's what he did when they got you."

"This is different. Roxy's different."

Charlie was suddenly overwhelmed with pain. His chest ached, his body trembling. He could remember this feeling, the sinking despair he'd suffered when he knew his wife was gone. It felt like he was reliving that day, but this was different. This emotion didn't belong to him—it was all his brother's. Rachel rubbed his arm, drawing him back to the solidity of the poky flat. Her eyes were inquisitive and fearful.

He squeezed her hand for his own reassurance. "When I met Sarah, John warned me I should stay away. He said it was only a matter of time before the Institute caught up with us. I didn't listen to him—I didn't think he understood. I was in love. And I'd tasted a life that was more than just surviving."

"He wasn't messing Roxy around, was he? He was trying to protect him."

"He's always known this would happen. The Institute will always exploit our biggest weaknesses. My worst fears were realised. Now, so are his."

Rachel swallowed. "I'll go talk to him," she said.

Charlie stopped her. "No. It should be me."

The early evening had already swallowed the buildings and pathways around the flat. The single light fixed above Mooney's door flickered, fighting a losing battle against the darkness. In a momentary surge of light, Charlie made out a shadow darker than the others. He moved towards it, climbing up the steps towards the pavement, meeting John halfway.

John clasped the railings, his head hanging low. Charlie stood at his side and placed a hand on John's back. With the contact John's utter despair consumed him, and his own heart started to race. He took a breath, steadying himself against the grief.

A long silence elapsed between them. Years of history contaminated by the Institute stretched across their past and seemed destined to continue into their future. It wasn't fair. And it made Charlie furious. They'd been children. They hadn't done anything wrong. They didn't deserve the torment, the nightmare, of living in the shadow of that facility.

"I can't leave him there. I won't let them kill him," John said.

"I know. So do they. That's why they took him."

John turned his head. His eyes were filled with cold calculation. Charlie recognised his brother's destructive mindset. John intended to take them on. He would go after Roxy, and he would sacrifice himself for Roxy's survival. But Charlie couldn't let him. He wasn't willing to lose his brother, not like this. If they could rescue Roxy, John had a shot at something more in the world. And didn't he deserve a chance at happiness?

He stood before Charlie a man, but Charlie could still remember the sharp-eyed boy looking to him for answers. For hope. He'd promised that boy that there was a world for them away from the Institute, that they were more than lab rats. He'd promised John that he would take care of him. He'd let that promise slide, allowing himself to be distracted by his own ambitions. Not anymore. The only thing that mattered, that had ever mattered, was looking after John. Charlie could do this. He could do what needed to be done. He would make sure John had a future. That would be his purpose.

"John, listen to me. We're going to get him back. We are going to go in, and we are going to get him back." Charlie leaned on the railings; they were violently cold. "And afterwards, whatever happens, you're going to leave. You're going to take Roxy, get out of the country and as far away from the Institute as you can."

"We're supposed to bring them down."

"For what? So we can sacrifice everything we love for revenge? It's bullshit, John. It was a pipe dream we had, to keep us going when times were rough. And we allowed it to keep us shackled to that place when we should have just let it go. The way we beat them is by living. By you living."

John looked for a second like he was going to object; then he surprised Charlie and let out a low sigh. The light caught him again, and he was a different person. He seemed older, or maybe Charlie was seeing him for the first time as a man rather than the infant soldier in the Institute. It dawned on him that there was a whole part of John's life he didn't know and that there was little time left to truly understand his brother.

"How long has it been going on between you?"

John swallowed. "Since the Grandchester."

"Wait a minute. That was before we met Sarah."

"He was raiding the safe when I got there. Bumbling fool set off the bomb that caused the explosion. We spent hours crawling through that building looking for an escape. And then afterwards… it was supposed to be a one-off." John sighed again. "Sarah introducing us was fucking awkward."

"All this time? You guys have been together all this time?"

"Off and on."

Charlie was so surprised he laughed. "How the hell did Roxy manage to keep this quiet for so long?"

"I guess he knew what was at stake." John's lips twitched in a sad, fleeting smile. "I was so fucking livid with you. When you got with Sarah, I wanted to smash your face in. You were putting her at risk. I couldn't believe you were being so stupid. But when Roxy showed up, I didn't push him away either. You were living in gaga land—you didn't think anyone could touch you. But I've always known this would happen. What excuse do I have?"

"That you love him."

"That's no excuse."

"You're not to blame for this. The Institute have done this, not you. And Roxy knew the risks. Especially after Sarah."

"I can't lose him," John whispered.

"You won't. I promise." He put his arm around his brother.

"Going after him is suicide."

"Maybe. Maybe not. I think it's time the Institute realise what they created when they put the two of us together."

30

Roxy's cheek stuck to the piss-stinking floor. He tried to move and his body revolted, explosions of pain bombarding his senses. He couldn't breathe. His chest constricted against his lungs, his throat burning with the lack of oxygen. *No, no, no, no, no. Not like this.* His gasping became more frantic. He didn't want to die like this, pathetic and afraid and conscious. *Breathe. Bloody breathe, you bastard.* His racing heart pounded in his body. *Breathe,* he told himself again and focused on the pounding, concentrating until it started to slow.

Pain was manageable. And this wasn't his first beating. He had to stay calm. Keep the air in his aching lungs. Keep the blood pumping. He was alive. For now, at least. His future depended on where he was and the damage already done to him. He started with his fingers. Moving the little ones first, then the others. Three were broken. His wrist too. He flexed his toes, and his knees started protesting angrily. There was no chance of walking out of here. And as the thought dawned on him, he succumbed to the panic again.

Breathe. He heaved in air, fighting through the pain in his chest. Broken ribs too. Even getting upright was going to be a struggle. Roxy closed his eyes and swallowed blood from loose teeth. *You're still alive,* he told himself. But it was little comfort.

He should be dead. He should be dead, but he wasn't. It meant they wanted him alive. And that knowledge was worse than any pain he was suffering.

A shoe scuffed against the floor behind him. Roxy froze at the sound. He wasn't alone. A shadow settled over him. He felt suddenly very cold.

Hands grabbed him, hurling him upwards. He cried out as he struck a plastic chair and found himself seated at a metal table. Violent shudders racked his body. The room blurred, and for a second he wondered if they'd overplayed their hand, if this was the end of him. It was an optimistic prospect. Before he could conjure a profound final thought, he felt a prick in his arm. His vision started to clear.

He blinked as he took in the room: the pale, stained walls; the scuffed, filthy floor. Then the man standing in front of him. Roxy recognised him from the alleyway, but there was more to him than just a memory. The man's sharp features, his robotic coldness, his expensive suit—he was another agent from the Institute.

Roxy swallowed despite the pain and straightened himself. The agent stood over him and flicked open a sharp penknife. Roxy refused to be intimidated. He clenched his jaw. He could take it. He would take it. The agent was unreadable, distant. Even if Roxy wanted to reason with him, he was sure it would be a waste of time. The man leaned forward and pressed the tip of the blade to Roxy's chest.

Then he ran it downwards.

Slicing through Roxy's bloodied shirt.

Exposing his bruised chest.

They did this to Sarah. He couldn't stop himself thinking about it, about her final moments. Had she been as afraid as he was? Did she try to hold her nerve? Afraid of death, but more afraid of a long, drawn-out end.

Breathe, he told himself. When he dared to look at the agent, he frowned. The man had put the knife away. He had his back to Roxy, his attention now fully on a metal briefcase resting on the table. Roxy's hands were shaking. He clasped the arms of his chair, steadying himself for whatever he was about to face.

The door in front of him opened. He looked up and then his heart sank. The Institute Bitch had arrived. She'd changed since the trap in the alleyway, replacing her hooker dress with a crisp black suit. Her hair was pinned back, makeup expertly applied. But Roxy could still make out the sickly yellow taint affecting her skin, the greyness of her recessed eyes. Having her lackey doing the hard work was starting to make sense.

"You're looking surprisingly well for a dead man, Mr Roxton."

"Which is more than I can say for you. You look worse than I feel."

The male agent struck Roxy across his temple. His vision blackened. He thought— hoped—he was about to pass out. But he didn't. He blinked until the room stopped spinning, then lifted his head, ready to face the woman that murdered his best friend.

Scarlet pulled out a chair. She sat down slowly, as if the movement pained her.

"It's not contagious, is it?" Roxy asked.

Her partner raised his hand, but Scarlet shook her head. She was weaker but still in control.

"Sarah Smith was your lover," she stated. "At least until Charlie Smith stole her away."

Roxy kept his swollen lips shut. Sarah had given up on him long before Charlie came along, but he had no intention of correcting her. The less she knew about his history the better.

"She was a stubborn woman. There was no need for her to suffer, and yet her capacity for pain—well, it's not often we get to experiment the way I did that night."

Breathe.

"Do you think you have the same dedication? The same tolerance."

You can do this. Roxy tried to sit straighter in the chair. He dismissed his racing heart. He clenched his fists to keep them from trembling. And he stared straight into her cloudy eyes.

"You can do what you want, love. I'm not telling you anything, so you can fuck right off."

She smiled, stretching her lips until they bled. "You're an interesting man, James. The son of the notorious Lulu Roxton. Linked to numerous robberies and cons, and yet your criminal convictions are only petty misdemeanours. No jail time whatsoever. You're obviously a smart man, so please just tell me one thing. How could you have been so incredibly stupid?"

Roxy frowned, unsure where she was going.

"We believed you were dead. You were off our radar. And yet you show up at a well-known journalist's home address, as though you hadn't even considered she could be under surveillance."

Now he was confronted with it, he had to admit it was bloody stupid. When he'd mentioned Li to Charlie, it hadn't even occurred to him she was part of a bigger game. He closed his eyes, furious at himself. This whole mess was his fault. He deserved this. He deserved whatever they were going to do to him.

"It was a very foolish error," she said.

"I've made worse."

"Oh, I doubt that you have." She leaned closer, her putrid scent invading his nostrils. "Do you think they will forgive you?"

No. Roxy swallowed. He couldn't show her how rattled he was. "Maybe. I can be very charming when I want to be."

"So I've heard. Do you think John will forgive you?"

"John hasn't forgiven me for spilling wine over his new coat, and that was six years ago. I'm not worried."

"Not even when you know he's going to put his freedom at risk, coming to save you."

"He isn't going to come for me."

"Are you so sure?"

"John will be glad to see the back of me, I promise you."

She still wouldn't lose the smile. "I thought that Sarah would be Charlie's weakness. I was sure that he would see her suffering and immediately give up his brother. But he didn't. Do you think you'll talk after my partner is finished with you?"

"Oh, I'll sing like a canary. You just name the song. If you hadn't smashed my hand up, I'd have even played you a bit of piano jazz. But I'm not giving them up, so you might as well get it over with now and stop wasting our time."

"That's what I thought you'd say. You see, if you were true to your record, a carefree opportunist looking for his next rush, you'd sell them out in a heartbeat. But you sit here, ready for death, preparing yourself for torture. The question is why. You could be a Reacher groupie, one of those evangelical lunatics. But you don't strike me as the sort. Or it could be that your connection with the Smith brothers runs deeper. That they are more to you than just comrades. Let me ask you another question. If John Smith had returned home that day instead of Charlie, do you think he would have given up Charlie to save Sarah?"

"I haven't given it any thought."

"What if it had been your life on the line, kind of like it is now? Who would John choose, you or his brother? Don't worry. I already know the answer."

"You don't know anything."

"I think you're John Smith's weakness, James. Am I wrong?"

"You are so far off the mark it's embarrassing. John doesn't have a weakness. Terrible taste in men, maybe, but he's not going to risk everything to save a misguided conquest like me."

"And yet there's a part of you that wishes he would, isn't there? A part of you that believes John Smith is more than a heartless soldier. That he cares for you enough to come for you."

Roxy didn't want this. He didn't want John coming after him. He'd stumbled into the snare. It was his fault he was going to die. John couldn't follow him. But would he? Roxy could pretend to the others that John felt nothing, that *Roxy* was nothing to him. But deep down he knew; he had always known. John would come. And when he did, he would die. Roxy couldn't let that happen.

"I hate to burst your bubble, pet, but John Smith is as damaged as the rest of you Institute lab rats. And I don't mean bugger all to him, just like I don't mean bugger all to you."

Scarlet rose. She circled around Roxy's chair, a huntress toying with her prey. She grasped his shoulders, her clammy hands sticking to his exposed chest. He tried to shake her off, but despite her sickness she was unbelievably strong. Her lips touched his ear and he retched, desperate to be away from her.

"You're a gambling man, James. Do you want to wager what he'll do?"

Her nails scraped over his ribcage. His stomach lurched. His skin burned under her touch.

"I know what he'll do. He'll kill you. If you haven't keeled over first."

"We've got a surprise for you, James."

The male agent turned. He held a metal, star-like device. Roxy started to squirm. Scarlet's grip tightened on his shoulders, fixing him in place. He felt the metal in the centre of his chest. It was cold, sharp. Then it moved. The agents released him and the star took hold, piercing his flesh. He cried out, squeezing his eyes shut, hoping the pain would end. That he would die. But he didn't. They weren't done with him yet.

31

A sheet of hail smacked the van windscreen, forcing John to slow down. His hands gripped the wheel tighter, his eyes sharpening on the disappearing road. So far he was calm, focussed. But the calculating soldier could easily become a berserker when provoked. If they crossed into enemy territory to discover the worst… well, Charlie didn't even want to think that far ahead. He sucked in a breath, knowing this could very well be the final stand.

It wasn't what they'd planned for, but Charlie was ready.

The station stood near the border like Scotland Yard's inferior sidekick. Cops zipped in and out of the main entrance like frantic bees, frenzied by the rioting erupting all over town. The distraction would work in their favour. John drove the van towards the side of the station. The gates to the fenced yard that usually housed the police vehicles were manually locked—nothing Charlie couldn't handle—and the yard sat empty and exposed. At the back of the yard there was a single entrance with keypad access. It was all too easy, but then the purpose wasn't to keep them out.

John parked the van by the gate and left the engine ticking over.

Charlie put a hand on his brother's shoulder. "We find him, and you get him out of there. I'll keep them busy for as long as I can," he said.

"Five minutes," John told him. "Then you bail. We'll wait for you out here."

"I'll be right behind you."

What would happen if—when—Charlie fell behind hung between them unsaid. He knew what he was getting into. This was a sacrifice he would willingly make. He squeezed John's shoulder, regretting only the fact that he probably wouldn't live to see his brother happy.

"Let's go."

Charlie jumped from the van and winced as the hail hit his face. He pulled open the side door and looked to Rachel. She was holding the cop's hand while he cowered away from the light. Charlie still didn't trust him, but this wasn't the time to worry about that. He nodded at Bellamy and held his own hand out to Rachel.

She threw Bellamy a reassuring smile before she jumped from the van, uniting— where she belonged—with the brothers.

Charlie pointed at Mark. "Keep the engine running, and do not move from this spot. We won't be long."

He hooked his arm with Rachel's, and the connection between them grew. They'd only just started exploring their collective power, and he felt another pang that he would never really get to see what they could do together. When he looked at her, he could see she was thinking the same. This was a suicide mission. If any of them made it out, it would be a miracle. But Charlie had just pulled off a miracle. He could do it again.

"I want you to make sure, whatever happens, that Roxy gets out," he whispered to her.

"Isn't that the mission?"

"That's the priority," he said. "You make sure John sticks to the plan. I don't care about anything else. All that matters is they leave this place. Do you understand? Even if you have to use your powers on them."

Her lips were bluing in the cold. "I get it. But do me a favour and don't go doing anything stupid if you don't have to."

John came around from his side of the van. Hail bounced from his head and shoulders. It wouldn't stop him. Nothing would stop him. He took Rachel's other arm, and together they walked. The three most dangerous people in Britain.

Rachel's boots crunched on the broken concrete yard. *You can't see us.* The command projected from her almost without her having to concentrate. She held both the brothers tightly, overwhelmed with the compulsion to keep them safe and together. She understood what Charlie was planning, and why. And she hated it. It wasn't like she didn't have her own vendetta against the Institute. She could go after them herself. She could draw them to her, keep them occupied, and give the brothers more than enough time to get Roxy and get clear.

Was her life really more valuable than Charlie's? She didn't think so.

The entrance to the station caught her by surprise. No obvious cameras and little security. Charlie pressed his hand against the keypad blocking their path, and the door immediately clicked open. She went in first, reaching out with her mind for any prying eyes. The corridors were empty.

"Right, then, I'm going to go and have some fun," Charlie said, flexing his fingers. "Don't wait up."

Rachel wanted to say something, knowing this could be the last time they would see each other, but he was already pushing through the double doors leading to the heart of the station, pretending this was just another mission. She turned to John. He seemed momentarily lost. How would he cope without his brother? She shook the thought away. This wasn't helping. She had a job to do, and Roxy was still in danger. She elbowed John.

"Three flights, third door on the left," she said, repeating what Mark had shown her.

She gestured to the stairs. Walking through the station was unsettling. Mark had trudged up these staircases, and she had done the same in his memories. She felt the oppressive walls pressing against them. This was a bad place, filled with bad people on both sides of the cells.

John hit the first landing. He leaned against the door. Another empty corridor awaited them, this one littered with closed rooms and concealed corners. John stepped forward, but Rachel stopped him. She moved ahead, running her hand across the wall as she walked its length, feeling out any potential ambush.

"Come out, come out, wherever you are."

A door opened behind her. John fired two shots, bringing two officers down cleanly. Rachel touched the wall again, reaching out for anyone else. Nothing. It was too quiet. Too easy. Was Charlie going to stumble across the same? Or were they all waiting for him upstairs?

John tipped his head. They were wasting time. At the end of the corridor their destination awaited them. She gestured to the room Mark had promised would contain Roxy. For the first time since entering the station, John looked pensive. Roxy could be dead. They were both thinking it. Beyond the door could be nothing but pain. Rachel looked to John, taking in his clenched jaw. It was up to her to lead the way. She pressed open the handle and stepped inside.

A wide stretch of glass ran the length of the wall in front of them. Beyond the glass was a darkened room. She could make out a heavy shadow heaped in the centre. She recognised the curve of the shoulders, the mess of hair. It was him; she just couldn't see how bad he was.

John was standing by the light switch.

"If he's…"

"We go after Charlie and kill anyone that tries to stop us."

John hit the lights. The glare blinded Rachel. She blinked and looked again at the room. Roxy was tied to a chair, his body slumped forward, his hair covering his face. He was so still. So quiet. Then she saw the breath lifting his back. He grunted, raised a bruised face to the light, cursed, and fell forward again.

She turned to John, but he was already going after Roxy. He pushed open the adjoining door, checked for wires, and then took three purposeful strides towards him. He crouched down, and Rachel was about to follow but stopped herself. John lifted Roxy's head and waited for Roxy to open his swollen eyes.

"Oh, you stupid, pig-headed wanker. What are you doing here?"

"Sightseeing. What the fuck do you think we're doing?" John said and cut the ties binding Roxy's hands.

"It's a bloody trap, you twat."

"Obviously."

John reached out to lift Roxy, but Roxy batted his hand away.

"No, don't touch me," he said. "They've put something in me. It's under my shirt."

With the tip of his finger, John raised the edge of Roxy's shirt. His stomach was matted with blood, running from a wound in his chest. Rachel moved closer, making out the metallic instrument imbedded in him.

"Have you seen anything like it before?" she asked John.

His skin had paled. "A less-sophisticated prototype. It's an explosive. Remote detonator."

Rachel hovered her hand over the wound. "It's buried deep. I don't think I'd be able to cut it out safely."

"You can't get it out," Roxy told them. "John, I screwed up. I got careless, and they got me. This is all on me, love. Now, say 'I told you so,' and piss off."

"You seriously expect us to just leave you here?" John snapped.

"Yes. Bloody go. There's no sense in them getting us all."

"If you've got nothing helpful to say, fucking shut up." John rubbed his forehead. He was starting to lose control. Rachel pressed her hand on his shoulder, steadying him.

"I can't do it. We need Charlie," he finally said.

Roxy frowned. "Where is he?"

"He's gone after the Institute."

"Charlie? Your plan was to send Peg-leg Percy after them? Are you off your head?"

"Charlie's fucked. They're waiting for him. They're waiting for all of you. Call this off, John. For crying out loud, this is what they want. I am not worth all this."

John glared at him, stopping Roxy's ramblings instantly. He rose, and suddenly Rachel couldn't read him at all.

"You need to keep him still," he told her when he got to the door.

Even if she wanted to stop him, she wouldn't have been able to. He stood in front of her, and she remembered there was still unresolved tension between them. He was waiting for her to challenge him like she had done before. But she didn't.

"I'll look after him," she promised.

"No you bloody won't. John, you are not going after them! Do you hear me. Don't be so shitting stubborn. Rachel, please. Stop him."

"Good luck," she said, swallowing the lump in her throat.

His lips quirked in something like a smile, and then he was gone.

"For fuck's sake! You're an absolute nobhead, John Smith! Do you hear me?" He closed his eyes and let out a desperate sob. "Absolute, stupid, bastarding, shitting arseface." Rachel crouched beside him, clasping his hand in hers.

"They're going to kill him."

"You don't know that."

"I know this can only end with at least one of us dead. And I know that it should be me."

32

Charlie pushed open the doors to the station's reception foyer, readying himself for an onslaught of police. He stepped inside, arms outstretched. A solitary officer occupied the front desk, a thick gash running down his face, still embedded with broken brown glass. He held a dirty rag to his cheek, soaking up the worst from the wound. His rifle was on the counter. Charlie's fingers twitched; there were no bullets in the clip. The weapon was as useless as the man who had discarded it.

As Charlie drew closer, the cop seemed to recognise him. He snatched up the gun and pointed it at him. "Get back!"

Charlie flicked his fingers and the gun was whipped into the air.

The cop raised his hands. "Don't hurt me."

"Where is everyone?" Charlie demanded.

"Out there." The cop gestured to the entrance. "There's a fucking riot happening, if you haven't noticed."

The police were out of the picture, but Charlie knew the Institute were still waiting. He glanced above the cop, catching sight of the CCTV keeping watch over the lobby. Scarlet, he knew, would be watching. She would want to see it all unfolding before her, keeping track of where they all were. Charlie waved at the camera.

"Where's the viewing room?" he asked.

The cop said nothing.

Charlie clenched his fingers, and the counter started to rattle.

"Okay, okay. It's on the sixth floor."

"If I was you, I'd get out of here," Charlie said and headed for the stairwell.

A second camera monitored his ascent. His leg brace took the brunt of the steps. He grasped the banister, counting the floors. Sweat ran down his neck and back, but he felt stronger than ever. He could already see himself confronting her, the woman who murdered his family, who destroyed his life. He was ready to sacrifice himself, but he was taking her with him.

Fourth floor.

Fifth floor.

A thunderous noise rattled below him. Steps. Someone running up. Charlie turned, cursing himself for his overconfidence. He stretched out his fingers, preparing to make a stand. Moments later, John was standing in front of him.

His brother's eyes were dark and focused. He was too formal, too decisive. Something was wrong. Charlie's stomach started to sink. "He's not…"

"I can't get him free," John stated coolly. He was too tightly coiled, too controlled. This was not good. Then he seemed to check himself, vulnerability appearing beneath the mask for a moment. "I need you," he said.

Charlie couldn't remember John ever admitting he needed his brother. Even when they were kids, even when they relied on each other to make it through each unforgiving day. John was defiant, independent, strong. And yet, in the middle of the standoff they'd spent their whole lives dreaming about, he was barely able to hold it together.

He looked at the camera. Scarlet would be enjoying the show. Was this what she wanted? To have them in one place so she could take them all down? Charlie straightened his back. She could try to take them. If he couldn't get to her, then she could come to him. And then she'd know who she was messing with. Then she'd pay.

"Okay. Let's do this."

John didn't move. He looked up at the next floor. "She's up there?"

"Sixth floor. Camera room, I think."

"Makes sense."

"Leave her," Charlie said. "What matters is getting Roxy out."

"She's holding the detonator that will kill him." His voice was still cool, too cool. "If I don't get it off her, she'll fuck us all anyway."

"John…"

"She'll kill him when I'm watching," he said. "She'll do it to make sure it hurts, like she did with you and Sarah."

"So you're going to go after her, walk straight into her trap?"

"I'm going to kill her," John said. "I've had enough of this shit." He grabbed the banister determinedly. "You'll get Roxy out of here?"

"Of course. And we'll meet you outside," Charlie promised.

John nodded and hauled himself up the steps. Charlie watched him go and felt a pang of jealousy. He wanted to be the one to end Scarlet. He wanted to finish this nightmare. But as John entered the sixth floor, Charlie knew his brother was the one with the real power. He was cut from the same material as Scarlet, but he had the edge on her. Charlie had taught him how to survive—and maybe that was Charlie's purpose, to give John Smith the smarts to get the better of the Institute once and for all. That and to pull Roxy out of this sorry mess for good.

He grabbed the banister himself and started to run.

Two dead cops marked the corridor he needed to be in. He stepped over the bodies, recognising his brother's work. The door at the end of the corridor was open, and as he neared it, he could hear Roxy and Rachel arguing. He quickened his step. John would likely be in the surveillance room already. Time was running out.

When he looked in, he could see Rachel and Roxy through a glass pane. Roxy's shirt was pulled open, exposing a shining piece of metal protruding from a wound in his chest. Rachel inspected the wound while he berated her.

"You're not a doctor anymore. Right now you're a bloody murderer. Letting him go up there, that's murder. You get that, don't you? You're sitting here, pretending it's all going to be okay. Look at me, Rachel. Look at me! They have won. Don't you see?"

Rachel shook her head, exasperated with him but keeping her patience. Charlie crossed the threshold to bolster her.

"Oh, brilliant, here comes the sodding cavalry," Roxy said.

"How you doing, Rox?"

"How do you bloody think I'm doing?" Roxy spat out a loose tooth.

"It's clasped into his chest," Rachel explained. "We need to get it out of him, but I'm too afraid to touch it."

"No, you need to piss off out of here before it's too late. Come on, Charlie, for once in your sorry excuse for a life, be the voice of reason here. You know what they'll do to John if they get him."

"I know what John is going to do to them. Now we've got to hold up our end of the plan, because if we keep him waiting he's going to be fuming—and

I don't know about you, but I don't want to listen to his bitching all the way out of this shithole town."

Roxy leaned forward. "They're setting you all up."

"John is faster and smarter and stronger than anything they throw at him. He always has been—you know this. Why do you think they want him back so much?"

"Before he left, I called him a nobhead and an arseface. If they are my final words..." Roxy closed his eyes. It was strange to see him so defeated.

"Then let's make sure they're not."

Rachel took Roxy's hand. "It's important you relax and breathe. I'll take your pain."

"If this thing goes off, we're all dead," he whispered.

"It's not going to go off," Charlie assured him.

"You've disarmed one of these before?"

"Sure," Charlie lied.

He placed his hand on the device and closed his eyes. It was sophisticated and complex. Disarming it would take time, and they couldn't afford to waste the minutes. The only real option was to extract it from Roxy and run like hell. He found the grasping mechanism and hoped releasing it wouldn't set it off.

"Okay, I've got it."

"You're sure?"

"I'm sure."

"It's just, you've not been the most reliable teammate, pet."

"We can sit here and wait for it to go off, or you can be quiet. It'll be okay. I promised John I would get you out, and—"

"Oh, love, just do it. I don't need a sentimental lecture; I've been tortured enough."

Charlie nodded at Rachel and raised his knuckles. Roxy's body rocked in the chair, but his face was serene. Blood spurted from the hole in his chest as the device was freed. Rachel caught the wound with Roxy's shirt. Charlie caught the device.

They were all still in one piece—mostly. He'd done it. Gingerly, he placed the device on the floor.

"Is he okay?"

"He will be."

"Good. We need to move now." He rose. "Hey, Rox do you think you can walk?" "Better than you can, love."

With Rachel's help they raised Roxy up. He managed a step forward and collapsed to his knees, vomiting violently. Rachel rubbed his back, settling him down.

"We'll have to carry him," she said.

They raised him again, hooking his arms over their shoulders. He was heavy, a dead weight to drag through the corridor. Charlie pushed forward. John was going to owe him for this.

33

Even without Charlie's directions, John knew exactly where Scarlet was. In the past he'd ignored this piece of himself—it represented a history he didn't want to think about—but now it would be his advantage. He knew, if he could sense her, there was a possibility she could sense him too. It didn't matter. He had no intention of hiding from her. He took the steps casually, making sure his brother would have all the time he needed.

A scratched, faded sign marked the surveillance room. The door was ajar. John removed his jacket and dropped it in the corridor. He clicked away the tightness in his neck and shoulders. The movement seemed to dampen the other sounds in the building until all that remained was his pulse. A steady beat. Daa dum. Daa dum.

If he closed his eyes he was back in the Institute, standing with the others, waiting to prove himself. The same thudding in his ears, the same odds, the same enemy. But he was not the same. He was John Smith now, and he didn't follow the Institute's rules anymore.

He crossed the threshold into a long, dark room. The right wall was fixed with screen after screen. Empty corridors, abandoned rooms. Then he caught his brother and Rachel, crouched in the interview room, trying to liberate Roxy. Just a few more minutes.

"You almost had me worried for a moment. I thought you might have chickened out."

His attention fell on the figure perched in front of the cameras. Through the blue screen light, he could make out her dire complexion. Her face was gaunt, sickly. There was an odour to her; she tried to mask it under a vicious perfume, but John could still smell it. She was dying.

"That would imply I have something to fear," he said. "How long do you have?"

"Long enough. And you'll understand that I really have nothing to lose. Unlike you."

On the screen, Charlie had his hand against Roxy's chest.

"You'll be the last of us," she said. "Not that anyone will really care when I'm gone."

"If they didn't care, you wouldn't be here."

"Oh, you they care about, brother. They've always cared about you. The success. The one in ten that made it. You weren't around for the after-party. Do you know how lucky you were to escape when you did? You missed all the extra treatments and the dependency that followed. You're not tainted goods. The theory behind you alone has prompted huge developments in the Institute's direction. You are a living legend. They will always want you back."

"And you're going to do it, are you?"

A smile played on her grey lips. "Keep thinking, John, you'll catch up soon enough." She concentrated on the cameras. "He was ready to die for you, you know. I suppose that's quite romantic, in a tragic sort of way." She toyed with a keypad in her bony fingers—the detonator.

"Give it to me."

"Wait." She gestured to the screen.

Charlie did it. He removed the bomb from Roxy's chest.

"Looks like the old man still has some tricks left in him," she said and tossed John the detonator.

Charlie and Rachel carried Roxy across the screens. They were slow, weighed down and clumsy, but moving. This was all too easy.

Scarlet let out a sharp squeal of delight. "Oh, John, come on. Think about it. We want you back. Do you really think we'd just let you all walk out of here?"

"Try and stop me."

She shook her head. "No, not me." She pointed to the top-floor cameras. "They didn't stop with us, John. They used what they learned from you, and they tried it again. Another ten. Then another. Once upon a time there were forty of us in the field. There are two of us left. My partner happens to be in much better condition than me. He's younger, has a keen eye."

John watched the others move. Second floor. They were nearly clear of the building. He searched the other screens, and then he saw what she was talking about. In a room overlooking the loading bay a man was poised at the window. He was static, staring through the scope of his rifle. He was professional, patient.

"You can't make your van out on the screen, but believe me, it's there."

Charlie hit the first floor. John considered moving. If he was fast enough, he might get to the window before a second shot was fired.

That was unacceptable.

"Aha, he has it. The dilemma. Who gets to die first? It's not going to be Charlie. You boys are programmed to look out for each other. And obviously not the lovely James. So it has to be the girl. You'll watch her body hit the floor, appreciate she went quickly, then see the horror in the others' eyes. Then you'll wish we'd killed Mr Roxton first, that he went as cluelessly as Rachel, because now he's scared. Now he knows he's going to die, it's just a matter of seconds."

"Shut the fuck up and tell me what you want."

"Surrender. Surrender, and I'll let them all walk." She turned her chair to face him, amusement flooding her eyes. "The clock is ticking, John."

"You're not going to let a grade-five Reacher walk," he said.

"For you, I'd buy them all first-class tickets to Hawaii." She picked up her radio. "They'll be in view in twenty seconds. Take them out at will."

"No," John said. "You do anything and I'll kill you."

Scarlet laughed. "Well, I've been looking forward to my slow, painful death, but okay."

Charlie was at the door. The screen flipped to the car park. A figure was running towards them—the cop, Bellamy. John clenched his fist. The fool could have pulled the van nearer, given them some cover. Instead he'd left twenty feet between the door and refuge.

Scarlet picked up her comms again. "Take them out."

John felt his heart beating faster. He felt his breath quicken in his chest. He didn't want to exist in a world without the people he cared about. He couldn't. Wouldn't. There was supposed to be a fight; he'd been ready for it since the moment he left the laboratory. There was supposed to be a monumental battle that justified everything he was. But he was more than just a soldier. He was a man. A friend. A brother. A lover. Fear was fuel, and he used it to spur on his new purpose. He knew what he had to do, and he knew he would not fail. He thought about Charlie. About Rachel. About Roxy. This was how it could end. This was right.

He couldn't reach the shooter. But he didn't have to. His thumb brushed the detonator. And his mind was made up.

34

Their exit beckoned. Rachel bore more of Roxy's weight, allowing Charlie to open it. He grasped the handle and pulled it. Icy wind whipped at his face. Hail pounded against the cracked tarmac. He could make out the headlights of their van at the edge of the lot. There was still so much ground to cover, and this station was just too damn quiet. All around, sirens blared; smoke billowed through the hail. Charlie scanned the lot, expecting at least an attempt at resistance. All he got was Mark Bellamy hurrying towards them on foot.

"He knows he's got a van, right," Charlie said to Rachel. There was a lot of distance still to cover, the weather and exposure making Charlie uneasy. "Go, I'll cover your back."

"Gee, thanks," she said and dragged Roxy out into the open.

Charlie checked the empty corridor behind them. John should have made it out by now. And as soon as the thought occurred to him, he felt himself shudder. He pressed his hand against the wall, gasping for breath. The thoughts in his head didn't belong to him, and they were so loud, so overwhelming he couldn't comprehend them.

Danger. They were all about to die.

When he looked up, Bellamy was reaching out for Roxy, ready to help Rachel carry him across the yard. The scene slowed. Bellamy's head arched back, the top of his skull shattering above him. A halo of blood and bone crowned his body as it hit the dirt. Rachel stopped moving. She pirouetted with Roxy, dancing in red puddles as she tried to find cover.

Charlie leapt from the door, his brace striking the ground with force. He reached out his hand, feeling for the van. He pulled forward, and the van hurtled towards them. The second shot was meant for Rachel. It hit the van's taillight instead. Rachel crouched behind it, covering Roxy with her own body. Charlie dived after her, hitting the freezing tarmac on his hands and knees. He pushed open the side door of the van and helped Rachel throw Roxy inside. Roxy hit the floor grumbling.

"What the bloody—"

Another shot hit the windscreen. Charlie ducked and slammed the door closed, trapping Roxy inside. He slid down the van beside Rachel. She stared at the body in the yard, halfway between the station and them. Bellamy's hands were twitching with the hail.

"Shit, he's still alive," Rachel said.

It was just a reflex. She was in shock and not thinking clearly. She moved before Charlie could stop her, her body suddenly exposed in the open. Charlie dove after her, catching her by the waist. He felt a bullet burn a hole in his trouser leg. Another shot. They were running out of luck.

"Get in the van," Charlie yelled.

"He's alive," she cried and cowered forward. "Look!"

When he turned, everything stopped. The shooting, the sirens, the hail. He saw Mark Bellamy's body, spent. He saw the empty doorway they had run from. Rachel hung from his arms, determined to save a dead policeman. Then, when he looked up, he could see the window the shooter was sitting in. A bright light blinded him. This is it, he thought.

The force of the blast struck him. Rachel was whipped from his grasp as they both slammed into the bonnet of the van. He rolled, falling face down into the dirt. A shrill hum filled his ears, his head thundering with the sound of his own blood pumping. He blinked, feeling a sharp heat on his face. Rachel was on the floor, her hand raised as she touched a wound on her head. Seeing her reminded him of the shooter.

He scrambled to his aching knees and stared up at the window. Only it wasn't there. Half the station had collapsed on itself. Flames clawed hungrily at the building. Another small explosion spread the fire southwards. In seconds, smoke billowed from the open door they had fled through.

Charlie grabbed hold of the van and then of Rachel, pulling her closer as the fire roared. It struck him more violently than the blast. His brother was inside. More than that: John had caused this.

"What the fuck just happened?" Rachel shouted, her voice a distant whisper behind the humming.

Charlie closed his eyes. John had survived this before, he assured himself. He would be inside somewhere, relatively unharmed like he was at the hotel. Somehow, he'd get out. Charlie remembered the certainty he'd felt the last time, when he stood outside the Grandchester, when he was sure his brother would be okay. Now he felt something different.

John was not walking out.

He shook his head. No. This was all wrong. He wasn't thinking clearly, that was all. He tried again. Reaching out with every power he had, searching the rubble.

"Was John still inside?" Rachel mouthed. Her lips quivered at the possibility.

She pushed at Charlie in a foolish attempt to go after John. Charlie caught her. He couldn't let her go there. He couldn't lose them both. Lost. John was lost. He was gone. Charlie felt tears rolling down his face. His body ached with emptiness.

It was supposed to be me.

Another burst of flames erupted from the lower windows, pushing them back. Charlie felt a flash of memory penetrate his shock. He'd felt things that didn't belong to him. They'd hit him at the door, before the sniper, but he hadn't had time to process them. Now, in front of the devastation, he could recognise his brother's warning. John had used the connection they shared to let him know that this was the only way. He had done this to save them. To save Roxy.

Red and blue light flashed against the surrounding buildings. The attack on their hive had drawn the police back.

Save Roxy. The thought had overridden everything else, and no matter his other feelings, that was all Charlie could do.

He clasped Rachel's hand and pulled her towards the van. She shook her head, pleading with him to at least try and look for John. But it was pointless. John was dead.

He forced her into the passenger seat and took the wheel for himself. *John is dead*, he told himself. *My brother is gone.*

35

Li's case was heavy. Her shoulder, cushioned under two cardigans and a thick jacket, protested at the weight. She hurried quickly down the stairs, not looking back at the flat that had housed her these past weeks. Snow swallowed her boots, betraying her journey. The street was empty, the Union supporters conquered by the cold. Spring would come eventually, then the seeds would sprout, and who knew what would grow in the new garden. Li swapped the case to her other shoulder. Time would tell, she thought. Time would tell.

[Transcript from the final broadcast of *Starr Talks*]

It's the first of December. Snow is falling thick and fast over the south. The sky is heavy, purple and bruised with winter's rage. Our time is up. Warm blood will freeze. We will not all make it out. We never do. Many have already fallen: men, women, children. There's no certainty for any of us. And this is what I want you to remember: it could be any one of us.

We are all still at the mercy of fate and misfortune. Our security is a façade, our power fleeting. There are those of you who have risen over the months, who have claimed positions of authority. They are not safe. Just like those they usurped were not safe. We are all teetering on the edge, pushing and being pushed. The only certainty is instability.

It could be any of us.

Our government had vicious ideas. Ideas that they made fact to profit and grow rich and powerful. It became gospel to us inside and outside the wall. Compliantly we obeyed their laws even though their cruelty was obvious. We are faithful sheep after all. Working men and women. Good people. Honest people. At least we were.

The line was drawn by them. It was built in concrete and iron, and now we have redrawn it in blood. Yes, I say we. I say we because there are no neutrals anymore. There is the old way and the new. The ones that have and the ones that will soon have. London is coming to an end. Which side are you on? Do you know yet? You should.

We must remember: our government, those people who we put our faith in, lied for power. Reachers are dangerous, they said. The Institute will protect us. And so we rounded up anyone who had potential to be better than us. We sold out our friends, our family. Let it be them. Not us. And now the Reachers have been decimated. Their help, which could have changed everything, we denied because we were afraid. The government sold us the lie, but we bought it. Their blood is on our hands. And we will never wash it clean.

After the Reachers, they came for the poor. For those in S'aven, desperate and hungry. We were labelled degenerates, blamed for poverty and ignorance. You could slip through the gates, climb the grime-covered ladder to become something more than a S'aven slum rat. But you were still tainted by the stench of your beginnings. You were never allowed to forget that you were raised swimming in London's shit-spill. That they are better than us and always will be.

I remember. I remember standing in a gleaming London street, and I remember the whispers they said about me. What they still say about me. Judged for the colour of my skin, the callouses on my hands, the holes in the clothes I wear. Their words are now irrelevant because *they* are now irrelevant. Power fades as quickly as it rises. Remember that. It's unstable, fickle. Kings are overthrown as many times as they are crowned.

We hold the judgement, my friends. We hold the power. Are we fit to take it? That's still in question. But take it we must. And as we move forward we must carry the burden of our birth with us, because it will be an anchor that will delay a despot ruining the world again. I came from nothing, I will return to nothing. So will you. But for this moment in between, I will carry you. Will you carry me?

I ask you now. Which side are you on? You people who have nothing, you who suffer. And those of you who were lucky. Those of you who have lived merciful lives, who have comfort and warmth and hope still, in this darkest hour. We have been divided, but we can redraw the lines. We can reshape this city, this country in our own image. We can be fair and just and righteous.

But first we take responsibility. We take the burden of the Reachers we have killed. We take the burden of the weak we have put upon, the workers we ignore. And we join together. In unity. We are the Union. But we stand no chance unless we organise.

This is a battle, my friends. Not all of us will make it. Many of us will fall before this war is won. But it will be won if you join us.

My name is Carson Mooney, and I am a Union man. Which side are you on?

[End transmission]

Static.

36

The first real blanket of winter snow had already touched the west. Winter had laid her claim on the country, and soon all would be hers. Charlie's breath frosted in the open air. He watched the sunrise over the farm, twisting shadows across the turbines. Somewhere inside the cottage an argument was brewing, shattering the otherwise still Welsh countryside.

The front door opened and closed. Footsteps crunched against the snow. Rachel hooked her arm in his, resting her head on his shoulder. He held her closer, trying to fill the void. A fortnight had passed since the explosion, and each day was harder to see through. Rachel cried often, but he had lost the ability to mourn. Sarah, Lilly, and now John. What more was left for him? Then Rachel would hold him tighter, and he would remember they were all each other had. More so now.

"He won't change his mind," she whispered.

"We can't keep him here against his will."

"He wants to walk back to S'aven in the middle of winter. He's not thinking straight."

He let her go. "I'll speak to him."

An open fire roared inside the cottage, making it unbearably warm. In the kitchen, his hosts were fighting over a broken engine dripping oil on the table. He climbed the stairs slowly, relying on his crutch for support. The leg brace had been retired. It was designed to keep him moving, but Charlie had decided his running was over.

There were two bedrooms upstairs: one for Hannah and Jay, one for the others to share. Charlie stepped inside the guest room, ignoring the bed his brother had recovered in so many months ago. In the far corner, Roxy was tying up his bags, ready to head out. Rachel had patched him up, but he suffered more pain than she could treat here. There was no way he'd make it more than a couple of miles before his body gave out on him, but Charlie suspected that might be the point.

"I expect she sent you up here to talk me out of going?"

"Something like that."

"Well, don't bother."

When Roxy looked at him, the wealth of unsaid words hung between them. He blamed Charlie for what happened, almost as much as he blamed himself. Once upon a time, they were good friends, but it was impossible for two people to suffer such loss and remain close. Charlie understood his reasons for leaving, and in many ways, he was glad Roxy was going. Seeing him was a constant reminder of John and the fact Charlie had failed him.

"I wasn't planning to." But he still cared for Roxy, more so now he knew how important he had been to his brother. He wanted his friend to be at peace and move on from the miserable lives the Smith brothers had lived. For John's sake, he wanted Roxy to be happy. He reached into his pocket and pulled out the keys to their van. "We restocked it. Hannah repaired the glass. Full tank, with a can in the back. Should see you to S'aven or Blackwater, or wherever you want to go."

Roxy hesitated, then snatched the keys before Charlie changed his mind. "You're letting me go, just like that?"

Charlie sat down on his bed and stretched out his weak leg. "When we were with the Institute, me and John developed this connection. Kind of like Rachel's powers, but just between us and, I don't know, more primal I guess. It's not like I could read his mind, but I've always known if he's been in trouble, and him me. Back at the Grandchester I knew he was fine, just like I knew he was gone at the station." Charlie's voice started to break. He told himself every day John was gone, but when he spoke it aloud it felt like he was hearing the news for the first time.

"Like how he knew you were in trouble when they got Sarah?"

"Exactly. And sometimes it's been more than just a sense of wellness. When we were kids it was second nature. We could just communicate. Not with words exactly, but if he wanted me to know something, then I would just know it." Charlie toyed with his crutch. "At the station, before the explosion, he told me we were in danger. And the last thing he thought about was you."

Roxy turned away in a feeble attempt to hide his pain.

"I don't know what went on with you guys. But in that one moment, I got a sense of how important you were to him. He wanted to keep you safe. And you have a much better shot at life away from us. We both know that."

Roxy nodded and rubbed the sadness from his face. He was good at masks and bravado. Charlie took it as a cue to continue to leave the words unsaid. It was best for them both that way.

"Do you know where you're heading?"

"Yeah, back to S'aven first." He pushed back his hair. "I'm going to check in with Li. See what the damage down there is. Then find a boat, or a plane, or something, and head out to stay with Mother. Start again, out of this shithole country."

"Sounds like a good plan. You're always welcome here. You know that, right. You're still family."

He scoffed. "No offense, Charlie, but having seen what has happened to your family, I'm not sure that's such a good thing." He grabbed his bags. "What are you going to do now?"

It was a question that had been haunting Charlie. All his plans, all his ambitions circled around John. Without his brother he was nothing. "I don't know. Ride out the winter here. Take stock in the spring."

Roxy regarded him for a moment. He had always been able to see through Charlie's lies, recognise his weaknesses. "I asked Rachel to come with me. She won't leave you," he said.

This he already knew. He'd overheard Roxy begging Rachel to get away, and deep down he hoped she'd see sense and go with Roxy. But the connection between Reachers overrode all common sense. She was bound to Charlie, as much as he was to her. She would be with him until the end, no matter the heartache in their future. And eventually he would be the death of her, just like he was the death of everyone else he loved.

"I'll look after her," Charlie assured him.

"She'll look after you." He moved towards the door and stopped himself. "Don't get anyone else involved, Charlie. Take Rachel, and just leave the world alone." Then he left.

Charlie heard the stairs creak and then the door slam shut. From the bedroom window he could see the yard. Rachel clasped Roxy, sobbing violently into his shoulder. He patted her back. Already there was distance between them. He wiped her tears, whispered something, and briefly glanced back up at Charlie in the window. Then he was climbing into the van and driving out of the yard. The shadow of the transit merged with the countryside as it pulled Roxy onto a new path, unburdened by the Smith brothers and the trouble that followed them.

Defeated, Charlie sat on the bed nearest the window. He flexed his fingers. The power now seemed insignificant. Father Darcy used to talk about the brothers' potential, about how they were destined for greatness. He never warned them about the possibility their futures could be squandered for nothing.

Epilogue

Dreams moved like clouds in her mind. In her waking hours her sky was blackness, empty of shape and colour, but when she slept her subconscious awoke into a brilliant daylight. The faces she saw could be dismissed as strangers, yet something told her they were more than the imaginings of her creative brain. A mother. A father. An uncle. Family? They had names, names she knew but couldn't place. While she slept she explored the images, drawing out truths.

The strongest was always the woman. She danced in a kitchen, ran through a small garden; she sang off-key, pulled faces. There was love in her eyes. Fear, anger, heartache, but always love too. Sometimes she spoke. Sometimes the words stayed.

Then the chimes rang out and she was awake and by her bed, the last traces of the dream dissipating. But there was a word—a name—that stayed with her. Lilly. It was familiar, and in the second before the wardens came she grasped its meaning. Lilly was her name from before. Her chest rose triumphantly. She was certain now. There had been a time before. But as the seconds slipped by, her certainty floundered. The door to her cell opened, and she was led to the examination chamber. By the time she made it, her memories were lost and she was once again just a number.

END

Dear reader,

We hope you enjoyed reading *The Rising Fire*. Please take a moment to leave a review in Amazon, even if it's a short one. Your opinion is important to us.

Discover more books by L. E. Fitzpatrick at https://www.nextchapter.pub/authors/le-fitzpatrick-science-fiction-author

Want to know when one of our books is free or discounted for Kindle? Join the newsletter at http://eepurl.com/bqqB3H

Best regards,

L.E. Fitzpatrick and the Next Chapter Team

Acknowledgements

As always my thanks to my long suffering family for putting up with writer mood swings, long hours at the computer, and weird late night conversations. Huge love and respect to Alicia, the queen of editing and turning my non-sensical ramblings into something publishable. Tip of the hat to those at Next Chapter, keeping the dream alive and developing the series into audio books and beyond, thank you Miika and team. Finally, a special acknowledgement to my dearly departed friend Li, whose enthusiasm for this series supported me more than she realised. *I wish I could have written this sooner for you.* Thank you to the readers still following the series. And to any readers who have picked up this book on a whim – have you heard about the others books? Reviews are a godsend and keep us in coffee. Thanks guys.

About the Author

L E Fitzpatrick is a writer of dark adventure stories and thrillers. Under the watchful eye of her beloved rescue Staffordshire Bull Terrier, she leaps from trains and climbs down buildings, all from the front room of a tiny cottage in the middle of the Welsh countryside.

Inspired by cult film and TV, L E Fitzpatrick's fiction is a collection of twisted worlds and realities, broken characters, and high action. She enjoys pushing the boundaries of her imagination and creating hugely entertaining stories.

Other Titles by L E Fitzpatrick

The Reacher Series:
　The Running Game
　Border Lines
　Every Storm Breaks

Reacher Short Stories:
　Safe Haven
　Family

www.lefitzpatrick.com

You might also like:

Storm Portal by Michael R. Stern

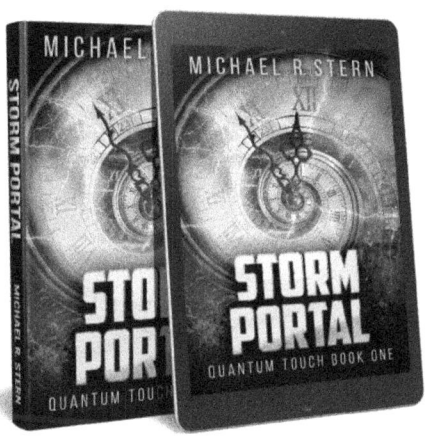

To read first chapter for free, head to:
https://www.nextchapter.pub/books/storm-portal

Lightning Source UK Ltd.
Milton Keynes UK
UKHW011845190521
384027UK00008B/374/J